MADE
IN L.A.

MADE IN L.A.

Vol. 4: BEYOND THE PRECIPICE

MADE IN L.A.
Vol. 4: Beyond the Precipice

FOURTH ANNUAL ANTHOLOGY

Cover design by Allison Rose

Visit Made in L.A. Writers online at
www.madeinlawriters.com

ISBN: 978-1-953954-01-5
Library of Congress Control Number: 2022902200

Published by Resonant Earth Publishing
on behalf of
MADE IN L.A. WRITERS
P.O. Box 50785
Los Angeles, CA 90050

CONTENTS

Introduction

INTRODUCTION

We tell each other stories to live within visions of the world that communicate essential truths. Sometimes our tales are uplifting, often devastating, but always we aim for a mix of both recognizable and surprising.

Made in L.A. Vol. 4: Beyond the Precipice is not a pandemic-era anthology. Many of the stories were written before the initial outbreak, and much of the editing was completed in early 2022, a time when "what's next?" was on many people's minds. And yet, how could the tumultuous and pervasive changes throughout the world not affect how these stories are received? The inspiration for the title comes from the vistas these stories portray: looking forward, moving past a point of no return, and wondering what there is to find just out of sight.

Some stories feature characters that shake like trees in a Santa Ana windstorm. In the story that opens the anthology, "Burnt Tortilla Sugar" by Tisha Marie Reichle-Aguilera, we get to know a character who can't move on, who obsessively compares the past to the present, and who looks for glimpses of hope in dark places. The rediscovery of joys, both unexpected and unearned, also runs through "Stealing Away" by Cristina Stuart, which features a woman drawn toward transgressive adventure. The young protagonist in "Two Trunks" by Kate Mo learns of family tragedy, secrets, and the transposition of generational trauma. "Requiem" by Aatif Rashid asks us to live with grief and ghosts intertwined and shows us what lengths we might go to for tenuous resurrections.

Characters who find themselves at the threshold of possibility, one step away from new lives and dreams, abound in this anthology. Lucy Rodriguez-Hanley's "Huevos Fritos" is a frantically humorous and ultimately empathic glimpse of a woman awaiting test results — for pregnancy, not Covid. In "(Just) A Girl in the World" by Amy Jones Sedivy, we witness romantic and professional urges that tear apart a friendship and reckon with the gap between our intentions and our impact. "What I Left Behind" by Deborah Weiss manifests a dilemma: when wildfires threaten a woman's home, she must decide what she can save and what must stay in the path of flames. And "Where We Make Home" by Hazel Kight Witham explores communities that take root, even when hope and survival are at risk.

The changes brought about in some stories are positive, with characters heading in unexpected directions in pursuit of hope. We see an Olympian at the height of her career question her choices in "Finish Line" by Sasha Kildare. In "Living, Dead, and In-Between" by J.P. Higgins, the struggle of a homeless man is told from a unique, idiosyncratic perspective and shows what grace can be bestowed by radical empathy.

This anthology makes room for the dark side of change as well. An exploration of longing and loss gives Karter Mycroft's "Bathypelagic Doubleshot Blues" poignancy in the midst of delusional conspiracy. Likewise, Nick Duretta's "Pandemic Salon" explores what happens when a character is unmoored from normalcy and set adrift in strange times. "The Long Drop" by Rachael Warecki takes us back in time and examines violence and the price of survival in a cutthroat world.

The anthology closes with two L.A. tales of friendship, love, and loss. "Boys on Mulholland" by Janna Layton imagines two social media influencers reunited one evening in the Hollywood Hills, and the pain that comes from a loss of control. The sharp and poignant final story in this anthology, "Lover's Leap" by Catie Jarvis, sees a woman at odds with herself, her heart pulled in two directions, who goes through a decisive change in circumstances on a sunny California day.

We hope these stories resonate with you. We hope they give you glimpses of what Los Angeles was, is, and can be. We hope we stay connected and find each other again under a blue L.A. sky.

With love and peace in our hearts,

Made in L.A. Writers

Sara Chisolm ¬ Gabi Lorino ¬ Allison Rose ¬ Cody Sisco

BURNT TORTILLA SUGAR

TISHA MARIE REICHLE-AGUILERA

My eyelids flutter, struggle to adjust to the darkness inside the bar. It used to be smoky here, even though cigarettes in bars haven't been a thing since 1998. Smokers would congregate by the back door, half in and half out so they could keep eyes on their table, make sure their opponents didn't cheat. Smoke wafted up and around, rose to the ceiling only to be blown back down by lazy fans. If anyone needed a joint, they were more discreet, it still being illegal in 2010. They'd sneak down the alley behind El Camaguey, post up between the dumpster and the refrigerated truck that picked up meat from Belcampo on Broadway. But back then, even through the haze of smoke, there was light. Fluorescents overhead, the neon glow of Pabst and Miller Lite, Corona Extra and Budweiser. A blue hue cast on cheekbones and foreheads seemed to linger until the beer buzz wore off. But now, a few years later, the bar is dim, the air HEPA-filtered. When I see better, I scan the place for the woman I love. We've been on a break for a few months, but it's her birthday, and I came by to celebrate with her.

When my pupils are fully dilated, I focus on each face for someone familiar. Can't imagine this space on Venice Blvd. without her. I see faces many shades paler than mine, a little lighter than hers. Folks in shoes bearing names I can't pronounce, suits, and designer athletic apparel. My

1

jeans were thirty bucks at Old Navy, and she once said this denim shirt made the color of my eyes pop. I have on new shoes, though, with better arch support than my old Adidas. We don't belong to this new crowd. The faded Dodgers jersey and acid-washed jeans she wore then would not match the shiny black leggings and tight tank tops the servers wear now. I'm not clear how that costume fits with the décor, how they stay walking so fast all night in those delicate high heels.

Inside the bar now, shiny wood-paneled walls and tree stumps in the ceiling simulate a Big Bear ski lodge, which doesn't make sense, since, if you want Big Bear, it's only a two-hour drive from Los Angeles. Last November, we had our first weekend away together at mi tio's cabin there. I built a fire. We never ventured outside until it was time to go back home. A fresh dusting of snow covered my truck. Maybe that's why she still works here; it reminds her of us.

Antlers surround the disco ball over the dance floor, a juxtaposition right out of an eighties horror flick. I squint through the dimness, worried I might see a serial killer, a new Richard Ramirez, who caused many young women like me sleepless nights back in the eighties. I feel chilled, despite my long sleeves, and move a little in time with the noise coming from the back corner. The dance floor is empty except for a few people standing around its edge, waiting for a table. They barely tap a foot or nod in time with the music. In the far corner, where the black metal security screen to the alley used to be, a gray barn door stays closed until the live band packs up fiddle, accordion, bass, keyboard, and drum set. Neighbors on Veteran must've complained. The band's van waits in the space where I used to park.

On Sundays, TVs once blared games instead of the arty videos they have on now, and Paco would set up his taco stand. Asada and al pastor perfumed the air then, but

2

tonight the odors of lust and luck hover. Both are better than the stale cheap beer stuck to the bottom of my shoe, which will still be there after I walk a mile to my apartment on Rose and Overland.

There are no more pool tables, just two long cages where freckle-faced bros throw axes at giant wooden targets on the wall behind where the jukebox had been. There are spotlights pointed at the targets, but the rest of the bar is lit with twenties-style pendant lights, and a fireplace that frames a candelabra with a battery-powered glow.

When we were here every weeknight, before the new ownership, I could get a bottle of beer for two dollars. Now there's a different craft on tap each night, and it's five bucks during happy hour. Their specialty is whiskey-based cocktails with silly names like "Smoked on the Slopes," "Manhattan Snowstorm," and "Bedtime Slippers." But on special occasions, like today, diez y seis de Septiembre, Mexican Independence Day, they've changed it up with a tequila tasting: tiny glasses to sip, not slam, and one signature cocktail. Tonight's is something called "Dulce de Tequila," which includes cognac, a cream float, and a burnt tortilla sugar rim. The thought makes my teeth hurt.

The band has kept things thematic. They play "Jose Cuervo," which is not served here, and no one here is a "friend of mine." They try "Straight Tequila Night," which is slow and sad, makes me want to fight the whiny guy on the guitar. I don't think it can get any worse until he starts singing a song I don't think I've ever heard. It takes me a few lines to realize he's singing in Spanish. Ay dios mio! Thankfully, it's a short song. They play one more, an acoustic version of "Whiskey Mama" by ZZ Top, which I only recognize after they've sung a whole verse.

"They shoulda kept the jukebox," I mutter.

A woman nearby says, "That's my brother's band."

3

"Sure hope he has a day job." I give her a knowing smile.

On the band break, my ears pick up the drone of conversations about investments and housing markets, wineries, and Airbnbs. Back in the day, this was the place where folks shouted about point spreads and upsets, campsites and fishing holes.

We met here on her birthday two years ago. Before the renovation, this was our spot. Tonight, I want to take her away from all this fake-ass fancy and go somewhere we used to love. A place where the appetizer of the day isn't quinoa chips with green pea guac or herbed flatbread with white bean hummus. Some hole in the wall, like El Abajeño, where we had chilaquiles, not just for breakfast. Or a joint like JR's on La Cienega, where we shared slow-cooked ribs that fell off the bone and greens so garlicky we didn't kiss until the next day. She loved their coleslaw, while I chose fried zucchini as my veggie. Maybe she'd like to try someplace new for this birthday celebration, but someplace real, like Humble Potato, where we could eat chicken katsu sando or pork belly bahn mi or share the Da Kine plate and reminisce about our week in Maui that New Year's, eating Spam fried and wrapped in seaweed. We could sit on metal stools on the patio, listen to songs we recognize, and sing along when we know the words.

We loved singing together, to harmonize lows and highs. It fixed the worst of our fights. Like that time she dropped my hand when we ran into her mom's neighbors on the Venice Beach Boardwalk. Or after she introduced me as her roommate to the cousin in town for a tech conference near LAX. She reminded me how Catholic her friends and family were, that they wouldn't understand. Wasn't it better for us to be our secret? She made me dessert when we got home. We sang "Secret Lovers" by Atlantic Starr and "Our Lips Are Sealed" by the Go-Gos, danced around my living room, and collapsed on my faded red sofa. For six months, we shared that tiny space. We walked down to The Overland Café on Sunday mornings just minutes before bottomless mimosa brunch ended. We never ran into her holy family there, where she fed me strawberries off the top of her waffles and I placed bites of my omelet gently on her tongue.

I step away from the door as another group of unfamiliar faces enters the bar. Then I see her. She walks out of the bathroom, wipes her still-damp hands on her shiny black thighs, tosses her long golden-brown hair behind her shoulders, and stands straighter before she picks up her empty drink tray. As she makes her way back to the floor, I stare at her breasts, accentuated by the fitted black, ribbed fabric. I imagine her naked, next to me on my sofa again. She laughs at some guy's joke as she takes the order for his table. She touches another guy on the shoulder when she checks to see if he needs anything else. Back at the bar, she leans on its edge while some long-haired dude pours, ices, shakes, garnishes. He has on a black, loose-fitting button-up shirt and, I'm sure, comfortable shoes, even though I can't see them.

She deposits the vari-colored glasses on a table across the room, turns to head back, and her eyes smile. She must've seen me. She sets the drink tray in the return space and takes a sip from her metal water bottle that had been behind the bar. She presses her lips together, pulls lipstick out of her pocket, and colors them bright pink.

Gross. She knows I hate the way it tastes, like I hated the thick layer of foundation she'd spread all over her face that left pale greasy smudges on my clothes.

She struts over to the stage as the band returns to their spot and takes the microphone.

I make my way through the crowd and sit on a barstool.

Bartender tilts his head as if he recognizes me. "What'll it be?"

"What tastes like Corona?"

He snorts. "Nothing behind this bar." Tilts his head the other way. "Try a blonde ale."

"I don't like blondes."

He gives my dark curls and hazel eyes a closer look. "You sure about that?"

I scowl, lean away from him so that I can see around a tall suit, and stare at her mouth as it forms the words of "Tonight Is the Night" by Betty Wright. I'm tense until I get my drink. One sip and its bitterness breaks the spell. I turn my focus to her clenched abs and heaving chest, feel her words vibrate into my heart, and know she's thinking about our first time together. She'd never been with a woman before me. She was accustomed to men taking what they wanted and had asked me to be gentle. I'd helped her relax with a massage and music just like this. She'd trembled. I'd trembled. We'd lain still, our toes entwined, her head on my chest, until the sun peeked through the sheer turquoise curtains.

Applause brings me back to reality, and I take another draw of the bitter beer. She sips from her water bottle again, and a few drops glide down her chin to her throat. She moves the mic to the left, and the bass player sets his instrument in its stand. The rest of the band starts intro chords. Bass dude steps up next to her and leans over the microphone to kiss her. More than a peck. They surround the mic like it's a third lover and duet a double-time version of Aaron Neville and Linda Ronstadt's "Don't Know Much," but she sings Neville, and he hits Ronstadt's high notes like I never could.

I don't taste the last of my beer. Ask for a double shot of top-shelf tequila, a label I don't recognize. During the instrumental break, they kiss. Longer this time. More tongue. I tilt my head back and open wide, the burn coats my throat. I slam the glass on the bar, rim down, and it shatters in my hand. Shards I don't feel. Blood I see.

No one hears the crash. The applause is too loud. The guy next to me shifts away, as if my pain is somehow contagious.

I can't clap.

Long-haired bartender scoops up some ice and tosses me a towel.

I thank him, continue to stare at her. I get it. She's performing for this crowd, fulfilling the actress fantasy she came to Los Angeles for twenty-five years ago. None of this is real. She still loves me and, when her set is over, will celebrate her birthday with me. Not that guy.

Bass dude moves to sit at the keyboard behind the accordion, and accordion dude picks up his guitar. She starts slow, moans into the lyrics. She belts out in Spanish, "I gave you all my love and more," and stares across the bar in my direction. She knows I love Selena.

But that song, "Si Una Vez," is about regret and yesterday's mistakes. So, it's clear she's not talking to me.

(JUST) A GIRL IN THE WORLD

AMY JONES SEDIVY

Do you know what the Ninth Circle of Hell is? If you haven't read Dante (English major here!), then perhaps you don't. It's the lowest circle. What would you imagine it to be? Reserved for murderers? Child molesters? Rapists? No. They are further up. The Ninth Circle is for Betrayers. Judas, for example. And Brutus. "Et tu, Brute?"

Kelley thinks I belong there. I am pretty sure that's where I'll end up. Also, she only knows about it because I told her.

⌐

We were sitting at Little Sheep Hot Pot, happily cooking our meat and veggies in the hot broth, dipping them in sauces before eating.

"I could always eat like this," Kelley said, holding a shrimp above her tilted head and dropping it into her mouth. This was childish, but because she was so beautiful, it was, instead, captivating. How do I know? Besides being captivated myself — even after so many years of friendship — I looked around. Every man and many women watched her, mouths open in half-smiles. Transfixed.

"You say that at all the good ethnic restaurants we go to," I said. I ate my shrimp on the end of a fork, parallel with my mouth, which was aiming straight forward and not capturing anyone's attention.

"Anna. Don't say 'ethnic,'" Kelley said.

"Don't say … why not?" I waved my empty fork at her. "We go to restaurants that don't serve American food. We go to Thai and Chinese and Afghani and Persian. Those are ethnic restaurants."

"But it sounds racist."

I loved Kelley. She didn't go to college, but to a for-profit art school that offered no humanities classes. What should have been a waste of money with second-rate teachers gave her the freedom to explore her vision, and within three years of graduating from one of the worst institutions ever, Kelley hit it big in the L.A. art world. She was a Major Artist. So what if she didn't know the kind of things I knew? Me with my almost-PhD in Literature.

"Recognizing ethnicity is not racist." I started organizing a mini lecture in my head. Kelley usually enjoyed these. Usually, she said I was so smart, and she was lucky to have me for a friend, and there was so much she didn't know, and wasn't it wonderful to have me teach her, et cetera and blah blah blah. But this time, as she slithered a noodle from her chopsticks to her mouth in a slow sucking motion, she muttered something.

"What?" I asked.

"There is a circle of hell for people who are racists," she said once she swallowed the noodle. "And another circle for people who do hate crimes."

"Actually, there isn't, even though there should be." I didn't bother to mention that people committing hate crimes are a priori racists. But I switched gears from a lecture on racism to one on the circles of hell.

"First circle is Limbo, for those people who don't accept Jesus. Second is Lust. Third is Gluttony. Fourth is Greed. Fifth is Anger. Sixth is Heresy. Seventh is Violence. Eighth is Fraud and Ninth is Treachery."

She put her chopsticks down, sat up straighter, leaned forward, and said, "What is Heresy? And what is Treachery?"

"Heresy is speaking against God. Treachery is betrayal. I mean, at least that's how Dante means it."

"Who's Dante? Other than that annoying new artist at the gallery?"

"Dante is the Italian poet who wrote Inferno, which is a long poem and has the nine circles of hell."

"Damn, Anna, you just know this shit. Betraying is number nine, huh? Where are murderers? Are they at ten or eleven?"

"Nine is it. Nine is the bottom. The worst. Except for Lucifer, the devil. He is in a pit below nine. Murderers are at, um, level seven. Violence."

Kelley continued slurping noodles, and I looked sideways at a man who leaned over his soup to watch her, ignoring his tie as it sopped up the delicious broth.

Whenever we had these mini lessons, I got immediately tired. I changed the subject as soon as I could, and I knew right then I didn't want to talk about hell, and I sure as hell didn't want to talk about racism.

"Your retrospective," I said. "Did the museum agree with your idea? Are they going to …"

"Project my film? You bet. Otherwise they wouldn't get a single painting. That film has to be projected against my big blue panel or else it doesn't make sense."

We finished the vegetables. The shrimp and pork slices were gone. The broth was nearly empty. Soon we would walk out, and she would go to her electric BMW and drive to her studio building ("her," as in she owned the whole building) in downtown L.A. where one of her boyfriends — probably Steven B., as opposed to Steven L. — would eagerly await her. I would get in my twelve-year-old Jeep and drive to Highland Park, to my airy studio apartment on top of a commercial building — airy because the windows had to be open or else I might die — and then I would miss her. I would miss her as soon as we hugged and walked our separate ways. I was in love with Kelley just as much as I was in love with Franklin, the man I would eventually marry (I was certain of it). For years, she and I had had a symbiotic relationship where the ties that bound us together braided and strengthened until saying goodbye felt like tearing out a part of my soul. Or my heart. Or maybe my guts. Something tore, and it hurt as if it were physically happening. Kelley felt this way too. She had, anyway, once upon a time. She said so. Once. Now I was feeling unsure, but I put her easy breezy wave and her sudden turn away from me down to the fact that she was preoccupied with the show. It was in less than two months, and it was important. A museum retrospective combined with her new work, work that had taken a drastic left turn (or maybe it did a 180. Or a 360 — except that would mean it came back to where it was. Math concepts were not my strong point).

I called Franklin while I walked to my car. It went to voicemail because, no doubt, he was in the studio playing drums for some famous person. Everyone had interesting lives. With an eventual PhD in "Romanticism and the Aesthetics of Beauty and Terror," I was trying to make my life interesting too so Franklin would be proud of me. But more because Kelley would approve.

Franklin came to my hot and breezy apartment late that night to tell me he was offered a gig with a band that was about to go on the road.

"I'll see Europe," he said, "and Brazil and some other places in South America I never heard of."

"How is it you've never heard of … never mind." I thought briefly of buying a world map to share with him before he took off on whatever this adventure was.

"How long will you be gone?"

12

"Sixteen months." He had the decency to look abashed.

"Sixteen? As in six and teen? A year and a half?" I did not have the decency to keep from shouting.

"Well, technically a year and four months."

"Do you, like, get to come home every so often?"

"That wasn't mentioned. Can you take it, babe? Will you wait for me?"

I went to stand by the hot breeze that blew in the window and listened to the radios in the cars below. Most of them were playing ranchera music, but one played "Bohemian Rhapsody," and I hated that. At that moment, I hated rock music, rock bands, and rock drummers, and I wondered why I ever thought it was a good idea to fall in love with a rock musician of any kind. This was my third. Or fifth, really, but one didn't count because he OD'ed, then survived, then went home to Tucson to sell insurance. The other one didn't count because he was famous, and it was a one-night stand. So, three.

"Like you're a soldier going off to war and I'm the sweetheart left behind wondering if I'll be tying a yellow ribbon around some palm tree."

"It's an oak tree."

"Well, the palm tree is out front, so it would be that, wouldn't it?"

"Not like a soldier." Franklin came to the window and wrapped his arms around me. "No one is going to shoot at me, I don't have to wear fatigues or bulletproof vests or carry an AK-47. I am just playing drums."

"For sixteen months."

"Yes."

"On the road."

"Well, yes, that's the idea."

"And after each show? Backstage? Girls and drugs and booze and girls, and I'm supposed to wait for you? Will you wait for me?"

He squeezed me a little harder, I think to hide the fact that he was not going to answer that question.

After waiting longer than was necessary, because it was clear what his answer would be, I said, "I might wait, and I might not. We'll see."

He kissed the back of my neck. "Please?"

We ended the night with no promises, and when he left in the morning, he took everything that belonged to him.

¬

"I hate Dante," Kelley said as we drove toward her gallery in Santa Monica.

"Who? The Italian poet?"

"No, of course not, I don't even know who that is."

"He's the poet, I told you about him, he wrote …"

"Dante is the new artist at the gallery. Lois is enchanted with him. She loves his work, she loves his explanations, she loves his hair, she loves him."

"So, what is he like? Why do you hate him?"

I wanted to point out that she was sort of driving in two lanes on the 10 freeway and cars were passing and people were giving her dirty looks, but I knew from long experience to never, ever comment on Kelley's driving.

She veered into one lane and stayed there, so I relaxed while she enumerated the ways in which she hated Dante. It was a long list, but it boiled down to two things: he was not attracted to her, and he was poised to become a Major Artist and she didn't like having competition. I was, however, fascinated with her description of his hair, and I hoped he would be at the gallery when we got there so I could see this amazing, waist-length multicolored wonder of a hairstyle.

Do you see where this is going? I did not. So much for an almost-PhD in romantic literature, which should have tuned me into the vagaries of the human heart and psyche and should have made it abundantly clear to me that I was falling into a romance trope that would cause great pain and suffering. But I digress. At this point, in that car, on the 10, three miles still to go, I was only thinking of what multicolored hair would look like and how long it would take for this man to realize Kelley was what he, of course, wanted.

Kelley is just over six feet with long, long legs, and she wears skirts to show off those legs. She is narrow where she should be and rounded in other places that are appealing. She is very rounded in the boob area. Instead of low-cut necklines, Kelley favors very tight T-shirts so there is that stretched wrinkle that goes across her chest, as if the T-shirt is just barely keeping those boobs in control. Kelley has luxurious (and weaved) blonde hair, big blue eyes, a full mouth with only a bit of lip plumper. She is so beautiful that she is almost a caricature of beautiful. Kelley only had sex because everyone wanted to have sex with her. She'd had "relationships" with a few well-chosen men. One of them was Franklin, but she got tired of him about the same time I found him interesting, so that worked out. All my relationships with men ended up being compared to my relationship with her and so, obviously, since they couldn't know me the way she did, they all fell short. Franklin had an advantage; he had listened to Kelley talk on and on about me when she was complaining or explaining or just chattering. I felt like I got him ready-made in that a) he understood me, and b) he had already had sex with Kelley, so I didn't have to deal with any unrequited lust.

Anyway, she is gorgeous, and I wondered what Dante's deal was that he wasn't attracted to her. I had seen her at gallery openings and parties where literally everyone in the room was attracted to her. I shouldn't use literally; I'm an English major for God's sake. But I think it may be accurate.

She is like a shining beacon of beauty and sex and everyone around gapes at her and, in some way, wants her.

Kelley parked her car in the fire lane in front of her gallery and hopped out. I followed. And, oh boy, I saw a man facing away from me, and all I saw was absolutely gorgeous long hair in a rainbow of colors cascading down his back. I didn't know anything about the man, but I wanted that hair. On me. I wanted it on me.

"Oh, it's Kelley," he said, turning around to see us come in, then turning back and speaking directly to Annalisa, the young gallery intern behind the front counter. I was offended, and Kelley, well, she went into Kelley-charm.

"Dante! It's good to see you. I wondered if you would be here. I heard they are hanging your show and thought you might show up to help out, and let's see the work; I've heard so much about it." At which point, she grabbed his elbow and steered him into the large room where paintings leaned against the wall, making a march of vivid colors all around the floor. I saw that his hair was part of his vision; the paintings were rainbows of color that should have been too garish and childish, but they were not. Instead, they were masculine, hard-edged, abstract shapes with glimpses of recognizable objects. Strongly masculine. Dante was clearly a man's man, a macho man. Ignore the waist-length hair and the pretty face with high cheekbones and green eyes. (I was having a hard time ignoring those things.) His feminine face had nothing to do with his raging masculinity. Then I thought perhaps he was trans, and then I was more interested in everything — the work, the man. So, with that floating in my head, I tuned into Kelley and Dante trying to talk over each other.

And it was boring. Both spouting many art theory terms, both claiming to be free from art theory as they both accused the other's work of hewing to art theory. I walked around and studied the paintings and chatted with Annalisa, who was somewhat wide-eyed at the conversation.

"Two big names," I said. "Evidently there is only room for one of them at a time in this place."

"It's magical," she said.

"It is?"

She went on. "Just like my theory professor said at Art Center. The center of theory is found on the fringes of life."

"Oh," I said. "And what else did he say?"

"Just what they are saying! That structure of necessity is formulated beyond the borders to defeat expectations."

I wondered if I asked her to repeat it, she would be able to. I did not ask.

Kelley came bouncing past me, anger emanating from her like a force field. Annalisa was saying something else, and stupidly I turned to hear her. So, Kelley drove away without me.

Calling her on her cell had no effect.

"There's the train," offered Annalisa. "It stops right here and goes downtown. Or Uber."

"Or I can give you a ride," said Dante, coming over to the counter. "Since I drove your friend away, it's the least I can do."

"Don't you have to hang your work?"

"The hard part's done. Now it's just physical labor, and we hire someone to do that. Where do you live?"

Fortunately, Highland Park was not a stretch, since he lived in downtown L.A., and we drove through the city (he refused to take the freeway), talking all the while about things that were not art or theory or Kelley.

⌐

The next morning was coffee and Mexican pastry at La Monarca, then a sweet goodbye kiss and a promise to text later. I found myself sitting in my favorite (and only) chair in the middle of my apartment and smiling like some kind of fool. I wanted to tell a friend about my fun and wildly interesting night. Franklin was in Berlin and probably would not appreciate the information, even if he was reading the text while in bed with a hot German girl. So of course, there would be Kelley and, in fact, I was supposed to be at Kelley's favorite dive diner in an hour. I could tell her then. I drove downtown knowing there was nothing I could say to her that would cause her to congratulate me on my spectacular evening.

On the far side of downtown, in some land that is not considered East L.A., but is considered — by me anyway — warehouse-land, there is a diner painted bright orange (to make it stand out from all the beige and grey blocky warehouses?), and as garish as it is outside, the food is super bland inside. Kelley loves this place and mostly because, IMHO, the other customers are truckers and warehouse workers and one-hundred percent male. Also, it feeds her sense of the starving artist, although she is netting six figures for her bigger paintings, so "starving" is a psychological concept at this point.

Why was I friends with this woman, one might ask? One might not know that Kelley was not always this way. We met in middle school. She was not gorgeous then, but the proverbial ugly duckling, while I was pleasantly unremarkable. She was tall and gangly and did not have all those round parts that developed or were enhanced later. Braces, zits, the whole nine yards. (What is with nine yards? Is this a sports metaphor and if so, isn't ten yards a more realistic number? Like, in football, the field isn't striped off in nine-yard increments. And that's about as much as I know of football.) We were both creative, geeky, and spent hours together daydreaming of greatness. We put our energies together and made fanciful zines that we shared with a couple of other friends, gathering great praise. We listened to classic rock and '80s pop and '90s sad songs. Our teenage-girl sensibilities were well matched, and we told each other everything. And we continued to, I thought. I knew about the surgeries she had to make herself more beautiful because she truly believed that she was not. I knew about the one guy with whom she did really want a relationship but who went off to New York and might as well have gone to Mars. She knew about me, how I wanted to be the next Ursula Le Guin, or at least a published writer, and how the one guy I wanted in my life disdained monogamy to quite an impressive degree. Of course, I had to tell her about Dante.

The diner was empty; we'd missed the morning rush. There was only one older man in the corner to admire Kelley, but he was facing the wrong way. The waitress, about seventeen and looking like the whole world depended on her paycheck in this lousy job, brought me a menu, refilled Kelley's coffee, and walked away.

"I'm still so angry," Kelley said.

"About Dante?" I tumbled his name over my tongue. I liked hearing it, I liked saying it. I smiled.

"You think it's funny that I hate him." She grabbed my wrist. "You don't understand. He is the antithesis of what I do and what I think and how I paint. It's like he studied my work and purposely decided to paint the opposite, to make my work meaningless."

"But Kelly, there are so many artists that do work different from yours."

"He is evil. Vicious. He is out to destroy my reputation."

"Really?" I sat back and shook my head. "I don't think he —"

"You don't know. You don't know him."

I thought, well, I know him pretty well after last night, and I didn't see anything evil or vicious or even someone who had any interest in Kelley at all. "I don't understand. Kelley. Start at the beginning and explain."

She knew him in art school. Of course she did. He was two years behind her, he was Danielle then (I had already learned this) and she was a dilettante, rich mom and dad sending her to art school. She was a thoroughly uninteresting artist, and when the seniors were tasked with doing a crit of the sophomores' work, Kelley told her so.

"I told her, uh, his work was banal and boring and basically bad," Kelley said to me. "That it was the work of someone who had no clue what art was about, yet couldn't even just paint pretty pictures. Garbage. I told him he was wasting his parents' money. He cried, although of course it was a girl crying then, not Mr. Masculine like he is now."

"Wow. That's kinda harsh."

"Art school. People need the truth. Anyway, he dropped out. I forgot about him. Then last year, there he is, all changed and happy and so damn forceful. And spouting off all this theory to explain his work, when really it's just a malicious attempt to completely ruin my career."

"Ruin your career? I just don't think there's that intent."

"There is! There is. You can't see it; my stupid gallery can't see it. The insipid art critics can't see it, but they are playing right into it. Look at this."

Kelley slid a sheet of paper to me, a printout of how her gallery would publicize Dante's show.

Just as I read it, skimming over superlatives that certainly described Dante's paintings but offered no clue to Kelley's insistence that her work was being attacked, just as I was reading his name, Dante texted me. I grabbed my phone from the table and put it in my purse.

"I don't want us interrupted," I said. Kelley's focus was on the paper, so she didn't see Dante's name flash on the screen.

"Well," I said, trying to find soothing words, "this is pretty over the top, I agree. Like he's the second coming of Picasso."

"That's what I mean. I hate him. I hate my gallery. I'm going to his opening, and I'm going to make sure people look at me and realize that I'm the real artist. I'm not the dilettante. I'm not fake, and I'm not trying to get my fame by screwing over someone else." She sipped her coffee, then said, "Your phone keeps pinging. Who wants you so bad?"

"Franklin," I lied. And so began the lies that continued for the next few weeks, every time we were together: yoga, dinner, a party at LACMA, lunch, a walk on the beach, an intense therapy session at her studio (her talking, me listening) … all the many hours the two of us spent together. Then, in the hours of the night when Kelley worked in her studio, I was in Dante's bed, which was a really nice bed in a super-beautiful modern loft in downtown with a view of all L.A. and from which I could even make out Kelley's building off to the east.

⌐

I am a terrible student of literature for many reasons, and one was because Dante's opening was approaching, and I wondered how this would play out. Would I go with Kelley or would I go with Dante? Should I go alone and then see what would happen when I got there? Did I think anything at all, or was I so enamored with Dante that I thought Kelley would see this and back off her attack? Would she congratulate me, hug me with tears in her eyes and welcome Dante into our hug and everything would be beautiful, with rainbows and roses and violins playing sweet, sweet songs? Any novel could have pointed me in the direction things would actually go.

The day before the opening, a deadline nagged at me; my thesis advisor wanted to see a chapter and wanted to see it that day. When was I supposed to work on my dissertation if I played all day with Kelley and played quite differently all night with Dante? I pulled notes together; I typed madly and managed to write twelve pathetic pages about the pathetic nature of romantic ideas of beauty. My advisor wouldn't pick up on this, but all my descriptions were of the beauty of Kelley and of Dante, and ultimately it was an allegory about my pathetic romantic love for each of them. I'm sure when she read it, she would have a good laugh, then figure out how to defund me.

The opening was ugly, but it was short, fast, over quickly. I went alone. I got there late, near the 9:00 end of 7 to 9. I walked in and saw Kelley with a rather large contingent of acolytes surrounding her as she spouted off all that was wrong with Dante's paintings. I saw Dante with a slightly smaller contingent, all grinning, laughing, and shaking their heads. And then Kelley and Dante saw me at the exact same moment. But Dante was closer and he took several steps and embraced me, then kissed me, leaving no doubt to anyone what kind of relationship we had. Kelley stopped. Full stop. Then she walked past us and left the gallery. Some of her ardent fans followed her out, calling her name, asking what was wrong.

I felt funny in a way I never ever felt before. An entirely new feeling. I felt lots of love from Dante, a warmth from him I had never felt from any other lover, and an excitement about what could happen and where this could go — and also a sense of grief that my longtime friend-love affair with Kelley was probably, certainly, at an end. I felt terrible that it happened and that I caused it and that I lost her after so many years. All of this swirled in my brain, and I guess I looked confused or addled, because someone offered me a chair, and someone else brought a bottle of Evian, and Dante kept his hand on my shoulder. The life of the party, that's me.

So the opening ended, Dante was congratulated, many paintings had red dots next to them (Sold! Sold! Sold!). I recovered enough to stand up and insist I could drive home. Dante wanted me to come to the after-party, but I begged off. I wanted nothing more than to be in my hot box apartment, listening to the trumpets of whatever local mariachi band was playing at a nearby party, and thinking about my place in the world. I made my choice, and it was a choice that surprised me, that I thought I would never make … could never make.

I sat and listened to several versions of "Guantanamera" and thought about Franklin, and I thought about Kelley, and I thought about Dante. And then I thought, what would the Romantics do? I got in my car, weaved through the late-night traffic on Figueroa (the mariachis heading home to East L.A.), and went straight to Dante.

⌐

So, I am in the Ninth Circle of Hell with Brutus and Judas and Cain. I have broken through borders, defeated expectations, and floundered in the fringes of life. In the weeks that followed, things happened that were not my responsibility, but I felt like they were: the museum show had the unfortunate effect of Kelley's work being badly curated; art critics criticized the outdatedness of her oeuvre; the film was excoriated. Meanwhile, Dante's name and face and hair and paintings were everywhere, like really: every art mag, art section of every paper, and even on the evening news. My face was often next to his in the photos as we became some kind of "it" couple. I wondered if I was a muse, if I was a good-luck token. If I was a good person.

A good friend. Every time someone took our photo, every smile, every flash, I thought of how I had betrayed Kelley.

There is no exit from a circle of hell. I looked it up. Dante — the Italian poet, not my lover — never described anyone moving out of hell or moving up from a lower circle to a higher one, at least not from the ninth one. You get in a circle and you stay there. I would like to explain this to Kelley, to sit at some ethnic restaurant and tell her, over and over until I'm certain she understands, that even as I fly to New York or Paris or Berlin, even as I attend the Met Ball or the Venice Biennale, I am forever floundering in the ninth circle, heartbroken that I broke the heart of my first and best love.

BATHYPELAGIC DOUBLESHOT BLUES

KARTER MYCROFT

These two girls work at the massage parlor next door. When I'm taking out the recycling I'll see them out back, smoking and checking their phones. I sneak them coffees sometimes. I'll ask them things like how's business or can you believe how bad traffic is or has anyone you know gone Sinking or how do you like the coffee. My coworker always teases me for trying to fuck them but I'm not. I mean I'm not gay or anything, I just think of them as friends.

The tall one's name is Muzi and I've never seen her without a cigarette. The shorter one is Maggie. I don't think Maggie buys her own cigarettes, but she asks Muzi for one sometimes. Muzi runs the massage parlor. Maggie works there part time and studies biology at the university. I'm in the fine arts program, so we probably won't ever have classes together. Also my dad donated all his money and went Sinking, so I don't know if I can even stay in school after this semester. Mom says I'll need to get loans, but I'm not sure that's worth it.

It's busy today and I'm late because I was up all night drinking. My brain and throat hurt. I don't really smoke cigarettes, but I only have two left in the pack I bought last night. My coworker looks frazzled when I slide behind the counter, he's stabbing the ice machine like he wants to kill it. He says I smell. I ignore him and start making iced

Americanos and milk bubble teas until the line dies down. My coworker mutters that it's always Koreans ordering iced Americanos and always Chinese ordering milk bubble teas. That sounds racist to me but I don't say anything.

Eventually the shop clears out, and then someone comes in chattering with his hand on his ear. It's an older white guy in a tweed blazer, looks like he was just airlifted out of Pacific Palisades, and I can already tell he's going to do the thing where he orders while talking on the phone.

"Oh my God, I know, unbelievable. The service you get around here. Uh yeah, hey. White mocha for me."

"What size?"

"Yeah you're telling me, Jimmy. Huh? Size? Oh. Large. Doubleshots, too. Yeah, I'm back. Sorry, I'm getting coffee."

"You want doubleshots of espresso or doubleshots of the white chocolate?"

"I know, it's insane. Forty fucking dollars for a massage and the girl's *crying* the whole time. Hang on a sec, Jimmy. Yeah, double espresso. Can you handle that?"

He drops his credit card on the counter, and I almost forget to swipe it. I want to ask him what he meant about the massage, but instead I ring him up and tell my coworker I'm going out back for a smoke.

"Dude you just got here."

"Sorry."

"Fucking freshman. Ha. Just kidding."

Outside smells like spring flowers and garbage. It's too bright. The slick facades of Westwood's luxury apartments bake under the empty L.A. sky. I glance up the alley, and Muzi waves from behind a puff of smoke. There's a lighter in my pocket but I ask for hers anyway.

"Hi Jonas. You look tired."

I take a drag and my stomach coils like an angry cobra. "One of those nights. You know."

"I know," she smirks.

I wonder if she'd ever buy me alcohol if I asked. I start feeling a nicotine buzz.

"Where's Maggie?"

Muzi exhales slowly through her nose. She glances at the back door to the parlor. "She went home early."

"She's sick or something?"

Muzi takes out another cigarette just before finishing the one in her mouth. She's a chain smoker. Camel Turkish Silvers. I could never smoke that much.

"You like her, don't you?"

"As a friend."

I sound embarrassed, but it's true. Like her style is great, she's always wearing these weird jackets that match her nails and shoes. Sometimes I kind of wish I could pull off her look, although obviously I can't since I'm a guy. And she's pretty. I'm just not interested in dating her or anything. I don't feel like explaining all this to Muzi.

Her smirk melts off a little. "You said your parents went for the Sinking, right?"

"Just my dad."

"I'm sorry."

"It's fine."

"Well, Maggie's parents did too. Both of them. They just left this morning."

My stomach quivers. Cobra's ready to spit. "Fuck."

"Yeah. And she's an only child, and the rest of her family lives in Beijing. So I think she doesn't know what to do."

"Did she know they were planning on it?"

Muzi shrugs.

I remember when Mom told me Dad had made up his mind. I was pissed off but sort of weirdly glad. We'd never gotten along great anyway. It must be worse for Maggie. Having to hear your parents — both your parents — tell you

27

they're headed out on a ship that'll never bring them back. I feel queasy, even though the nicotine's settled down a bit.

"Do you think you could give me her number?"

Muzi raises an eyebrow. "What for?"

I take a drag and taste filter. "I dunno." I flick the butt behind the dumpster. "Like. Maybe I could talk to her since something similar happened to me. I definitely wish I'd had somebody to talk to when my dad left."

"Huh. Okay." She narrows her eyes. "You better not try anything with her."

"I won't."

"She's really hurting right now. And I know how you college guys are. Opportunistic."

"I really won't." I start to add something like *I'm not like other guys*, but the words feel wrong in my brain so I just shake my head. Muzi bites down on her cigarette and takes out her phone. She shows me Maggie's contact info and I start a text to her number.

The back door to the coffee shop swings open behind me. "Yo. Whenever you feel like doing your job." My coworker sounds somewhere between annoyed and big mad. I tell Muzi thanks and head back inside. Before I tie my apron I send the text.

> *hey maggie*

I spend most of my shift checking my phone, constantly feeling it vibrate even though it's not. The possibility of really talking to someone about the Sinking settles in my brain until it's all I can think about. And Maggie always seemed so easy to talk to.

Around dinnertime we run out of milk tea powder, so customers are annoyed. Normally that would stress me out, but today I think about Maggie and my dad and this docuseries I just rewatched. Crowds of olds in purple cloaks praying on a stripped-down luxury yacht. The narrator uses the word "syncretic" to describe how the faith was born out of ideas from Judaism, Shinto-Buddhism, Earth Liberation, and the Voluntary Human Extinction Movement. It was originally called the Church of the Blessed Descent, but now there are many sects with different names. Anyone can join at any time, but supposedly you have to be fifty-five to go on the boats. Dad went at fifty-two.

"You don't have milk boba?"

"We *just* ran out."

"You guys run out all the time."

"Yeah. Sorry."

"Do you have Thai flavor?"

"Sure."

It's sunset when I clock out. My hangover is almost gone, and I think maybe I should see if any of the guys want to drink again. I pull out my phone and re-read the text I sent Maggie. It looks stupid by itself so I text again.

> *this is jonas from the coffee shop btw*

No response while I clock out. I steal a couple shots of espresso for the road. I'm halfway back to the dorm when my phone vibrates.

> *Hi Jonas!*

I respond immediately.

> *how are you doing?*

> *I'm fine. How are you?*

> *good … i saw muzi out back today but you weren't there*

At this point I feel desperate. I don't know why but I need to talk to her right away.

> *i dont want to be intrusive but i heard about your parents and i'm so so sorry. the same thing happened to my dad like a month ago. just wanted to say if you felt like talking about it i'm here*

I wait on the sidewalk for a few minutes. UCLA's campus hums ahead of me like it's trying to distract me.

Nothing from my phone. Eventually I head back to my dorm and lie on my bed and stare at the text thread until nighttime. Mostly articles about the Church. No response from Maggie. I realize I probably made her feel way worse. What was I thinking? This just happened to her *today*, and here I am making shit even more complicated. I have to stop thinking about it so I start walking to my friend Rich's room to see if his brother can buy us vodka.

Maggie's text comes like a wasp in my pocket.

> *OK. Thanks for reaching out.*

I run a hand through my greasy hair. I haven't showered today. I hate the communal showers in the dorms. They always feel so awkward and when I'm hungover I can't even handle it. What the fuck am I supposed to do about Maggie? She doesn't want to talk. She probably doesn't even want to be friends anymore. Why am I feeling so weird? I need a drink.

> *I'm at the library right now if you want to meet me here.*

˥

I'm halfway down the street before I realize I've left the dorm. It's dark, but there are plenty of students out. My stomach is eating itself. I text Maggie a few more times while I walk. I assumed she was at the big campus library, but it turns out she meant the public one in town.

Westwood Village is morphing fast into nighttime, and it's Friday so everybody's drunk already. I shuffle down Wilshire, past the sushi restaurants, the power-washed storefronts, the bars where crowds are getting rowdy outside. The hookah bar, the frat bar, the hipster bar, the sports bar, the other hipster bar. I should get a fake ID. I speed up past the marble pinstripes of the Hammer Museum to the library. It's closed when I arrive.

> *hey im here. it's dark and empty lol*

"Hey!"

I whirl around. For a second I'm not sure it's her. But there she is. Her cropped bangs and glasses poke out from the cracked window of a blue Prius.

For some reason I get in the back, diagonal to where she sits in the passenger seat. "You scared me."

"My bad." I can tell she's been crying from the eyeliner on her long pink sleeves.

"Yeah, so, sorry if this was super random, I just talked to Muzi and —"

"No, it's fine. I'm glad you texted when you did. Hey, do you have a cigarette?"

"Ugh sorry," I start instinctively. "Wait. I do have one left actually. We can share it."

"That would be amazing."

I let her light it. She inhales and just sort of holds it in, like it's weed or something.

I can't decide whether I should bring up the Sinkings. "Is this your car?"

By the time she exhales there's barely any smoke left. "I don't have a car," she says. "My boyfriend dropped me off. He's at the bars."

"Nice."

"He doesn't know about … anything." She takes another drag and holds it for a while. "So, your dad?"

"Yeah." The sick slithers through me. "He was into the Church for a few years. Honestly I saw it coming." I motion for the cig and she takes another puff before handing it over. "I was really sorry to hear about your parents."

She shakes her head, and her eyes get watery. "I knew it was coming too. They were hardcore. They took me to services."

"I always wondered what those were like." I try holding in smoke like Maggie and the buzz comes fast. "My mom

31

never let Dad bring me with him. She didn't want me to get indoctrinated."

I giggle out some smoke.

Maggie gives me a weird look. "What's funny?"

"Sorry. Just thinking about how bad he would whip my ass if he saw me smoking."

Probably worse than the time he got into my browser history. I'm not even into that stuff, I was just clicking around online, but Dad always thought I would turn out to be some giant queer. I had bruises for weeks after. But he's gone now. Dressed all in purple in the middle of the Pacific. Or maybe he's already gone down.

"Your dad hit you?"

"Oh fuck yeah." A long drag. "He stopped though, toward the end. I guess the whole Church nonviolence thing got through to him eventually."

She wipes her eyes. "I tried to talk my parents out of it. But it's different when you grow up with it. When it's everybody you know. My first words might as well have been *From Below we have arisen, to Below we shall return.*" She made a quick crossing motion with her thumb on both sides of her neck.

I pass her the cig at about its halfway point. "I didn't know you grew up in the Church."

"Really?"

"Yeah, no idea."

"You ask about it all the time."

"I do?"

She takes a long drag and hands the cig back. "You don't know why I'm here, do you?"

I glance out the windows at the barren library parking lot. Only a single emergency light is on inside. "I guess not."

"There's a service tonight."

"A service? Like a Church service? Here?"

"Yeah. The university got some laws passed to keep us from recruiting students, so there's no brick-and-mortar parish. One of the librarians hosts services after hours. My parents always said I had to go or they wouldn't pay for school. I usually found ways to skip it. But now they're gone, and I just … I felt like I needed something familiar, you know? I even called and told them I was coming, but then you texted and —" She's crying all the way now. "I don't know what to do anymore."

I feel my heart speed up. She's actually talking about going to a Church meeting after what happened to her parents. "I'm sorry," I croak, trying not to sound anxious. "I didn't know what to do when Dad left either."

"At least you have other family. At least you have someone to talk to. Sorry. Fuck. It's not a contest. I shouldn't have said that."

I want to tell her there are actually plenty of things I can't talk to anyone about, but I realize I'm not sure I know what they are. I finish the cig and toss it out the window.

"I'm just lonely. I'm so fucking lonely." Her crying has a kind of giggle to it. I listen to her cry for what feels like a very long time.

A pair of headlights pull up across the lot from us. A big white Porsche. Maggie's gaze darts up as two men in long, purple robes step out and walk around the side of the library. The same robes Dad would wear.

"Maggie." I put a hand on her shoulder. "All that stuff about saving the planet and returning to our ancestral home and a Heaven Below and all of it? It's bullshit. It's a fucking death cult. You have to know I'm right because you got away, or you tried to anyway."

She rotates her head in a way I'm not sure is a nod.

"Look, what happened to your parents is fucked up. Don't let it happen to you too." I unlatch the back door of the Prius. "Come on. Let's go back to campus right now."

She gives me the most miserable look I've ever seen. She isn't crying anymore though.

"You know," she whimpers, "they know I talk to you."

My heart feels like it might blast through my chest into the cupholder. "What?"

"They keep really good track of people. They've asked me to bring a friend before, thinking it might convince me to come. They've mentioned you and Muzi and my boyfriend, basically everybody I talk to. But I've never asked. I thought maybe I'd ask you tonight, since you texted. Or maybe I hoped you'd talk me out of it. I don't know what I thought. They're definitely interested in you, though, and whenever we talked you seemed so interested too —"

"I'm interested because I think they're fucked! They should all be in prison. I mean I hated my dad, but he didn't have to die. Your parents didn't either. No one does."

There's a long, churning silence. Maggie glances over her shoulder at the library, then back at me.

"Everyone does have to die, though."

I want to throw up. My throat tastes like metal. My stomach is all fangs. Two more cars pull into the lot.

"Maggie, come on. Let's get out of here."

Four robed figures pass by as we sit in silence. Maggie takes a deep breath. The figures round the corner. A light flicks on inside the library.

"Maggie."

She looks at me and nods.

I spring out around the car and open her door. We start across the lot toward town. She's breathing heavily, we both are. My heart is pounding and I'm thankful we're moving.

A man's voice calls out from behind us. "Hey there."

34

Maggie turns.

I put an arm around her shoulder and guide her along. We make our way to the main drag, bathed in the noise of drunk kids and muted music, the dull glowing zoo of sandwich shops and pizza joints and taco trucks. We don't speak. There's time for that later. I just need to get her away from the library, away from the Church. Someone pukes in a trash can on the street, turns around, and heads back into the bar.

We're almost at the edge of campus when Maggie stops walking.

"Oh my God." She slaps her forehead. "You know what I just remembered?" She gives a smile that's somehow darker than all her crying faces. "I have to pick up my boyfriend from the bars. That's like, half the reason I'm out."

My heart sinks.

"Maggie."

"Seriously. He lives all the way on the east side and I don't want him to drive drunk. I completely forgot. You go on ahead."

"Please don't go back."

"It's fine. I'll just wait it out in the car. Might get some more cigarettes." She grabs my hand. "Thank you for talking to me. Really. It helped a lot."

"Tell me you're not going in."

"Don't worry." She whirls around. I want to chase her down and drag her back to campus, but I know I can't. I stand still, stunned, watching her go. I imagine her Sinking, naked in the freezing ocean, watching the sun shrink away up above. Maybe I'm imagining my dad too, the last bubbles leaving his lungs as the stone drags him down. I wonder if he regretted it or if he really thought he was plunging into heaven in his final moments. They say drowning kills you one of two ways: either you hold your breath long enough to pass out, or panic takes over and you hyperventilate seawater. I'm imagining my dad flailing, screaming, sucking in brine until he bursts. Maybe I'm imagining Maggie's parents, too. Maybe I'm imagining myself, plunging into the crush of that cold pressure, trying to claw gills into my neck. Look up, Dad, I'll be there soon.

Maggie's lost in the crowd.

On the way home I try texting Rich about vodka but my phone dies before I hit send.

¬

A week later I'm back at the coffee shop, making Americanos for the morning crowd. Espresso and water. Nice and simple.

I haven't heard from Maggie. It's taken everything I have not to text her. I'm trying to focus on school and work and drinking. I'm trying to stay out of the articles and the documentaries, trying to forget the Church and the Sinkings and Dad and all of it, trying to move on with my life. But I can't. When I take out the recycling, I have to force myself not to ask Muzi where Maggie's been. We talk about coffee and massages and it kills me. The whole time I'm thinking about her. Did she go back to the library that night? What was the service like? Did the cultists cross her neck and promise her parents had been delivered to Heaven? Did anyone notice the eyeliner stains on her sleeves, or did they throw a purple robe on her and lead her in prayer? What would have happened if I had gone with her?

I finally hear from her on a cloudy morning, a couple minutes after the white mocha guy comes in. He's on his phone again. Thankfully I know his order now, so I don't have to strain out the relevant words. The text comes right after I swipe his card.

> *Hey Jonas. Hope you're doing OK.*

I try to ignore it. I try not to think about the library or the color purple or the finality of consciousness upon death. I try not to think about anything at all except the fucking mocha. But my phone keeps vibrating, and every time, I check it.

> *Just wanted to let you know I did go to the service the other night. Honestly, I think it helped put a lot of things in perspective. I'm still skeptical, but I think I understand some things better.*

I slide a sleeve on a large paper cup and set it under the espresso machine.

> *I know you had a lot to say about the Church. Trust me, I get it 100%. I'm still processing a lot of what you said + my own thoughts about why I left.*

I pull two shots of espresso.

> *That's partially why I wanted to ask if you'd come with me next time.*

I squirt three pumps of white chocolate sauce onto the espresso.

> *I know it's a pretty crazy thing to ask. Especially from me. The thing is, they understood when I told them why I'd tried to leave. They really listened to everything I had to say about my parents, my doubts, everything. I think it might help you to have some of your thoughts heard, even if you don't like their answers.*

I stir the chocolate into the espresso.

> *Just so you know, they're totally accepting of all people too, no matter what.*

No idea what that's supposed to mean. I fill three-quarters of a stainless steel pitcher with whole milk and prime the steam wand.

> *It's totally noncommittal. If you come once you never have to again. I don't know how many more I'm really down for myself.*

I steam the milk. The angle has to be just right. Not too much foam for a mocha.

> *But I think I do want to try. Just until I get a handle on things. Especially if you come with me. I'd really love to hear how you feel about everything.*

I pour the steamed milk onto the chocolatey espresso and stir.

> *So yeah. Sorry for the novel. Just let me know!*

I spray the top with whipped cream and drizzle on more white chocolate. I hand it over to the customer and he stomps out, still on his phone.

On my break I let smoke drift away from my lips like a slow stream of bubbles.

WHERE WE MAKE HOME

HAZEL KIGHT WITHAM

When I wake, it is smoky dark and cold. I open my eyes to a night that doesn't yet hint at dawn. I feel the firm pad of the triangled flag below my head. One arm snakes out of the warmth of the sleeping bag. I run my hand along the rough concrete. It is cold. It is coarse. It is a tiny landscape below my palm.

Though the day will grow SoCal warm, at night the temperature plummets, especially here along the river.

I imagine the workmen who drove the concrete pourers, the smoothers, whatever big machines cemented over the earth and created the false banks of our sorry urban river. Below my hand, somewhere, maybe six inches, maybe a foot, maybe three, there is dirt that died for humankind's need to contain the world.

Along the river, the sludge of the city moves slowly. We are aching for rain, always. Ducks forage in two inches of water, nudging along the surface, their yellow feet unable to paddle.

This is the place I now call home. This place that is cold ground and open air and a canvas for whatever comes next.

⌐

I have to be the first one up. Once I know the night-black is blueing, I slither my arms out of my sleep clothes, and shimmy the binder up from my feet. I smooth out all the folds and press myself flat into boy-chest. Once I'm contained, I pull a warm shirt from the bottom of the sleeping bag, where I tucked it before sleep. I pull it over, slide out of my sweatpants, put on jeans, roll up the sleep clothes and stash them at the bottom of the bag. Near me, others are dreaming and free, and they will probably stay that way for at least a couple more hours.

My bare feet find the rough, cool concrete. I can feel the feathery leaves of the Chinese elm below me. I stay still for a moment to make sure no one is awake and then walk off a little ways, behind a bush to pee. When I return, I double up the sleeping bag and sit, my back against the cinderblock wall, the cold coming through my clothes to my skin.

The city's morning smells are these: dust, exhaust, and a hint of salt from the ocean a few miles downstream. I lean against the wall and breathe for the first ten or fifteen minutes after waking. Some might call it meditation. I call it peace. This time of day there are no threats, and the grief hasn't hardened into stone. An occasional car along the Overland Overpass is a small wave lapping the shore. The sky is brightening somewhere over the hills to the east, and no one is stirring, and I don't have to listen to anything but the last murmurs of night. Soon I hear the birds, their wakeup calls, their stories of surviving the dark.

My stomach is twisting itself into a pretzel of want. I pull on my shoes, roll up my bag, and stash it inside Eamon's tent. Time to get breakfast. I gather my hoodie around me and set out along the river. We are year three or four into what may be an epic drought, and I can't remember when rain last came. Certainly not since I've been outside.

A still-life is laid out before me, cast in grays and blues and blacks and purples, splashed here and there with streetlight. There is the bridge that spans the river, edged with gilded green guardrails. The looming condos that back up to the bike path. The chain-link fence beautified by purple bougainvillea that stretches up fifteen feet. The swan-necked streetlights craning over the yellow-dashed lines and sleeping cars. The now-and-then pairs of headlights carving the earliest hours.

The chain link is sharp on my hands, tight on my Converse toes. The morning rattle of the lock and chain; the thud of my feet landing on dead crabgrass. The whisper of some nocturnal creature ending its long dark day and settling in for sleep as its bright night approaches.

Two long blocks over, the Ralphs glows in its insomnia. The delivery trucks are just arriving.

Recon is the most important part of any mission. My mom taught me that long ago. You lie in wait, watching from the shadows, or mill about innocently, like you're trying to find what you need while you case the place — the longer the better. This morning, I'm watching, wedged between the dumpsters at the far side of the rear entrance.

To be a good thief, you need patience.

I didn't just develop these skills once I was living outside. I learned my thieving skills when I was housed, or semi-housed, during times we were so broke that my mom needed me to help. In times when money wasn't so tight, it became my secret act of rebellion; secrets were what kept me sane. Now I put these skills to good use.

I wait. I watch. I become part of the air of the place, invisible. And then, I strike.

As soon as the store swallows up the delivery guy with his loaded dolly, I scoot to the edge of the dumpsters, do a quick survey, and dash to the truck with my duffle bag. I am inside the truck before he has taken the first box inside, and I set to work with my box cutter on the Entenmann's box in the way-back. I only have time to slice open the top before I have to stop and wait. I can hear the Ralphs door open and some dude laughing at something someone said inside. I hear him come back up the ramp and pause, perhaps to consult his clipboard, then he moves closer in and pulls a few more boxes.

I am wedged in tight between the croissants and the muffins, box cutter in hand. He loads and goes, and then I slice the box down one side, put my open duffle next to it, and shove all the contents inside. Boxes of morning pastries. I slice the other side of the box, flatten it and fold it once, twice, three times as I hear the back door open again. He should only have one more load, but I'm good on time. As he heads in with his third load, I shove the folded box in with the goods, zip, and zoom.

By the time the delivery guy slams down the rolling door to the truck, I am charming Abigail at the Denny's across the parking lot, my bulging duffle tucked under the counter chair and a hot chocolate with a whipped cream skyscraper steaming in front of me.

"What's it gonna be this morning, Rio? Is it your birthday again? And what's that you're always carrying?"

The things we carry are the flotsam and jetsam of the city, as though we are the very river we so often sleep beside, carrying things that others have left or lost. The things we carry are scattered, sacred, and ever shifting.

Lost books are my treasures, but everyday things have a kind of shine out here too: shoelaces, duct tape, bungee cords, pennies, nickels, dimes, quarters, Metro cards, empty cups, empty water bottles, markers, cardboard. The things we carry are our beds on our backs, or we carry the weight of wondering if those beds will still be where we stashed them, if we choose not to carry them during daylight.

Among the necessities are hats, bandanas, sunglasses or reading glasses, sweatshirts or sweaters, socks, and shoes. We carry things in common sometimes: a Coleman stove, propane, a pot. We carry private things: pictures of our past lives, mementos. Eamon carries a lock of his daughter's hair from her baby days. Alonzo carries a small carving of a snail, made from some rock of the earth. Fareed carries a Spanish-English dictionary, even though he can't read. I carry a sketchbook and pencils, Sharpies, and oil sticks. I carry six-inch ACE bandages and an old-school Mariners baseball cap, even though I can't stand sports. I like the trident logo and the conversations it sometimes sparks with people who do care about organized athletics.

Ollie carries an old-fashioned shaving kit, the kind with the brush and metal tin cup that he wraps up with a thick hand towel to protect it. He is fastidious about his appearance in certain respects. He can't stand to have stubble, but his clothes go weeks without seeing the inside of a washing machine. He also carries a flipbook of autographs and well wishes from eighth grade graduation in the inside pocket of his long beige trench coat, which he wears in all weather. I've never seen his knees.

We carry towels, some hand, some bath. We carry hotel soaps and hotel lotions, tiny and too soon gone. We carry packs of baby wipes or Handi-Wipes swiped from KFC; some of us call the sludge from the river good enough. We carry the things we carry in backpacks and shopping carts and duffles. We carry the knowledge of secret places that are safe for sleeping, both day and night. We carry knowledge of bathrooms where we can wash up without being hassled, until one of us goes too far and gets us all banned or locked out by keys that are carried on key chains that say, "Restroom for Customers Only," or on keychains that are cow bells, blasting our business throughout the café.

And this: we carry our escapes, our tiny freedoms. Some of the men carry their needles or their pipes, their lighters or their matches, their rolling papers or their bottles, their belts or their grime-gray tourniquets pocketed from the free clinics and used again and again. They all carry the possibility of oblivion close to their chests, and when they don't, they carry a kind of panic only an addict can know — panic I witness, stand far from, and walk away from when I have to. When they are dry, they are rabid, and the others grow guarded with their own stashes.

Because they carry these things, these men that I have come to love, that I have come, in only three short months, to care for, I refuse to carry any escape of my own, or rather, any escape in the form of intoxicants, that fleeting ingestible danger-laden freedom. I find mine in the pages of my sketchbook, or on the little patches of concrete I sometimes paint into an alternate universe of promise, a place where there is a flicker of the possible. I seek my escape in the careful typed lines of books that I borrow illicitly from the library, books that I devour as rabidly as the drugs consumed by the men around me. One of those books: *The Things They Carried*, by Tim O'Brien.

And the intoxication of those handheld worlds is as dizzying and liberating as the highs that my guys seek. When I finish a book, I have to block off hours to soak in the glow of the story, the words still sparking, the scenes smoldering within me. I seek out parks or green spaces where few people go so that I can lie on the earth and look at the sky and marvel: some wordsmith under this same sky built a world from nothing, from air, and pressed it into life, into me, to help me experience someone else's anguish for a time so that I might have new hope for my own small, weary life.

My most recent trip was to Vietnam, carried by the words of O'Brien, into the soil and sorrow and horror of a place that so many of the men I see have been and have never really returned from. Eamon told me to get the book, told me it would help me understand better the things he carries, and the things Dustin, who served in the first Iraq war, sees when we have to tackle him and zip him up in his sleeping bag and sing Elvis tunes to him. Eamon says *The Things They Carried* conveys the travesty of the war better than anything he's read.

And so, last week when I went to the Julian Dixon Library for my school hours, I found it and settled into my favorite window nook, the one that looks over the parking lot, the river, the walking bridge, and the elementary school. But I was so lost in that first chapter, reading and rereading, I couldn't come close to finishing, and I found it was one of those books I couldn't let go of, couldn't leave without. And since I can't use my old library card anymore, and I couldn't part with it when closing time snuck upon me from nowhere, I had to take it.

There are only a few books I have had to do this with. Most I can stand to leave overnight, secreted in some spot where there's no threat of someone else getting it and checking it out. But some call to me, speak to me so fiercely I cannot have them be away from me. This is my addiction. Books that grab me by the throat, take me far away to more important places. They are my life rafts.

Books are also my education right now. And as Eamon promised, *The Things They Carried* is a masterclass on the impact of war on men, or women, or a people, or a person. The day I got my hands on that book, I carried it with me everywhere, lost in the jungle and rice paddies of Vietnam for a time, lost in an apocalypse of our own creation, aching right along with Lieutenant Jimmy Cross for his beloved but never-will-be-loved-by Marcia. That first chapter I read again and again, swept away by the burden of objects, and how parallel my own world is now with those men humping their homes on their backs. They carried their homes, as we do, they carried their protection, their hopes, their dreams of return.

That is something all of us carry, and it is more fragile than any of the men in O'Brien's regiment: the dream of return.

The dream of being visible again.

¬

After my fifth birthday breakfast in the past three months, I leave Abigail the biggest tip I can manage — $2.36 — and head out with my extra-large go-cup of black coffee and duffle into the dawn-cracked morning. By now the men are stirring and hungry. They are bleary-eyed and waiting. They are finishing their water bottles and pulling on clothes, relieving themselves under the shade of the trees along the south side of the river, where we have been stationed for the past few weeks.

No one has bothered us yet, though sometimes you see people over on the north side bike path peering over and pointing, squinting, and staring. I wonder who will press the cops to move us along. This is my favorite spot along the river so far.

My first night outside was three months or so ago, early June, about three days after my mom overdosed. It had been bad for a while, and I'd thought about leaving often, but I couldn't stand the thought of having to retake ninth grade, so I white-knuckled it through finals, and then once grades were in, I loaded up my father's old backpack from his Sierra hiking days. I shaved all my hair off, letting my old life float down around me in clumps onto the rose-tiled bathroom floor. I strapped a sleeping bag onto the bottom of the backpack frame and stuffed the pack with three days' worth of clothes, about four hundred dollars I had managed to squirrel away, and what food would keep for a few days. I grabbed my skateboard and hit the street one morning when I should have been watching movies in my English class.

I took buses from my old home in Silver Lake to the west side, the route burned in my brain from studying maps online. I knew that the 201 to the 204 would get me to Venice and Vermont, and from there the 733 Metro would take me straight to the ocean. The bus was full of students and people heading to work, carrying briefcases, backpacks, purses. I couldn't believe how careless so many were with where they dropped their bags while they became entranced by phone screens or fussing or, more rarely, reading a book. I people-watched and felt a calm take over my whole body, this wave of certainty that I hadn't felt ever. I watched the flow of people, on and off, on and off, for more than an hour as the bus drove and stopped, drove and stopped. A rhythm emerged: dings for stop requests, the great sighing of the doors opening, the squeak-squeal of them shutting. I was so present, so in that moment, no longer consumed by worry and anxiety. I pulled my Mariner's cap low, leaned my face against the glass, and dozed, my pack firmly wedged between my legs, my skateboard a shelf for my arms.

After I got off, I spent the early part of the day at the beach. It was just me, leaning against my pack, on cool soft sand, watching the grays of sky and water, the thick marine layer. I ran my hands through my newly shorn hair, marveling at the feel of fuzz. No one was there, since school was still in session and the tourists hadn't yet descended.

I had never felt so free, so alive, and yet also so aware of the depths of my grief, vast as the ocean before me. But somehow, being there, I could finally see it, take it in, along with the rush of my first taste of true freedom after the prison of childhood and adolescence, of being my mother's daughter. I sat and watched the surf lap the shore, lulled by the back and forth, back and forth. I couldn't remember the last time I was at the beach.

I never planned to be out as long as I have. I thought I would start classes when they rolled around mid-August. I imagined I'd hitch out somewhere to where distant family might step up and take care of me. Turns out no one seemed to look for me at all, especially when I started passing as a guy to be safer out here.

Instead, I found people who needed me.

Those first nights I could have slept at friends' houses, but I quickly felt the rush of freedom catch hold of me, and I didn't want to seek out yet another living arrangement. I wanted to be in charge. I had tasted what I thought was freedom, and I wanted more.

So, that first night I slept in a graveyard, a kind of test to see if I could do it. Holy Cross Cemetery on the hill overlooking Culver City, the Westside, a few miles away from the beach I'd spent the morning at. I walked in around dusk, when the pedestrian gate was still open, and wandered amid the tombstones awhile, calculating the ages of death. I paused at the ones where the birth and death year were too close: 2001–2004; 1974–1982; 1995–2010. My body ached at the untold stories, the young gone too soon. I wrote my brother's headstone in my mind:

Soren Ellison, 1992–2014

Son, Brother, Soldier, Beloved.

"Be a Lamp/Or a Lifeboat/Or a Ladder."~ Rumi.

An enlisted man with heart of a poet. He knew so many poems; would get that dreamy look in his eye just before reciting some jewel of a line. I keep trying to remember ones he once quoted or find them on my library days: a scattered and scavenged legacy.

In the cemetery, I found myself a perfect spot, under a tree near the top of the hill. There were just a few people wandering around and no one paid any attention to me. When the sun fell, after eight, I gazed out over the new space that seemed to be my life: a ghost-littered green land, full of haunting memories and waiting spirits.

Soren came to me that night. The flag they gave us when they brought the news was the pillow below my head. My brother. Long lost and still somehow with me. His voice in my dreams:

Riley, what are you doing? You can't make it out here alone. You need to go back home. You need to forgive. You need to hang on, just three more years, get your degree, go to college or enlist — scratch that, don't enlist. Get a job, get out. You can do this. I know you can.

But he's wrong. He's dead and he's wrong. I can't go home. My home is gone. Mom is gone. Riley is Rio now, a river in motion, bound for the sea.

That first night, I rolled out my sleeping bag on the cold grass underneath a tree near the top of the hill, where a few big mausoleums gave a little shelter, and I tried to sleep.

It was a long, long night surrounded by ghosts.

⌐

Eamon found me about a week in, when the shine of street freedom was wearing perilously thin.

I was lying on the grass in Carlson Park, where moms bring their infants who don't need play structures to enjoy outside time. The big houses surround three sides of the park; there are well-maintained bathrooms and tons of Chinese elms, palms, and drooping firs. It was the greenest place I could find in my new neighborhood, and easy to tuck away under a tree somewhere and sleep without fear.

It was probably about 10:00 a.m. when I felt a presence nearby. My stomach was growling at me anyway, making my nap a fitful one, my loneliness a hollow ache. I was curled around my backpack like it was a lover, my head resting on the roll of my sleeping bag, my face covered by a black T-shirt to block out the sun. I heard a humming nearby, and I found the thread of the song familiar. I pulled my tee part way down my face and peeked out. Two trees away was a long thin man with a mop of salt-and-pepper hair, doing a kind of slow-motion dance under one of the elms.

I listened and watched, and realized it was one of those martial arts, jujitsu or taekwondo. The man was humming his tune slowly and moving his arms and body even slower. He seemed to have left the petty world around us. I noticed his shirt was threadbare at the collar, his pants a bit ragged at the hems. His feet were bare, his eyes were closed, and something made me love him. Maybe it was the wisdom I could feel, even with his eyes closed, maybe the peace spread so smooth across his face, that made me think he was the grandfather I wish I'd had.

I lay there and watched him, feeling again the freedom of no one to answer to and nowhere to be. That feeling had been fleeting over the last week. It had thinned and thinned, until there were only a handful of moments each day when I could summon it. I'd even started thinking of going to the Valley to find my mom's sister somewhere in Encino or Woodland Hills, a woman I hadn't seen in at least eight years. But as I stared at this stranger, I decided against that, for now. I wanted to know what this man knew.

When he reached the end of the routine he stood quietly, his hands in prayer position, and waited for at least five minutes. Then he lowered himself to the ground and lay down, looked up at the sky for another ten minutes or so. I couldn't remember ever being so content to just watch someone as I was with this man. For some reason, he made me think of Soren, but in a good, "everything's gonna be all right" kind of way.

And then he was walking toward me, smiling, like he knew me from long ago. I pushed myself up from the ground and sat. Waiting for what? I wasn't sure.

"How are you, young friend? Enjoying the trees?"

I was caught, not knowing what to say, but then, dropping my voice to its raspy lower octaves, I answered: "I am, this park is so nice. What were you doing?"

"Oh, just my waking-up salutation. Some people rush into their day a little too quickly, I think. Breakfast, coffee, shower, without taking a minute to say hello to this world and life that is so astounding, don't you think?"

I smiled, stood, and stuck out my hand. "I do. But thank you, I think I needed reminding. My name is Rio."

"Hello, Rio. What a perfect name." He broke into several songs and a little shimmy: "Let the river flow. Many rivers to cross. Her name is Rio and she dances on the sand." He shook his head, like coming out of the music, and I wondered if he knew I was a she, like that Rio on the sand, if he already saw right through me.

"Most days I'm Eamon. Would you like go scare up a cup of coffee with me?"

And that was it. He just knew that we would get along, that we had something to offer each other. I shouldered my pack, envying his empty handedness, and followed him not to a café but a church nearby. Grace Lutheran: the place that posted funny messages on their announcement board, things

51

like, "Jesus turned water into wine, not whine. Come worship with us." I'd seen it in my explorations of the neighborhood, but never thought to go inside. My family was never very churchy.

On our walk, Eamon told me the history of Culver City, that it arose in response to the movie studios in Hollywood, that Henry Culver hoped it would become the "Hollywood of the West." Because of careful city planning, he said, these streets were his favorite in Los Angeles, with the trees that are all the same on each block, Chinese elms arching their twisted branches over the asphalt, or tall firs standing sentinel. He acknowledged that it was nothing like nature, which craves diversity, but that he liked the uniformity all the same; it let you really appreciate each tree for itself.

Eamon walked into the lobby of the church, empty of people at this time of day on a Tuesday, and went straight to a table that had a coffee maker, a tower of Styrofoam cups, and bowls of creamers and sugars. He poured his black. I made mine pale and sweet, and we took them outside to the bench in the church courtyard.

Eamon took a slurp and exhaled out the heat, and with it: "Rule Two: always know where you can find a decent cup of coffee, gratis."

I blew on my coffee. "What's Rule One?"

"First rule is find your people, of course."

I sipped. Did he know I was staying outside? I looked down at the backpack with the sleeping bag cinched to the bottom. I hadn't had a decent shower in a week, just sad little sink baths when no one else was in the bathroom at the parks I'd started to haunt. It wouldn't take a Sherlock to figure it out. I decided to test him out.

"And Rule Three?"

"Rule Three. Find the best places to get a good shower. Never go more than three days without one. You start to feel a little feral."

I stared at this man, his youthful eyes that crackled with laughter, his easy smile and lanky limbs, his gestures that were like a trained actor's. I felt like he could read my story without me offering a word.

┐

After coffee that morning, Eamon took me over to a condo complex right next to the river and across from the Julian Dixon Library. I'd been loitering in the library already. Found I could slip into the bathroom if I lingered by the water fountain and grabbed the door as someone was going out. I tried to stay invisible there, but it wasn't easy.

But the complex Eamon took me to had a shower off the pool. He showed me how to get in through the gates just after some car got in, and where to stash my giant pack, near the dumpsters (unless it's a Monday). He showed me how to get into the laundry room through the window, if the door was locked, and put in a load before hitting the shower. We took the back paths to the rec room, which was usually open, as are the restrooms. It was perfect — not too many people around, plus I had the cover of anonymity and could pretend I belonged in this giant complex. The shower was attached to a separate sauna room, and I was relieved when Eamon said, "Maybe another time."

That hot shower was one of the most exquisite pleasures of my life. A thing so simple, once withheld, can become a kind of paradise. I had been whittled down to so little in that first week that my appreciation for small things like showers or hot coffee or safe sleeping had exploded. The new shifting of priorities was surprising.

Afterward, we gathered my now-clean clothes, and it was a relief to have something that smelled fresh on my back, warm still from the dryer. My short hair didn't feel like there was earth embedded in it. We got my pack and left by early afternoon, and I felt brand new.

I felt like I'd figured out not just Rule Three but also Rule One.

┐

As I return to camp, the morning is pale and cool, but not for long. I stop before hopping the fence again and pull out two boxes of the baked goods, keeping the rest in the duffle so the guys don't gorge on them. I'd like the loot to last a few days. A week is a miracle. But it's okay; it's what it's here for. We are hungry.

When I have the offering ready, I whistle for Eamon. In a minute I hear him sweeping his feet through the leaves, and then he is here: long and lean like a willow, eyes still drifting inside a dream. I hand Eamon the pastry boxes and coffee, and he says in a quiet purr, "You're a prince, my friend. A prince."

I smile and wish those simple words didn't mean quite so much. Eamon's round glasses glint in the dawn light, and stubble speckles his face. With some attention, a good shower, a little of Ollie's shaving kit, and a suit, he could pass as a college professor. His voice is always gentle, and he is the one man in our crew I don't feel I have to take care of, even though I still find I try. He was a disciple of Timothy Leary way back in the late '60s, and he's been living the bohemian wanderlust life ever since.

Now the cemetery is months back, and I am encircled by more grounded spirits. The difference between us and other outside encampments is that we actually feel like a little community. Maybe I am being idealistic, though. Maybe my band is just wasted, wounded, once-warriors and I am trying to be the glue. But there's something to this.

I toss my duffle and scale the fence. When I land, Eamon puts a hand on my head. "You are a good kid, you know that? But you need to get your shit together, you hear? I can get my own coffee. Rule Two."

I smile and scoot out from his hand, shoulder the duffle, and set about getting breakfast to the ramshackle crew I belong to, along this paved river we've made home.

WHAT I LEFT BEHIND

DEBORAH WEISS

I was canning raspberry jam when I saw a funnel of dark smoke. We live in a remote part of the Santa Monica Mountains, on the ridge between the San Fernando Valley and Malibu, on the outskirts of Los Angeles. Our twisty dirt road is more akin to a trail than a street, with a steep drop-off on the west side and thick chaparral on the east, perilous for those unfamiliar with its narrow "s" turns and unpredictable potholes. The only public utility is electricity, and with the fire heading toward our property, I hoped our three water tanks were all full.

When I saw the flames dancing on the ridgeline through the kitchen window, I dialed 911, willing someone to answer the phone; no one ever did. But twenty minutes later, I heard sirens, then *whop, whop, whop* — the sound of helicopter blades. Then there were pink cascades of flame retardant ribboning down over the glow in the distance. Normally, I would have been mesmerized, but this was not a normal day.

My driveway looked like the freeway during rush hour, except instead of cars it was filled with every type of emergency vehicle.

"Ma'am."

I turned.

A firefighter with bright blue eyes said, "You should turn off the air conditioning, close the windows, and shut the doors. It'll help keep the ash out."

"Thanks, how much time do we have?" I asked.

The firefighter urged us to be ready to leave within the hour.

┐

I am an attorney. For nearly thirty years, I've been the problem-solver, the one who comforts clients by breaking down complex issues into digestible bites. But my lawyer hat must have been in the laundry when the fire started. I could neither slow down nor process what was happening. My plans were incomplete and confused. First, I grabbed documents, unsure what I was taking, running my fingers over the blue, mottled covers of our passports, opening each one. In a moment of clarity, I returned the expired passports to the safe and stuffed the current ones in my purse.

Then, suddenly, I remembered the animals: a pig named Julie, a poodle named Einstein, four parrots, fifteen chickens, and a turtle. I abandoned the safe, leaving papers strewn about, and left the duffle bags half-packed, to get the animals' carriers. This led to more pawing through my possessions, like a looky-loo at the flea market, and more indiscriminate grabbing, before finally rushing outside to begin packing the cars.

My son Tucker's black Hyundai sedan was already stuffed with three skateboards, an acoustic guitar, and a poster from a garage sale. Then, Tucker himself rushed past me, dragging the air compressor.

"What are you doing?"

"I gotta get the Navie running," he said without stopping.

Tucker was headed to my husband's old, bumper-less Lincoln Navigator with ripped seats and four flat tires. Tucker cherished the memories that car held for him and told me he was about to pump up the tires, charge the battery, and drive it to safety. After a short, staccato debate, Tucker agreed to focus on packing the functioning vehicles. The plan, such as it was, was for me to evacuate all the animals that could fit in my car, while my husband and son loaded the remaining animals into their cars.

My husband and son had other plans.

"We need to leave now," I urged.

"We have a better chance of saving the house if I am here. The firefighters will stay to defend the house," my husband insisted.

My husband's health, incidentally, was precarious at best. Ralph, sixty-one, my childhood sweetheart, was overweight and diabetic. Yet with one foot swollen from gout, he strode around the property like he had everything under control, oblivious to his obvious frailties.

"We don't need the house; we need each other," I countered.

"I talked with the firefighters and we have a plan," Ralph said.

Switching angles, I turned to my son, "Tucker, *you* need to leave. We can rebuild the house; it's too risky to stay."

"Like I'm gonna leave Dad here?" he said.

He paused, then continued, "The cars will be ready. If it gets bad, I'll make sure to get Dad out."

Tucker, twenty-three, with expressive deep brown eyes and olive skin, was fit and strong. And though he and my husband weren't saying it, both felt a visceral need to stay with the chickens, the two parrots, and a turtle that wouldn't fit in my overstuffed car. If the situation became dire, Ralph and Tucker would somehow make room for the birds and Speedy the turtle, leaving the chickens behind. I tensed my hands into fists as I watched my husband hobble away. He was imagining himself a superhero, saving the day. But in reality, he was taking what seemed to me to be an unacceptable risk.

My animals had no choice. Turning toward the chicken coop, I could feel my chest tightening. If I opened the gate, they would be killed by coyotes or bobcats. If they remained and the fire reached them, they would die a gruesome death. But not even a shoebox would fit in my car now. The chickens had to stay, even Ruth Bader Hensburg, a black bantam chicken with a white head, who loved to be held and eat from my hand. She was my therapy chicken; they all were. During stressful or difficult times, I sat in their enclosure, calmed by the clucking.

As a Californian, I have lived with the fear of fire my whole life. Growing up in Laurel Canyon, I remember my mother racing home across Mulholland Drive with my sisters, brother, and me in the car when we heard there was a fire heading toward our house. My beautiful mother, with her perfect auburn hair, styled in a Beverly Hills salon, pleaded with the police officer who had blocked off the road, telling him we had to get home to turn on the sprinklers. I now understood her urgent pull toward home.

Meanwhile, an endless stream of strangers was descending on our property: sheriffs and people with press passes, hikers and their dogs, and families with kids seeking a better vantage point for watching the flames. While they socialized, I continued to pack. Black specks coated every surface in the house and a noxious charcoal odor lingered in the air. My throat felt dry and prickly from the smoke. There was soot in my hair, under my nails, on my clothes and feet; my skin felt sandblasted in the hundred-degree heat of the June day, at nearly 7:00 p.m.

I could feel wrinkles forming on my face filled with ash as I slipped into the driver's seat. Then, in my rearview mirror, I saw what looked like a flying pig coming in my direction. My son raced toward us carrying Julie, all squirming hundred pounds of her, against a backdrop of smoke. Even though pigs are part of the even-toed ungulate family, Julie was more human than most people. With her soulful eyes and heart-shaped face, she looked like a person, except for her snout and black-and-white, bristly fur. She lived in our house and slept in her own bed. And, like me, she was feeling tense and vulnerable. As he ran, Tucker fought to keep Julie's flailing head still while she relentlessly sought to break free, screaming like only a pissed-off pig could.

"I froze a bunny just by staring at it," Tucker told me once, convinced that he could communicate with animals. But he didn't appear to be telepathically calming the pig.

Einstein, our scruffy poodle mix, was quiet, draped across the driver's seat while I played a lightning round of Tetris, trying to jam in as many bird cages as possible. Carriers were stacked on cages leaning on larger cages filled with parrots. I'd adopted three of the birds five years earlier from a former client of mine who'd died homeless and friendless. The fourth parrot, Babalouie, had belonged to my husband since before we married. Babalouie was jealous by nature, and we had never gotten along. Across the driveway, fifteen chickens stared at us from their enclosed yard. I had gotten them when they were a day old, and they lived in the house with Julie until they were old enough to go outside. As adult hens, they were tall and thin with large feather headdresses, and they strutted around their yard like Las Vegas showgirls, clucking and cooing, contentedly unaware of the rising danger. But there was no way to load them into the car with the dog, parrots, and pig. The Hobson's Choice haunted me. I could not get past the terrible feeling of choosing parrots over my chickens.

When the firefighters told us to leave, I scooped pills and insulin for my husband into a duffle bag. Later, I could not remember which duffle held the meds or which car the duffle was in. I was too mad at my husband to say goodbye. But before driving off, I glanced at my hens, mouthing, "It's gonna be okay."

I sped off like an avatar in a video game, maneuvering around fire trucks, hoses, and boulders. In the imaginary competition, I lost points if I collided with a firetruck or went off the edge of our precarious road. And like in a video game, there were numbers in front of each house — though they did not represent points. Instead, the neighbors had made signs to inform the firefighters how much water they had stored in their tanks.

I drove my menagerie to my friend's house outside of the mandatory evacuation area. When I arrived, Gemma rushed outside, anxious to help. She insisted that Julie could sleep in the guestroom. "We're about to remodel it anyway," she said.

Finally, separated from the fire, my mind returned to its normal speed. Then I remembered Julie had destroyed an old encyclopedia just that morning, pulling out the pages and crumpling them out of boredom. She had a sensitive stomach and was subject to bouts of vomiting; she could not stay in Gemma's guestroom. And without Tucker, I could not lift Julie out of the car.

So, Einstein and I followed Gemma inside while the other animals stayed in the car. She insisted again that we all stay at her house for the night.

"Think about it, have a glass of wine, and relax," Gemma said.

But by that time, the sun had set, the wind had died down, and the temperature had cooled. I called my husband, who said the firefighters had begun to contain the fire. It was time to go, so Tucker could put Julie in her own bed.

I thanked Gemma, backed down her driveway, and headed toward home.

Since then, there have been more fires. There always will be. For some, I've been well prepared; for others, less. Sometimes, I think it's time to say, "Okay, Mother Nature, you win, we're leaving." Instead, I bought a van so that my chickens won't be left behind.

THE LONG DROP

RACHAEL WARECKI

The blonde girl on the other side of the rooftop hadn't come dressed for a fight. She wore a white dress with faded green polka dots, in a style you might trot out for a picnic, topped off by her wide blue eyes and a button nose and ears that stuck out a little, like a moth tentatively spreading its wings in a flyswatter's shadow. She could've played somebody's daughter in one of those wholesome family pictures, the kind where no one ever drinks anything stronger than milk or says anything heavier than *gee whiz*. Instead, they'd put her up against me. I was stronger and heavier than any punch she could throw, on account of being about half a foot taller, and I stood to make some money if I beat her. Maybe even more if I beat her to death. Boyle Heights chisme said she'd set a foot wrong with the Cohen gang, and no one would shed any tears for a dead woman, especially one who'd left her common sense in her dressing gown pocket. There were more than enough of us to go around.

The girl's face spasmed as we looked at each other across the blanket that was our ring. She was plenty scared.

I couldn't face her head on, her or any of the other women who had come out onto the rooftop and settled themselves around the blanket like bloodhounds waiting for a fox. They had that purebred quality about them. Weak chins and hard eyes and enough money to act like weak chins and hard eyes were moral virtues. It was all I could think about anymore — how much everything cost. Just a year ago it was all anyone could think about. The Depression had hit Los Angeles as hard as anywhere else, but the papers said we were pulling ourselves out of it quicker, thanks to the way the movie people printed money. Now everyone was flush, except for me and my mother and the girl across the rooftop. No one cared if we beat each other's brains in if it meant they could throw their cash around.

I tilted my head back. A few clouds hung in the hot blue sky, as flat and false as a painted Hollywood backdrop, and overlaid with a sheen of smog to remind me where I was. Sharing the same sky, that was as close as most people in Boyle Heights came to Hollywood, outside of a theater. Hell, maybe even the sky over there was nicer.

I turned to my mother and said, "This is the best bout you could get me?"

"What did you expect, Margarita? Nine years you've been on the circuit, off and on. People don't want to step up just to get knocked down."

"You could've gotten me something with a bigger purse, for starters. Five bucks, and that's before it's split. Two-fifty might cover some of what daddy owed to the liquor store — or maybe we can throw it down the hole and the bank will take a nice deep breath before they start trying to blow the house down again."

She shrugged. Her brown eyes were as flat and faded as the haze above us. I had gotten plenty used to that shrug and the flat stare and her haunted, unsmiling mouth over the past few months. My father had died gambling at the racetrack. My mother crumpled when his friends from Santa Anita brought us the news, until she was as wadded and useless as the dollar bills my father had shoved at his creditors. It was a small tragedy any time a man died, considering how many we'd lost, but his death had ripped through my mother's life like a torpedo through the hull of the *Lusitania*. She had met my father when they were both seventeen, a pair of boxing gloves slung over her shoulders and brand-new immigration papers burning a hole in her pocket. He had been her entire life in America: her Boyle Heights and her Los Angeles and the whole damned country wrapped into one. He'd been a pretty poor example of it, if you asked me. All the same, I felt like a screw had come loose inside me. My father was dead and the old Californio families were trying to rustle up signatures for a secession vote to put on the November ballot and Eleanor Roosevelt was running for president and Hitler had invaded Poland seven months ago. Maybe a screw had come loose all over the whole damned world.

"That's just the purse you know about," my mother said. "So, the rumors are true?"

She shrugged again and stared at the girl on the far side of the roof. She could have been that other girl's mother instead of mine, at least in the looks department. She was small and honey-blonde and had fought as a flyweight when she'd been on the rooftop circuit. I was tall and dark-haired and looked a little like Gene Tierney, from the magazine covers. The both of us, mother and daughter, boxed like Midget Wolgast. We ducked, we dodged, we rolled. Or at least we used to. The last few years, I had started to use my height and my long arms to a greater advantage. The last few months, my mother had forgotten how to duck, dodge, and roll altogether.

"The rumors are just rumors," she said. "Chisme."

She had spent most of her childhood in northern Spain and Madrid, then a few years in Mexico City, and those places had left their imprints on her voice. "Nobody tells me the chisme anymore, not since your father —"

She turned away and looked out over the edge of the roof. Three stories down, Boyle Heights was preparing for the weekend. A stream of black-hatted, bearded men and modestly wigged women flowed down the sidewalk toward the Breed Street shul. For the rest of the neighborhood — all the Irish and Japanese and Mexican families — it was just another summer Friday afternoon. The smell of popcorn drifted up from the theater on Brooklyn and a warm-up band in the Rojo Room wailed a few octaves. Pretty soon the kids from Roosevelt High would start making their way to the main drive, the Catholics going home to their fish dinners, the Jews to Shabbat services, and the Shinto to their kamidana. It was the only kind of Friday afternoon I'd ever known. I'd missed it since we'd left, but with a childish longing, a kid prodding the gap where a tooth used to be, wondering what else she'd lose along the way to growing up.

"There's not enough money otherwise to keep this up," I told my mother's shoulder. "I'm twenty-five. Sure, people don't like it when I beat them now, but the tables will turn pretty soon. And then they'll like to beat me too much."

She didn't say anything. She kept staring out over the roof's edge, as if the fall could break her neck if she just thought about it hard enough.

"I'll leave school," I went on. "Go full time at the diner, pick up a few more shifts."

Below us, a pair of Orthodox women scurried down Brooklyn with their bags from the market. They didn't want to be caught carrying after sundown. It was how I had earned back some of the money my father had gambled away — carrying keys and opening doors and running errands on the Sabbath for several women who'd found that holiness had its inconvenient side, but it could be overcome with a small cost. I supposed if your mind was flexible enough, you could bend it through any loophole.

I said, "I've even been thinking about joining the police. They've got women detectives now. Better pay than the diner. A good pension, too."

My mother made a noise like a gull being strangled. "The neighborhood would never have us back."

"They don't want us anyway."

It sounded petulant, and I meant it to. Across the blanket, the timid blonde girl jumped and quivered and twitched at the sharpness in my voice. "It's not like widowhood's catching."

"Maybe not now." She plucked at the sleeve of her dress, a somber black number. "But before, you were just a baby — you couldn't know how it felt. Three years of war and then the flu, coming together like that. Sometimes it felt like every day someone's husband was dying, someone's brother, someone's son. All the neighborhood women, except me, hanging black curtains and planting poppies in their window boxes. Then they watched your father run around, drinking and betting on the ponies, and they thought maybe death should have caught up with him long before it did."

"Still, they could have lifted a hand to help us. And now where are we? In Angeleno Heights, living off John and Betsy. Think about it for a second, will you? John doesn't want his mother around, not with his new wife."

She settled back into brooding silence. The weight of her grief had become a physical thing, so heavy that I thought the force of it might pull her off the roof. I put a hand on her shoulder and said, "This is my last bout."

That startled her. "What?" she said, but her voice was distant, as if she had snatched it back from the edge of a long drop.

"This fight and then I'm done. It's not worth it. I can make more money other places, doing other things." I tightened my grip on her shoulder. "You taught me to fight because you said I needed it — would need to know how to be tough to make it anywhere in the world. We've got ourselves into a tough situation, so I'm doing the tough thing."

She plucked her sleeve again. Her gaze wandered over the women gathered around the blanket, and a small flame sparked behind her eyes. "This one will be worth it," she said.

I followed her stare. There were about twenty women with blank, bored faces, sitting around the blanket the same way you'd sit around a bonfire on the beach, waiting for something to happen and realizing the waves would only ever go out and in until the fire burned itself out. Several more women were standing, passing each other money and betting slips and laughing with forced heartiness. They were from some other neighborhood, there on a promise of a good show, and were impatient for it to get started. A few stood, keeping their own counsel, smoking and watching me and the blonde girl. One of them was Becky Cohen.

She was a small woman, a few years older than me, brown-haired and brown-eyed, compact without being dainty. Her brother, Mickey, was in Las Vegas, building up some fancy hotel under Bugsy Siegel's gimlet eye. Becky was watching over things while he was gone, bootlegging boys across the border from Mexico to serve as companions for all the rich, lonely American women. It was sort of a family business, run by a few kids who had taken all the wrong childhood lessons from the Old Testament — the parts where God went around smiting people who'd hacked Him off and feeding them to large fish. Mickey had gone to jail every so often, which meant he knew all the wrong people and had killed some of them, too. Becky had gone to college, which meant she knew the right words to smooth things over with the right people when the wrong people ended up dead.

Across the ring, the blonde girl was watching Becky with the nervous energy of a bank teller watching a customer walk in with a violin case.

"Is the purse really worth all that?" I asked my mother.

She made a listless gesture with her hands. "I don't care about the money. You were the one going on about doing the tough thing."

"Someone has to care," I said, but her expression had gone flat again, like someone had let all the air out of her personality. She went back to looking out over the neighborhood, the towering Sears-Roebuck warehouse and the squat Mexican market and the immigrant community center, picking out her memories of John Mitchell Sr. and fixing them to each place like stamps. It was the only currency that mattered to her.

The woman refereeing the bout rose to her feet. A decade ago she had fought as a heavyweight, going up against a lot of large, square women with enough muscle and horsepower to run a fleet of Cadillacs. Over the years, her opponents had battered her until her features had flattened into vague masses that every so often moved slowly toward each other to form something new, like continental drift.

"Rita Mitchell and Ruth Henderson," she said, "take your positions."

I strode to the near corner of the blanket. The blonde girl — Ruth — pussyfooted to the far corner. The sun beat down on our heads. It baked the roof, and the smell of hot asphalt was as familiar to me as a roast from Canter's or perfume from Sears-Roebuck. The muscles in my back clenched and relaxed and clenched again, warming themselves up. I felt a twinge along the tip of my right ear where some middleweight had clipped me back in '32, when I was seventeen and wild, and the dull ache in my left knee where I had twisted away from a bruiser trying to land a knockout. They were warnings or memories or lessons — all the things that could happen if I wasn't careful or ready enough. My shoulders loosened. In some ways I would never stop being ready for a fight. It was how my mother had taught me to be a woman.

The referee blew her whistle.

The blonde girl flung herself at me. She boxed like Midget Wolgast, too, but not because anybody had taught her how. She fought like anyone would fight if they wanted to stay alive.

She darted under the reach of my long arms and flailed a small fist in the direction of my ribs. She glanced a punch off my armpit before I could adjust my feet, flew free of my wingspan, and then threw a wild, desperate haymaker toward my chin. It connected. A small army of bees stung their way up my jawline, and I sat down hard.

When I got up, little blonde Ruth was back in her corner, and a few of the ringside women were booing. The referee pushed a wad of chewing gum around her mouth. She kept the rest of her face indifferent. The rules of our ring were loose. Her job was to count to ten when one of us went lights out — if she remembered how to count that high. Our job was to keep our fight in our fists and put on a good show. Other than that, we didn't give much of a damn for any Marquess of Queensbury. He had never had the joy of fighting on a rooftop.

I brushed myself off and Ruth charged at me again. I let her. I had always figured that boxing was sort of like being a lion in Roman times — you had to let the gladiator think he had a chance, for a little while. Ruth tried to dart in again, but I kept her at bay, jabbing at her like she was a speed bag, not putting too much weight behind it, enjoying the old familiar rhythm in my muscles. She tucked her arms in tight to her sides and flung her gloves up to shield her face. My jabs bounced off them. There was more booing from the sidelines. This time they were booing her. She was turning the fight dull.

"Ruin her face, sweetheart!" one of the ringside women shouted, shoving a handful of bills at the woman next to her. She herself had the kind of face you could only maintain with money. I let the girl dart in again. When she got close, one arm thrusting toward my sternum, I hissed, "What did you do to get in bad with the Cohen gang?"

She pulled the punch and looked up at me, blinking. I clouted her down low, near her hip, so that she wheezed and buckled into my shoulder.

"This isn't a tea party," I said, keeping it quick and quiet. "We're still in the ring. Act like it."

"The numbers," she whispered. She rapped the side of her head against my chin so that I reeled backward, and then she ducked back out of the reach of my arms. An ache settled into my jaw. The rank sweat of her fear filled my nose. When the referee blew her whistle for a break, little blonde Ruth came over to me. There was a curious look on her face — a bank teller beginning to believe that there might be a violin in the violin case after all.

"I thought you'd be wiping the floor with me by now," she said. There was nothing against fraternizing with your opponent between rounds, but she kept her voice low just the same. "Why don't you put your heart into it?"

"I don't have much to put in at the moment," I told her. "I'm feeling pretty heartless."

She chewed at the dry skin on her lower lip and squinted up at the sky and then down again. "I appreciate it, I guess. Not many people would go easy on a girl just because it's her first fight."

She didn't sound like she appreciated it at all. Her face had started its twitching and jumping act. Every so often she threw a glance over toward the audience. She was working hard not to look at Becky Cohen. The muscles around her eyes spasmed with the effort.

I led her away from the blanket, off to the side where it would be harder to hear us.

Becky watched us go. My mother stayed in my corner of the ring. She kept running her fingers over her dress to smooth the fabric, as if my father's ghost might show up at any moment and she needed to look her best.

"What did you mean about the numbers?" I asked Ruth. "Plenty of people play Italian bingo without rating a personal appearance from Becky Cohen. What the hell makes you so special?"

"Not me. My boyfriend. He played the numbers and got sunk, the kind of sunk you don't get out of. So, he decided to start over someplace the Cohens couldn't touch him."

"There's no place on earth the Cohens couldn't touch. I've heard they've got friends in New York and Chicago and Detroit. Hell, Mickey even boxed in Cleveland for a while. If they could get to a man in Cleveland, they could get to him anywhere."

"I believe it." Even breathing hard, her voice had that rounded *gee-willikers-mister* enunciation of children on radio programs. She was working hard to be ingratiating. She would get stuck in your teeth if you let her.

I glanced back at my mother. She was staring at something beyond us, out toward our old neighborhood. I let her stare. I said to Ruth: "What's this all got to do with you, anyways? You don't look like the type to fight the Cohens' battles for them."

"I'm collateral."

"What do you mean?"

74

"Becky put the word out. If my boyfriend didn't come back and start paying his debts, she'd put me down." She traced a finger up and down her arm and stared at the asphalt. "He hasn't come back, that I've heard."

"Sounds like Becky needs a better bargaining chip."

An emotion I couldn't read pulled the corners of her mouth downward. She looked like a fish that had swallowed a hook and now felt the yank of some invisible line. She reminded me of a woman in a poem I'd read at school, who'd gotten sick of staring at shadows and looked away from the mirror in her tower, trying to catch a glimpse of something real. She'd gotten an eyeful of darkness. She hadn't known what was coming for her, away from her pretty mirror with its gentle reflections, but she couldn't hand back the trouble she'd found. That wasn't the way trouble worked. Most of the time, it found you whether you'd gone looking for it or not, and half the time it was other people's trouble that they were happy to let you borrow, with interest. It was another kind of debt with another kind of cost.

"You know where he went," I said.

"I sent him a letter. I told him what was going on. I tried to explain, but I don't think he believed me. He isn't a very serious person, my boyfriend. He didn't take the numbers seriously at all, to begin with — it was all on paper, for the most part. He doesn't believe anything he can't see right in front of him, and because he couldn't *see* any bills, it didn't seem real to him."

"He took it seriously enough to get out of town and leave you holding the bag."

She caught her bottom lip between her teeth and bore down on it until it bled. Her mind was plenty flexible, but she was having trouble finding the loophole.

"I thought maybe if I let Becky hurt me, just a little, I could go to him and then — then he'd understand," she said. "He'd understand what he owes, and then he'd come back home and we'd work to settle it, the two of us together."

It was stuff straight out of a weepy program, but her eyes were large and shiny with sincerity. A vein started to pulse in my forehead, thumping away, getting good and worked up and sending flashes of red dancing across my vision, like a toreador waving his cape. All the men that women threw themselves away on, even now. I couldn't see why. Some neighborhood boys had taught me how to box a bigger opponent, but mostly they had grown up fighting to cling to whatever small power they could still reach — running out on their wives and spending their daughters' pocket money and passing around social diseases like a pack of cigarettes. And instead of writing them off as a bunch of bad jobs, their wives and daughters and girlfriends sat and cried until they came home. Now the men were busy gathering in bars and garages, wondering about the bigger fight they thought was coming now that Hitler was shoving his way into France. The papers said that if Eleanor won the presidency, she would start shipping boys over to Europe right away to help the Allied effort. I bet she wouldn't think twice about it. Two and a half million American men had died since 1915, between the flu and the first war. It had been a brave new world for women for twenty-five years, and sometimes I felt like I was the only woman brave enough to seize it. Me and Eleanor Roosevelt and Becky Cohen.

"You know what you get if you win?" I said to the girl. "Most of five bucks, if that. A little of it will go to me, and some will go to the referee and whoever organized this damned bout, and you'll get the rest. That's what Becky Cohen's decided your life is worth, at least in the public eye. A little less than five bucks."

She smiled at me. "You think I'll win?"

I didn't answer. She kept right on smiling as the referee motioned us back to our corners.

She was still smiling when the whistle blew, until I threw a haymaker that caught little blonde Ruth Henderson right in the sternum.

It felt good enough that I did it again. In fact, it was a wonderful feeling. A breeze whipped over the rooftop and sweat dripped down my back and the ringside women whooped at me to knock the blondie stiff. I set about with my knocking equipment. I was there to give them a show, after all. I forgot all about Midget Wolgast and fought like a heavyweight — I tried to put my fists through every one of the green dots on Ruth's pretty picnic dress. She doubled over, spat, tried to catch her breath. Bruises started to form on her chin and arms and collarbone, and I imagined her insides turning slack and pulpy. If she wanted to get hurt a little, I was happy to oblige. I had taken enough knocks. I was getting tired of trying to come back from them.

She tried to dodge the fifth blow, but the first four had put a stagger in her step. She fell down and got up and then fell again. I stalked toward her, and she scrabbled backwards toward the edge of the roof until her back was up against the short concrete ledge that kept anyone from wandering off the rooftop. Behind me I felt all the ringside women staring at us. I felt one gaze more than most. It occurred to me that a hard punch could send Ruth up and over and a few stories down. The drop was long enough. It would look like an accident in the heat of a bout. It wasn't a very nice idea, but I had run out of nice ideas around the time the first collector had come to our door. Nice ideas didn't pay off debt.

Ruth could tell what I was thinking. "It would be easier if you knocked me off," she panted. "Hit me hard, tip me over." Her eyes had a beseeching look. The sunrise purple of a shiner was swelling up around her right lid, and this time her smile hung crooked on her face, like a welcome sign on a cheap motel. She was trying to get me to borrow her trouble. "Please," she said. She sounded like she was about to cry. "It'd be quicker than whatever *she's* going to do to me. It would hurt less." She gazed over her shoulder at the fall waiting behind her, and in that instant she looked like my mother, plumbing the depths of her sad, small life, searching for the fastest way to get to the bottom.

I wiped the sweat off my face and looked down at her. If I won this fight, I would be in debt to my mother's suffering, and if I threw the fight, we would be further in debt to my father's creditors, and if I tossed Ruth off the roof, I would be in debt to Becky Cohen, in a way that she would remind me of every so often when it was least convenient. There was no way I could see how I wouldn't owe something to somebody. There would always be a cost. And I still had to look in the mirror every morning and live with what I saw. There was only one way I could see to do that.

I said, "Don't be so sure."

I stepped back a few paces and let Ruth lift herself to her feet. For such a small woman it took some heavy lifting. She was carrying everything with her, all the wrong choices she'd made, the knowledge that her boyfriend had left her high on a rooftop and no one was coming to lift the weight of the trouble she'd borrowed for him, and that Becky Cohen would kill her eventually, little by little or all at once. I should have felt sorry for her. Instead, I just felt sick of her troubles. I had enough trouble of my own.

This time, when she charged at me, I threw all my weight behind my right fist and drove it up and into the soft rounded point of her chin.

It was as heavy a punch as I had ever thrown. The purebred ringside women gasped as if they had one set of lungs, and in the silence that followed, there was the quiet pop of Ruth's neck snapping backward. The force of the blow buckled her legs and flung her toward the edge of the roof. Her head cracked briefly against the concrete ledge on the way down. That made a louder sound — a deep, soft thump, like the noise a body might make if it hit the sidewalk below. She hadn't fallen as far as that, just to the rooftop asphalt. A short drop, about the distance from the curb to the gutter. Her head rolled slowly to her shoulder. After that she didn't move.

I stood over her body and the ring suddenly felt very far away. My breath was heavy in my chest, the sun heavy against my back and shoulders, and the noise of Brooklyn Avenue heavy in my ears. I watched a lone woman hurry toward the shul, glance up at the horizon, calculate the number of minutes standing between her and trouble. Another Friday afternoon. The woman disappeared and behind me I heard the referee blasting her whistle, like she was sounding the horn to kingdom come. Becky Cohen was clapping. She certainly thought I'd done my best. My mother was still staring distantly, and for once she looked like all the other women there. To a woman, they looked haunted.

I didn't move. I just stood over Ruth and waited.

Underneath her pale delicate lids, the girl's eyes twitched. Her lashes fluttered. She took a breath. I watched as the world slowly came back to her. She didn't like it very much.

"I didn't die," she whispered.

"You didn't win, either." I pressed my gloves together, relishing the strain in my arms. Below us, the warm-up band in the Rojo Room took a long tour around a few lively scales. It was just the right sound for a summer evening. When all this was done and I turned my winnings over to my mother, she would go to mass at St. Mary's to pray for my father's ghost and I would go down to the Rojo Room and pass the word around that I had won my final bout. It would earn me a couple drinks on the house. For a few hours I wouldn't have to pay anything to anyone, and the only cost would be to myself. It was how I would live the rest of my life, if only the world would let me.

"You should've let me," Ruth said. "Win or die — you should have let me do one or the other." She still hadn't moved. She snatched her blue gaze away from the place where Becky Cohen stood and turned it up to me. "What am I going to do?"

"Well, you certainly won't thank me," I said. "But you won't owe me, either."

HUEVOS FRITOS

LUCY RODRIGUEZ-HANLEY

Amelia opened the door to her office suite on the seventeenth floor of a West Los Angeles high-rise and picked up the *New York Times*, the *Los Angeles Times*, and the *Wall Street Journal* that were slipped under the door. In about an hour, the other assistants would stroll in and she would pretend to care about their brunches, hikes, and weekend shenanigans.

She turned on the cappuccino machine, craving a cup, but she didn't want to caffeinate the embryo she hoped was growing inside her. She took a quick look in the cupboards and refrigerator and made a mental note to remind Paulette to order more seaweed and kombucha for the office.

With a single touch of a sleek remote control, the blinds went up, the sunshade came down, and the lights turned on in the conference room. She commanded Alexa to adjust the temperature and then watched the sun rise over the Wilshire Corridor. She said a prayer to La Virgen, wishing the Virgen was as compliant as Alexa.

Amelia was on edge.

Should she pee on a stick, even though the transfer was four days ago? She knew that it was possible to get a faint line. She also knew not to set herself up for disappointment. At her doctor's recommendation, but to her and Diego's unease, the doctor had implanted three embryos in the hope of getting her pregnant with one healthy baby. This was her third round of IVF, and she hoped the third time with three embryos would be the charm.

Should she pee on the stick and potentially ruin the rest of her week? Because once she started, there was no going back. Before the transfer, she bought three boxes of the expensive pregnancy tests, the ones that can detect the rising pregnancy hormone two days before the other pregnancy tests. She had two of them in her purse. She was going to hold her urine for another hour to give her body a chance to produce enough HCG to at least yield a faint line.

She stored her Marc Jacobs bag in the bottom drawer of her desk. She had yet to turn on her computer, and the phone was already ringing; she let the call go to voicemail. As the assistant to the two CEOs at a private equity firm, she was the right hand to a Masters of the Universe husband-and-wife team who made millions faster than traffic clogged up the 405.

Amelia heard the back door open; the clank of Manolos on the marble floor let her know that Campbell was early, even though Campbell was never early. She took a deep breath, and before she could exhale, Campbell's Birkin bag plopped onto the desk in the cubicle next to hers. Campbell took something out of her bag, hid it behind her back, and walked over to Amelia, giddy with the anticipation of a child about to sit on Santa's lap.

"Guess what!" Campbell squealed.

Before Amelia tried to guess, Campbell shoved an ultrasound picture so close to her face that her nose got a paper cut. Amelia tried to swallow the giant lump that constricted her throat.

"Congratulations!" Amelia said, mimicking Campbell's squeal, though her eyes started to betray her.

"Oh my God, are you okay? You're bleeding," Campbell said.

Amelia touched the tip of her nose and felt blood flow from the thin slice. She shook her head. "The paper cut, it really hurts." She reached into the bottom drawer for her purse. "I need to take care of this." She wiped the blood off but in a few seconds felt another thin line emerge from the tip of her nose. Before she made it to the bathroom, she had a full-on nosebleed. She reached into her bag hoping to find a Band-Aid, but all she had was a panty liner and a pregnancy test begging to get peed on. She stood in front of the mirror feeling sorry for herself; a panty liner on her nose and a pregnancy test whispering sweet nothings to convince her to open it. And now, she had to pee, badly.

Amelia raced to the toilet and struggled to open the pregnancy test. Her bladder wanted to empty itself, but the plastic wrapper was like steel mesh. She tried to bite it off and almost lost a tooth, but then the bag finally opened. Urine rained on the stick. Amelia crossed herself and the test; she willed it to return a BFP — a Big Fat Positive.

A memory of her younger self barged in. She said three Hail Marys, hoping to shoo it away and forget about the boy she slept with when she was seventeen, the one who was nice enough to come to her house and tell her that he had tested positive for chlamydia. The one who was now an A-list movie star. She had crushed on him when they met in drama camp in sixth grade. Amelia didn't see him again until they were seventeen, when Josh was a regular on the TV show her mother played the mom in. On the show, Josh was best friends with one of her mom's TV kids.

Amelia and Josh had sex in his trailer a couple of times. While all her friends fantasized about him, she had him all to herself while his girlfriend was away at college. It made her feel badass and grown-up, but she kept the relationship to herself because her mother would have killed her if she'd ever found out.

She sat on the toilet staring at a BFN, Big Fat Negative. Thirty thousand dollars wasted on three rounds of IVF was too much to take on a Monday morning. She often wondered if chlamydia was to blame for her lack of fertility. She should have gone to Planned Parenthood and gotten herself tested back then. Josh had offered to put her in touch with the set nurse, who recommended a gynecologist to his girlfriend and the other girls Josh slept with, but she was afraid her mom would find out. She was twenty-three the first time she went to a gynecologist; her pap and STD test came back negative, and she got the HPV vaccine as an extra precaution. It was likely Josh gave her chlamydia, and it was likely it went away, but she would never know for sure. Each time she was unsuccessful at getting pregnant, and after each failed IVF, she blamed herself.

When the bathroom door opened, she jumped off the toilet to pick up the wrapper from the floor. She threw the test and the wrapper in her purse. She heard Campbell puking her guts out two stalls down.

Back at her desk, Amelia couldn't get the BFN out of her mind. She felt like a gambler on a losing streak. Her and Diego's savings were evaporating quicker than the baby dust Campbell had stolen from her. She was going to try again, once she figured out how to get the money. Would she dare take a loan out of her 401(k), and then Diego's, if a fourth IVF didn't work?

Her thoughts were interrupted by a text from her boss, Joey Reeves, the much-younger third wife of Michael Reeves, CEO. Joey was twenty-eight, two decades her husband's junior, and the one with the money. After divorce number two, Michael had been broke. Joey inherited a small fortune, which Michael turned into a sizable fortune when he invested her money in their private equity firm, Lake

Geneva Capital, for which Joey was the majority shareholder. Joey's text read, *Be there in a few. Top priority assignment 4 u 2 work on!*

When Amelia heard Dolores, Joey's prized Wire Fox Terrier and Best in Show runner-up, racing and yapping down the hall, she knew Joey was in the office. Dolores beat Joey and patiently waited for her by Amelia's cubicle.

"Oh my gosh, congratulations! When are you due?" Amelia heard Joey congratulate Campbell in the kitchen. She tried to tune them out.

A few minutes later, Joey stood in front of Amelia's desk, her Lululemon pants and SoulCycle tank top slightly visible under a Diane von Furstenberg forest-green wrap dress. "I am super excited for Campbell! Add the baby shower to our events tracker; we are going to throw the best office baby shower this side of the 405."

Amelia swallowed her righteous indignation. "You have a top priority assignment for me?" she asked, hoping not to hear another word about Campbell's pregnancy or baby shower.

Dolores nipped Amelia in the ankle.

"Ahhhhhouch!" Amelia felt the cry from her soul, not from the pain in her ankle.

"Dolores Reeves! What has gotten into you?" Joey picked up Dolores and walked into her office, scolding the dog.

Amelia followed with pen and notebook. Joey put Dolores in the large playpen she kept in her office. Amelia hated the playpen.

"I need your help with a personal assignment, and I'd appreciate it if Michael didn't know about it."

Amelia was surprised. In the four years she had worked for Joey and Michael, she had never been asked to keep a secret from one of them.

"Dolores is going through something, as you can see from her aggressive behavior."

"She's just excited. Think nothing of it," Amelia reassured Joey.

"I think she's depressed, and her psychic agrees that something's up."

Amelia looked at Dolores in the big playpen, lost among all her toys. "Maybe she needs a playmate."

"I need you to find a sperm donor," Joey blurted out in a hushed tone.

That was not what Amelia expected and TMI. Why did Joey think it was okay to ask her do something so personal? Clearly her question was written on her face because Joey started chuckling. "Not for me, silly, for Dolores."

Joey bent down and picked up her dog. "I think it's time for her to be a mommy. Maybe that will take the edge off her, give her purpose. I need you to find me potential matches, pure breeds only, and a vet who specializes in canine artificial insemination."

Amelia looked at Dolores licking Joey's cheek as Joey voiced tasks to her phone. Did Joey, one of LA's highest-ranking angel investors under thirty, not think this was the most out-of-this-world, ridiculous task ever assigned to an assistant? This even topped the time Michael left his belt in the security bin at JFK and asked her to fly to New York, sift through lost and found at TSA, and find the belt because it held sentimental value for him. Amelia had been the one who purchased the belt for Joey to give to Michael as an anniversary gift. She called the store, ordered another one, and he never knew the difference.

"Isn't it easier if you get her a stud?"

"Absolutely not. Everything in my life is planned. I will not let some beastly animal have his way with Dolores.

Until we are ready to pull the trigger, I don't want Michael or anyone knowing about this."

Amelia nodded and smiled. As long as it was not illegal or unethical, she rolled with the ridiculous aspects of her job as an executive assistant to the one percent. However, this was going a little far.

"Email the medium and find out when is the optimal time for Dolores to get pregnant and don't do anything when Mercury is in retrograde."

"Got it." Amelia nodded. She owned her place as the assistant with the magic wand who could make her bosses' ludicrous wishes come true. Her family's dwindling finances depended on it.

When she walked back to her cubicle, she noticed the ultrasound picture on Campbell's desk. She picked it up and tried to figure out where the blob of dots ended and the baby began. She wished and manifested with all her might that, in six weeks, she too would have an ultrasound, but unlike Campbell, she would not share the news so soon or leave the first picture of her baby unattended. When she heard the click-clack of Campbell's Manolos, she tucked the ultrasound picture under her shirt, secured it with the top of her underwear, and walked back to Joey's office.

"Given the privacy you want me to maintain, are you okay if I work from home today?"

"Yes, send a text to the staff and copy Michael after you leave. Tell them you're running some errands for me."

Amelia snuck out the back door and hoped no one saw her. She ran into Susana, the building's Head of House-keeping who polished the door plates and handles with a gloved hand and held her phone with the other as she watched *El Clon*, an old telenovela that Amelia, her mother, and grandmother were addicted to when Amelia was in high school.

Susana followed Amelia to the elevator. "Viste el bebe de Campbell?" she asked, miming a pregnant belly.

Amelia gave Susana a fake smile and placed her hand on her abdomen, securing the contraband she had taken from Campbell, then pressed the elevator button.

"Y usted, no quiere bebe?"

"Maybe next year," she said, squeezing the ultrasound picture so hard she hoped the ink didn't bleed.

"Si su esposo wants a baby, you have to hurry up."

"I wish the elevator would hurry up," Amelia said as she sent a text to Michael and her coworkers.

Susana got the hint and went back to her doorknobs and telenovela. Amelia started her audiobook and made believe she was on the phone. She did not want to hear another word about Campbell's baby from the security guards on the main floor. The elevator stopped on the fourteenth floor, where two pregnant bellies in full bloom walked in, one behind the other. The two of them were so big they couldn't walk into the elevator at the same time.

Amelia smiled at them and texted Diego: "The whole fucking world is pregnant except me!" followed by a gang of angry emojis.

"I hope you didn't test, it's too early, I love you," he replied.

Amelia could always count on Diego to bring her down to earth. Diego was right; she was not out of the game yet. She patted her belly where Campbell's ultrasound picture was swaddled by her underwear on top of her four-day-old implanted embryo and smiled at the pregnant ladies. She let them out first and waved at the security guards as she pressed the down button of the garage elevator.

She drove west on Wilshire to Ocean and merged onto Main Street with her sunroof open, strands of hair flying. She told herself that she shouldn't have tested, that it was too early.

"Virgencita, please let me see a faint line when I pee tomorrow morning. I promise to send them to Catholic school and give them biblical names. I'm counting on you, please don't let me down, okay? I'll take them to church a couple of times a year — fine, once a month — and baptize them at the Cathedral of Our Lady of the Angels and pick really good Catholic godparents." She was so distracted with her supplications to the Virgen that she almost ran a red light. Amelia stepped on the brake fast and hard, and the contents of her purse spilled onto the floor. She tried to scoop everything up before the light changed.

When she picked up the pee stick, for a second, with the sun hitting it a certain way, she saw a faint pink line. The light changed to green, and the car behind her honked, but she was focused on finding the faint line again. She fumbled for her cell phone and aimed its flashlight onto the stick. She could almost see it.

Had it been some kind of mirage? She looked at the silver Virgen, the one her mother had Krazy-Glued on the dashboard of her brand-new Audi to keep her safe. The same Audi she wouldn't have spent last year's bonus on if she'd known she was going to spend their house down payment on IVF treatments.

The car behind her went around; the driver flipped her off as he passed. Amelia blocked traffic until the siren and flashing lights of a police car startled her back to reality. She drove through the intersection and merged onto Abbott Kinney to pull over. She waited for the cop to ticket her, still hypnotized by the faint line that she could see in a certain light. Amelia saw the officer in the rearview mirror and could tell she was pregnant; her intuition had gotten so good that she could smell pregnant women, and it also seemed that every female she came across was either pregnant or about to get pregnant.

"Motherfucker," she muttered under her breath as she took a full look at the pretty Dominican-looking officer. Her short hair was jelled back into a tight bun; her radiant complexion was so pretty, with the glow of someone almost out of the first trimester.

"Officer, my bag fell. Everything went on the floor and my pregnancy test was negative this morning, but now I think it's positive." Amelia showed the officer her the pregnancy test. "Can you see a faint positive? Am I imagining things?" She pushed the test closer to the officer, like Campbell had done earlier with the ultrasound picture.

"Ma'am, don't get so close with something you peed on, but yes, I do believe I see a faint line. I'm going to let you go with a warning. You can't be blocking the intersection like that."

Amelia was about to ask if the officer was Dominican too, but this was not the time to make friends. "Thank you, officer. I appreciate it."

"Take another one tomorrow and leave it on the sink for an hour before you look at it. It takes a while for the HCG to show up if you're newly pregnant." The officer noticed the silver Virgen on the dashboard, then reached into her pants pocket and gave Amelia a small pendant. "This is Saint Gerard. He's the patron saint of motherhood. He and the Virgen will take good care of you."

The reality that Amelia could be pregnant started to sink in. The pools in her eyes slowly overflowed. "Thank you, officer, I appreciate the gift." She clutched the St. Gerard in the palm of her hand. Her ugly cry turned to hideous wail, with *mocos* and mascara cascading down her face.

A call for a disturbance on Electric and California came in on the two-way radio.

"Take a few deep breaths, ma'am, and take your time before you drive off, okay?"

Amelia nodded. "Officer Hernandez, you should keep the St. Gerard, given your job."

"I'm good. I have one in my car and another in my wallet. Drive safely, okay?"

Amelia wanted to rush home. She took a couple of deep breaths as she stared at the pregnancy test and turned it towards the sunlight to see the faint line again. To her surprise, it wasn't hard to find. She didn't want to get her hopes up, though. Before she started IVF, her fertility doctor told her something along the lines of, "Your ovaries are dried, your eggs are fried." At least that's what she'd heard. At thirty-two, she had the egg quality of a forty-two-year-old. She drove for a couple of blocks and found rockstar parking two blocks away from her favorite gelato shop. She wanted something sweet to celebrate the occasion.

Abbott Kinney was full of pedestrians, mostly moms pushing baby carriages or wearing babies, and hipsters drinking cold brews on the sidewalk. She got out of the car and inhaled the vibe of her favorite block in the city. She wished that she and Diego could afford a cute bungalow in Venice. If they didn't need to sink more money into fertility treatments, they would be able to save for a house somewhere in the city, but they'd most likely have to buy out of the area. She loved their Marina del Rey apartment, but if they had a baby, they would need to move.

She wasn't going to think about any of that. She was going to enjoy the walk, people-watch from her favorite gelato shop, and figure out the best way to reveal the pregnancy test to Diego. Finding Dolores a sperm donor could wait a little while. She put her hair in a bun and hid her smeared eye makeup behind her sunglasses, even though June gloom was hanging around in the middle of September.

Maybe Campbell's ultrasound picture on top of her belly had conjured some baby dust and turned her BFN into a BFP, or maybe it was La Virgen. Amelia knew she was going to pee on the other stick when she got home; and the next day, she'd pee on another. She was going to live in the moment and enjoy being PUPO: Pregnant Until Proven Otherwise.

REQUIEM

AATIF RASHID

We came across a scattering of shells on the beach, just before the cove where Sarah and I were headed with our picnic of wine and sandwiches. I picked one of them up and wiped away the wet sand from its curved surface. The ridges were thin but finely detailed, and they fanned out in such a deliberate sweep that I imagined someone had chiseled them from a block of marble. Perhaps it was due to my state of mind, the weight of the last few months, the thoughts of Martin's suicide, but I began to marvel at the strange creative powers of the deity who must have fashioned such an object. I hadn't believed in any god since I was twelve, but I was a literary scholar and not a scientist, so I couldn't account for the patterns I saw before me, the gentle gradation of color from white to beige, the smooth, silk-like feeling of the shell's surface under my fingers, the way it had been lying in this careful pile on the wet sand, as if placed for me to find, without attributing it all to some greater intelligence — if not God, then some great cosmic novelist creating symbols to tantalize me and prompt the drifting introspection that I worried had become my signature character trait ever since I'd turned thirty-seven last spring. Whenever we had dinner these days, Sarah would ask me what I was thinking about, and I found it impossible to describe the labyrinth my mind had traveled through, the strange connections I would make after staring at an object as simple as a saltshaker.

It was impossible to look at the shell and not connect it to Martin, although I didn't understand what aspect of him I saw in that curve of ridges — they were like the folds of a miniature handheld fan, some delicate object carved by an artisan in sixteenth-century Holland and presented to a king's daughter as part of an elaborate dollhouse, an item to be held by one of the ladies of the Queen's court, whom I imagined as a sculpted figure reclining elegantly on a Rococo sofa before pink wallpaper, her legs folded coquettishly and a daring look in her dark eyes as some aristocratic painter stood nearby with an easel. After a moment, though, I realized that this woman of my imagination was none other than Martin's friend and alleged lover, Fiona. I suddenly remembered that pair of dark eyes, staring intently at me from the neighboring pew during the memorial service, and then later from the entryway of the chapel as she stood near Martin's wife, Claire, and offered her words of comfort.

Sarah looked up at me, having picked up a handful of shells herself.

"What are you thinking about, Ali?" she asked.

She must have seen the intense concentration in my eyes, something she'd come to recognize after all these years together.

"Nothing," I said. "Here, let me carry the wine."

"No, I can do it."

She tossed the shells back onto the beach and then picked up the tote bag we'd brought with us from the car. I stared one more time at the shell in my hand before I dropped it into my pocket and followed Sarah toward the cove.

We spread our blanket on a strip of sand shaded by an overhang of curved rock. From this vantage point, we could see the waves building in the distance and hear the tide come in over the rocks. We were sheltered from the heat of the sun, though, and the sand was mostly dry, with only a faint spray of seawater reaching our extended feet.

Sarah unwrapped one of the sandwiches we'd bought from the deli in Santa Monica, and I unscrewed the top of the white wine and poured two servings into plastic cups.

"Cheers," Sarah said, lifting her cup and smiling. "To finishing."

"Cheers," I echoed.

The wine was better than I'd expected: crisp, fruity, not too acidic. I'd bought it for twelve dollars from the hipster liquor store down the street from our apartment, out of a desire to save money, given my new financial situation. Being friends with Martin had made me accustomed to more expensive wines, though, and for a few years, I had been bulk-ordering vintages that he recommended. But times had changed in the months since he'd died. Sarah wasn't a big wine drinker, and I realized I'd been pretending to be someone I wasn't. Who was I, an English graduate student with a stipend of $25,000 a year, to spend $400 on a case of wine? Now, of course, my program had finished, and even that $25,000 would disappear.

Sarah handed me half of the sandwich and then sat cross-legged and took a small bite. Because the world beyond her was brighter than the cove, her figure was silhouetted in a strange darkness. I could see the ocean waves churning, and the way the sunlight reflected off the water, but Sarah herself was bathed in shadow, like a figure in a movie set where the gaffer had got the lighting wrong.

"Are you feeling okay?" she asked.

She must have noticed me staring at her, perhaps with a strained expression, my eyes narrowing to try and see her in this light.

"I'm all right. Just worried about money."

"You'll find something," Sarah said. "There are always teaching jobs. Anyway, we're here to celebrate, remember? Nine years!"

As we drank and ate and stared at the ocean, I pondered this strange number. Nine years. The wine itself wasn't even close to being that old — 2018 the bottle said. The grapes had been grown in a Napa winery, harvested, crushed, fermented, clarified, aged briefly, and then bottled and shipped to stores, all within a year. Meanwhile, I'd spent nine times longer languishing in a graduate program here in Los Angeles, working on a dissertation on the novels of W.G. Sebald that should have been written somewhere in Europe, in a place with a thousand years of history, with old country houses that had been requisitioned by the government during World War II, or eighteenth-century coffee houses that had been turned into dance halls and then later communist meeting spaces. Los Angeles had so little of that kind of grand history — barely anything was older than 1900. I'd been born in California, but I felt so disconnected from the values of this place, as if I were an ancient artifact dug up from soil somewhere far away and purchased by a wealthy industrialist for display in a museum, pointed to briefly by tourists in cargo shorts who inevitably moved on to gawk at an overcoat worn by an actor in a movie. I'd lived in L.A. almost as long as I'd lived anywhere in my life, and yet the city didn't feel like home. The times with Martin had been an exception, of course, but Martin was no longer here.

On our walk back to the car, we passed by the shells again. I wanted to stop and sift through them some more, but the water was coming in and Sarah said she was cold, so we made our way back to where we'd parked along the PCH. On the drive home, we didn't speak, and I stared out the window, at the pier of Santa Monica visible in the distance on my right, the great Ferris wheel spinning and spinning, like a symbolic object in a medieval altarpiece, upon which some poor saint was tortured and then executed.

⌐

At home, Sarah said she felt like having a bath. "Do you want to join?"

"I'm okay. You go ahead."

She began filling the tub and then hummed to herself as she tied her hair back and glanced at herself in the bathroom mirror. After a moment, she closed the door, and I heard classical music begin playing from her iPhone, a muffled and somewhat scratchy sound that through its imperfection gave the Beethoven symphony a grand and dignified air, as if Sarah had set up a wax cylinder phonograph and would soon relax amidst scented bubbles to brassy notes echoing from a flared horn.

Far from relaxing my troubled mind, the music only swirled my anxieties, like waves sweeping in along a beach. I went to my computer and opened Facebook and pulled up Martin's profile. I had read an article recently that one day, not too far in the future, as the site's use inevitably declined, the profiles of the dead would outnumber those of the living — and so I began envisioning a vast digital graveyard where people would come pay tribute to their loved ones, once a year, leaving likes and flower emojis. These seemed, at first, like insufficient tributes, too insubstantial to have real meaning; but the more I considered it, the more I realized that a digital graveyard on Facebook was a more permanent and therefore unsettling means of remembrance than other kinds of human ritual. The Greeks poured libations for their dead, the Hindus had cremation, Zoroastrians constructed Towers of Silence for the vultures — each was a ritual that ultimately left very little behind. The wine that was poured soon dried, the bodies decomposed or turned to ash, and even the Muslims and Christians who buried their dead did not truly imagine that these monuments would last forever. How many cemeteries across the world, after all, now contained unvisited graves? I remembered Sarah and I had visited the British Crimean War cemetery in the Haydarpaşa neighborhood of Istanbul, a small stretch of grass along the Sea of Marmara, near a mosque and not far from the Selimiye Barracks, where Florence Nightingale had treated many of the soldiers who now lay beneath these crumbling stone slabs. A hundred and fifty years later and who but tourists visited such a place?

Facebook, though, was no Haydarpaşa Cemetery. The profiles of the dead were not digital graves, dug with ritual care and marked with stones whose signs of erosion captured the frailty of human life, but lingering remnants of an actual life, false signs that suggested a still-breathing person — photos of smiling faces, biographical details, banal posts about their final passing thoughts, as if any minute now they might give another update, share another article, type out another carefully considered comment about something political. Looking at the Facebook profile of someone who had died didn't give you the comfort of a visit to a graveyard. There was no sense of closure, no ability to reflect, mourn, and then move on. The emojis you posted wouldn't decay like real flowers but would last forever, and each time you returned, you'd see those pixels as fresh as the day you'd created them.

Martin's profile photo was not particularly striking — he was at a restaurant, wearing an open-collared shirt, smiling and holding a fork in an awkward gesture. His wife, Claire, must have taken it, I thought, at one of their many extravagant dates, something Martin's salary as a lawyer could easily afford him. The background was too blurry, so

I couldn't see where they were, but the darkness and moody lighting suggested somewhere expensive yet hip, as befitted Martin's taste. I could almost hear his voice describing it to me over drinks: "Yeah, man, the food was good, but the pasta definitely wasn't homemade like they said. I think that bastard Jonathan Gold exaggerated in his review."

I clicked through a few of Martin's other photos. Eventually, I recognized one of them, from a night in 2015, when we'd all gone for drinks at the Glendon in Westwood after a creative writing class. Martin had been drunk but in that charismatic way we'd always found compelling, with a bombastic, explosive energy, ordering more food for the table, encouraging us to get more drinks, bantering with the waitress in a way that was flirty but not aggressive. In the photo, he was leaning back against one of the leather booths and smiling at the camera. He was a big man, not fat exactly, but tall and broad shouldered and with a physical presence that you felt even through a photograph. His blond hair had been long at the time, and he wore it tucked behind his ears, which made him look like some kind of Viking, a mythical figure from a distant past come to this present world to shake us all from our stupor. I noticed myself in the photo, a shadowy figure at the other end of the table, my expression distant and lost in thought, as always. Fiona was there too, sitting next to Martin, her hands cupped around her drink. She was staring up at the camera like Martin, but she wasn't smiling. Once again, I found myself drawn to those dark eyes and to the hair that fell in tangles around her singular face, those sloping cheeks, that hard slant to the eyebrows.

I searched Fiona's name, but then remembered she said she'd never had a Facebook account, so I went back to Martin's profile and started clicking through his other photos. There was another one with Fiona, also at the Glendon, this time from 2016, after I'd stopped taking classes with them. She was smiling this time, a wry, amused smile, and Martin was on her right, in the midst of explaining something to someone off camera, his arm out, his face contorted into an odd but simultaneously very humanizing expression. I felt my heart clench and imagined Martin alive before me, gesticulating through one of his many improvisational monologues on the state of American politics, or the problems with contemporary literature, or the existential difficulty of switching careers once you'd settled on something and been successful at it for twenty years.

I clicked past the photo, feeling too overwhelmed to linger on it, and found one of Fiona alone, a close-up that Martin had clearly taken himself. I couldn't tell where they were, but there was something shockingly intimate in the way Fiona looked at the camera. I imagined them kissing furtively in Martin's expensive Audi, or else having sex on the gray sofa in his apartment while his wife was on one of her business trips to New York City, the lights of downtown twinkling from beyond his balcony while a warm breeze rustled the palm trees outside his window. My heart began to race, and as I stared at Fiona's face on my screen, I imagined how she might have looked to Martin just after he took this photo, her head tilted back, her eyes closed, her mouth slightly open, her hand on his chest.

I let out a breath and closed the browser, and then closed my laptop, feeling a strange combination of emotions: anger, frustration, eventually a deep sadness. I heard Beethoven still playing from behind the door of the bathroom. Quietly, I picked up my phone and scrolled through my contacts until I came to Fiona's name.

Hey. I don't think I've talked to you since the funeral. I wanted to see how you're doing.

It was a more personal message than I'd ever sent her, and I felt a shiver of guilt and instinctively looked up to the bathroom door, as if expecting Sarah to suddenly emerge. I scrolled up to see what else Fiona and I had texted about. There were only a few messages, mostly questions about the creative writing class we'd both taken several years before, and then a handful more recently about grabbing drinks with Martin. The only messages from 2019 were from a few months ago, about the suicide itself.

Did you hear? (Fiona)

Yeah I did. From Claire. (Me)

I can't believe it. (Me)

Me neither. (Fiona)

I never thought he'd actually do it. (Fiona)

After a moment, my phone buzzed, and I saw that Fiona had responded.

Hey. Thanks for the message. I'm doing okay.

There was a pause, and then I saw the three dots appear to indicate she was still typing. My heart picked up. There was something about that symbol that was so invigorating — the way it would disappear for a second before appearing again to indicate that someone had deleted what they wrote and was starting again, or else linger for a while before the message appeared, suggesting that whatever was being written was something that required thought. It was a very human touch to a very inhuman method of communication, and it always reminded me that there was in fact a real person on the other end of this exchange, a person with warm fingers tapping their screen, human eyes that darted across the letters, a heart that could feel whatever you sent.

How about you? Fiona asked. *Are you doing okay?*

I hesitated. I'd been about to say I was, but I realized it was a lie.

Not really, I said. *I've been thinking a lot about Martin for some reason.*

I waited. Through the door, I heard the Beethoven symphony shift gears into its third movement.

That makes sense, Fiona said a few moments later. *To be honest, I have too.*

I can imagine, I said. *Given your history.*

I don't know why I said it, a sentence so fraught with implication. None of our mutual friends knew exactly what had been going on between Martin and Fiona, though we'd all suspected. I'd been on the verge of asking him once, at a party he and Claire had hosted at their apartment, when the two of us were outside smoking cigarettes on his balcony. But then Sarah had come outside, and I'd never had another chance. Martin would probably have told me the truth, but it was in my nature to be hesitant around such things. Maybe if I'd been bolder, I would have understood more about what he was going through and helped him wrestle with whatever drove him to do what he did.

I stared down at my phone. Fiona hadn't responded, and I was afraid I'd offended her into silence. After a moment, though, I saw the three dots appear.

I didn't think you knew about that. Did Martin tell you? No. But I guessed.

Another pause. I stared at my phone, my thumbs hovering over the screen. In the bathroom, Sarah was finishing up, and I heard the tub begin to drain, a sudden rush of water that drowned out the violins of Beethoven.

Do you want to talk about it in person? Fiona asked. *We could get a drink somewhere. If you're not busy.*

My heart was racing now, and I imagined sitting across from Fiona in the darkened room of a bar, two cocktails before us on small black napkins. I looked at the time on my phone: 8:27 p.m. It was Monday tomorrow, but aside from applying to jobs for the coming fall, I didn't have any work.

I'm not busy, I said. *Where do you want to meet?*

┐

Fiona named a bar in the Arts District downtown, one of those old warehouses that had been converted into a brewery. The surrounding street was dark and a little unnerving, with a fenced-off empty lot and a gravel path in place of a sidewalk, but after turning down a small side street, I came upon a twinkle of lights ahead, the illuminated sign of the brewery rising above the brick buildings, a gaggle of smokers clustered outside, the sound of laughter drifting from the tables on the patio, and eventually the smell of hops, like the aroma of some rare flower from childhood you recognize at a distance, at once comforting and promising, nostalgic and inviting, a scent that brought a flood of memories, of a big group of friends gathering at a table in a dark bar and then staying till closing, leaving a scattering of empty glasses like unlit candles on a church altar, Martin giving the waitress one last wave of thanks and an extra tip before we walked out into the cool night.

I'd been vague to Sarah about where I was going; I told her an old writer friend wanted to grab a drink.

"Who?" Sarah asked as she dried her hair with a towel.

"Aaron," I said. "He took a few classes with us back in the day. I think he wants to talk about Martin."

I don't know why I lied, but it came naturally, as if an animalistic part of my brain was taking over my decision making. Sarah had met Fiona once, when she came to have drinks with us after one of my classes, and perhaps I remembered the sense of unease she'd radiated as she sat uncertainly at the end of the table, noting Fiona's arrogant poise, and perhaps also how frequently my eyes would flick towards her, would watch her hands gripping her glass or her hair falling across her face whenever she looked down at her phone.

"Okay," Sarah said. "Just don't wake me up when you get back in, okay? I have to get up early for work."

I found Fiona seated outside on the patio, smoking a cigarette, with a tulip glass of hazy beer on the table before her, a third of it already gone and a faint smudge of her dark lipstick on the rim.

"Hey," Fiona said, standing and stubbing out her cigarette into the ashtray.

We gave each other an awkward hug. We'd never really hugged before and had usually just acknowledged each other with a nod or a wave. I caught a scent of her perfume rising above the cigarette smoke, like the flash of some olfactory firecracker that lit up the sky.

"Let me get a drink," I said.

"Sure," Fiona said.

I ordered an IPA and then sat down at the table in the seat adjacent to Fiona. She angled her chair towards me and crossed her legs. She was wearing black tights under a short, patterned skirt, and a dark olive-green cardigan that hung around her like an elegant shawl. I'd never learned exactly how old she was; she had the simultaneously casual and confident demeanor of someone who could be anywhere from her late twenties to mid-forties. I always assumed, though, that she was around my age, or perhaps slightly older, at that cusp where "millennial" felt too infantilizing but "Gen X" not entirely accurate. If anything, she transcended such arbitrary categorization, and I imagined that, like me, she rejected these attempts by demographers to delineate generational experiences, as if someone aged fifty couldn't have the maturity of a twenty-year-old, or someone in their thirties couldn't feel many decades older than their years.

When I'd first seen Fiona, she'd been seated not unlike she was right now, on one of the antiquated metal chairs in the UCLA Public Affairs building, one leg crossed over the other, leaning back slightly, an amused and somewhat disdainful expression on her face. We were among fifteen other students, part of the first creative writing class I'd decided to take. It was 2014, and I was in my fourth year of grad school and growing tired of thinking about literature in the abstract, theoretical, and inhuman way that an English department inevitably taught one to do, so I'd enrolled in a creative writing class to try and re-experience the passion I'd once felt toward books. I struggled, however, to unlock whatever creative potential I might have had. I couldn't escape looking at text like a literary scholar, and so everything I wrote was too self-conscious or ironic, clouded by an interpretive lens I was unable to remove and frustratingly distant from any real human feeling. Maybe I should have written about Fiona, I thought, the faint excitement I felt looking at her across the table, or about Martin, whom I also met in that class, and whose friendship came to mean more to me than even the books I'd devoted my life to studying.

Fiona lit another cigarette and moved the ashtray closer to her.

"How are things?" she asked. "How's your literature program?"

"I'm finishing this year. I filed my dissertation last week."

"Oh, that's great. What's next for you then?"

"I don't know yet."

A long silence then. I took a sip of beer.

"What about you? Are you still working at …"

"The bar. Yeah."

"How is it?"

"It's fine." She shrugged. "It pays my rent."

Another silence. I watched as Fiona lifted her cigarette to her lips.

"So, should we talk about Martin?" she asked.

"Sure."

She let out a smoky breath, which I felt faintly against my cheek.

"I was surprised you knew. I thought we kept it a secret."

I felt unnerved by the directness of Fiona's gaze. Behind her, the interior of the bar shone with golden light, and through the open doors came the sound of laughter. I watched the bartender, a man around my age, cleaning the counter in circular motions with a dish towel hanging from his jeans.

"Was it that obvious?" Fiona asked.

"No," I said. "But I could tell by the way he looked at you. And the way you looked at him."

Fiona gave a short laugh and then looked down at the table. I watched as the end of her cigarette crumbled slowly to ash.

"I felt bad about it, you know," she said. "Claire was so nice."

"She was."

"But Martin … well, I just couldn't say no."

I looked down at my beer and slowly rotated the glass, watching the liquid swirl. I wanted to ask Fiona how exactly the affair had started, but I didn't want to offend her. Still, her comment made me reconfigure what I had thought. For some reason, I'd imagined that Fiona had been the one to pursue him, that after a month or so of long looks across the darkness of the Glendon she'd finally turned to him as he was walking her back to her car and kissed him on the mouth under the awning of a gated storefront. But maybe it was Martin who'd made the first move — Martin mad with desire, tormented with guilt.

"When was the last time you saw him?" I asked.

"A little over two weeks before I found out what happened. I … was with him in my apartment. We'd planned to get dinner at some point, but we were both busy. He had some big case at his firm, and I was trying to pick up more shifts. We texted pretty regularly, though, right up until …"

She let out a small breath.

"What was the last thing he said to you?" I asked.

She pulled out her phone and showed me the message thread.

I was thinking about you today. (Martin)

Yeah? What were you thinking about? (Fiona)

What we did the other night. On the sofa in your apartment. (Martin)

What a coincidence. I was thinking about it too. (Fiona)

When? (Martin)

In bed this morning. (Fiona)

Did you touch yourself as you were thinking about it? (Martin)

Yes. (Fiona)

Did you cum? (Martin)

No. (Fiona)

Why not? (Martin)

I don't know. Maybe I can only come when you're here. (Fiona)

My heart beat wildly as I read the messages. I imagined Fiona, lying in her bed, her hair disheveled from sleep as she typed out these messages, and Martin in his kitchen, dressed for work and pouring himself a cup of coffee, while Claire ate breakfast at the table and read the news on her phone.

Fiona leaned forward so that she too could read the messages, and I smelled her hair and perfume once again.

"Does that sound like someone who would kill himself?" she asked.

"I don't know," I said.

The truth was I didn't fully recognize the Martin in these text messages. There was a sharp directness here that I never thought him capable of, a pounding lust that I never realized existed under the surface of that sanguine, charismatic demeanor. We'd never had the kind of friendship where we talked about sex or women, though one time Martin had commented that he thought the waitress at a restaurant was "smoking hot." She'd been tall and blonde and had walked with a crisp elegance that reminded me of a flight attendant, but she'd looked nothing at all like Fiona, had none of her dark, feline intensity. If anything, she looked a lot like Claire, who'd been in the bathroom at the time. She'd returned to the table and Martin had smiled and kissed her.

"Do you know why he did it?" Fiona asked, looking directly at me.

She was still leaning forward, even though I'd given her back her phone. There was only an inch of space between us now, and if I moved my leg, it would graze hers, and I'd feel the fabric of her tights against my thigh. I imagined Martin reaching his hand out and touching her between her legs.

"I have no idea," I said. "I thought you knew."

"I don't," Fiona said. "One day he's texting me things like this. A few weeks later, I get a message that he's dead."

"Did you ... hear about how it happened?"

Fiona looked away and over at her beer, which sat forgotten. She reached for it and toyed with it but didn't take a sip.

"I heard something," she said. "At the funeral. I don't know if it's true, but one of his relatives told me that he ... that he hanged himself."

Her voice broke as she said the words. I closed my eyes. I hadn't known, and the knowledge, true or not, made it feel so terribly real. I imagined Martin swinging from a beam on his ceiling, his long arms limp and his head twisted to one side. I thought I was going to cry, and I let out a shaky breath — and then I felt Fiona reach out and take my hand.

I opened my eyes and saw a faint wetness clouding her eyes. Her hand was warm, and I gripped her fingers in my own, the blood racing in my wrist. Despite the thoughts of Martin, I was conscious of how close Fiona was, how her body was only a few inches from my own. Gently, I reached my other hand out and placed it on her thigh. She didn't flinch or move but stared at me with those dark eyes, still faintly wet with tears. Suddenly, I felt myself growing hard, and I imagined her fingers reaching down and grabbing me through my pants. It was a lurid thought, and I felt ashamed for thinking it — but despite this, my erection didn't go away.

After a moment, Fiona pulled her hand away. I felt embarrassed and let out another breath. Fiona took out a tissue and gently wiped her eyes and then checked her face in a pocket mirror. I finished my beer and set down my empty glass.

"Do you want another?" I asked.

"I want something stronger."

"They might have hard liquor."

I stared at her, my eyes drawn to the spot on her thigh where I'd rested my hand. I imagined sliding my hand upward, up those black tights and under her skirt, just as Martin had once done.

"Or …"

I leaned forward, hesitating.

"Yeah?" Fiona asked.

She was staring at me, her mouth slightly open. My heart was beating so hard now I thought it would fly from my chest and shatter the empty beer glass on the table.

"You live around here, right?" I asked. "Do you want to get some whiskey and go back to your place?"

﹁

Fiona lived in an apartment between Chinatown and Echo Park, in one of those squat, square mid-century apartment buildings common across Los Angeles. She'd Ubered to the brewery, so we drove back in my car. On the ride, we were silent, but the air was thick with anticipation.

There was a spot in front of her building, and once I'd parked, we stepped out of the car and looked at each other briefly. The street was dark except for the faint light of a distant streetlamp, but I could see the strained anticipation in Fiona's expression. She led me up the stairs and fumbled briefly with her keys as she unlocked her door.

Inside, I sat on the sofa while Fiona went to the kitchen to pour us the whiskey. Her apartment was much smaller than mine and Sarah's, a studio instead of a one-bedroom, with a single lamp that cast insufficient light across the space and IKEA furniture that looked old and worn. In addition to her sofa, there was a small desk near the window, an office chair with a gray T-shirt hanging over it, and her bed, which made the room feel far too intimate. In the kitchen, I heard Fiona rustling through her cupboard, and after a moment she entered with two glasses half-filled with whiskey.

"Cheers," I said. "To Martin."

"To Martin," Fiona said.

She drank half hers standing up, and then sat down on the couch next to me and crossed her legs. Her perfume was even stronger now, and in the stuffy space of the apartment, the scent enveloped me like a shroud. There were still a few inches between us on the couch, but Fiona had angled her body towards me, and so our legs were almost touching. She'd taken off her shoes, and her foot, encased in her black tights, hung like a pendulum in the air beside me. If she moved it just an inch to the right, her toes would rest against my leg.

"He talked about you a lot, you know," Fiona said. "Martin, I mean."

"Really?"

I was surprised. I was never sure how much of an impression I had made on Martin. I considered us close friends, but he was one of those people so confident in himself that it seemed he never valued friendship like I did, never needed it as much. Of course, given what happened, perhaps my impression of him had been wrong. Maybe Martin too suffered lonely nights lying awake in his bed and staring at his ceiling, wondering how his life had ended up the way it did.

"What did he used to say?" I asked.

"Lots of things. That you were the smartest person he knew. That he really respected you." Fiona hesitated. "I think he looked up to you a lot," she said.

I stared at my whiskey, unable to comprehend what she was saying. It didn't make any sense. I was the one who respected Martin. I was the one who looked up to him. His life was so full of energy, lived to an extent I could only dream of. How was it possible that someone like him looked up to me?

"Where was he the last time he was here?" I asked. "When you two ... you know."

Fiona uncrossed her legs and set her whiskey down on the coffee table. I could hear my heart beating as she leaned towards me.

"He was on this couch," she said. "Sitting like this."

She put her hands on my shoulders and adjusted my body so that I was facing her, with one of my legs bent across the couch. We were close enough now that I could see her lips in microscopic detail, the lines caked with lipstick, the flash of her teeth through her open mouth. Her breath smelled like the whiskey she'd been drinking, and I felt my head spin.

"And how were you sitting?" I asked.

Fiona stared at me for a moment, and then leaned towards me, across my folded leg. She placed one of her arms around my neck and rested the other on my thigh.

"Like this," she said.

My heart was beating wildly now. I thought of Sarah, back home with a sleep mask over her eyes, ambient ocean sounds from her iPhone lulling her to sleep. But even that thought wasn't as strong as the feeling of Fiona's hands and body, the smell of her breath and hair.

Slowly, I leaned my head towards her and kissed her on her lips, tentatively and softly. She pulled away and frowned, and I felt a sudden wave of shame. Had I gone too far? Had I misread what was happening?

"Don't kiss me like that," she said. "Kiss me like Martin would have."

I let out a breath, half of relief and half of a complex emotion I couldn't begin to describe. Then I leaned forward and put my hand around Fiona's neck and pulled her towards me, pressing my lips against hers with force and pushing my tongue into her mouth, as I imagined Martin must have done. I felt Fiona's body responding instantly, her muscles tensing, and then she pulled my head towards her and pressed her mouth against mine. I ran my hand up her leg and, without hesitating, rubbed her between her legs. I felt her breath catch, and she closed her eyes and moaned softly.

"Oh Martin," she said.

This only made me more eager, and I reached up and pulled down her tights and then put my finger inside her. She was wet enough that it went in easily, and she leaned her head into my neck and bit my skin. I would end up with a hickey, and I worried at first — but then I thought of what Martin would do and realized that he wouldn't care, that he would let the moment unfold without letting his mind interrupt his feelings. And so I pushed all thoughts of Sarah aside and focused on the sensation of Fiona's wetness gripping my finger.

We had sex on her bed, with our clothes still on, my pants around my ankles, Fiona's tights in a ball on the floor and her skirt pushed up.

"Condom?" I asked, breathlessly.

"We never used condoms," Fiona said.

The way she said it, the gleam in her eyes, made me even more aroused. Without letting myself stop and think, I leaned my body over her and pushed myself inside her. I had placed a pillow under her, something I'd seen once in porn but had never tried with Sarah, and the angle made her come in less than a minute. She cried out Martin's name, and when she did, I came too.

Afterwards, we sat on the floor, leaning against the sofa and drinking our whiskey, the smell of it mingling with the scent of our fluids. Fiona lit a cigarette and smoked it without speaking. I avoided looking at her and focused on my breathing. I had expected that now that it was over, the shame of what we'd done would overwhelm me in a sudden flood, but I didn't feel anything except exhilaration at what had happened. It was the first time I'd cheated on anyone, and all I could think of was the sensation of it, Fiona's lips, her body, the warmth and wetness of her around my cock, her hips pressing upward into mine as her body shuddered in sensory ecstasy.

"I want to see you again," Fiona said, after her cigarette was done. "Just like that."

"Okay," I said.

"But next time, can you dress like Martin?"

"In a suit?" I asked.

"Yeah," Fiona said. "Blue if you can. No tie. Open collar."

"Okay," I said again.

We started seeing each other every week after that, and then multiple times a week. Sarah wasn't suspicious, but I knew it couldn't last, that the intensity of it would lead me to ruin, and that soon I'd make a mistake, leave a trace of Fiona's lipstick on one of my shirts or forget to hide a hickey with makeup — and after that, I'd not only be a man without a job, but someone who'd thrown away the partner he'd built his life with. I imagined myself in a Day's Inn somewhere out on the outskirts of Los Angeles, waking to a cup of watery hotel coffee and spending each morning looking at Sarah's profile on Facebook, clicking through photos of her and her new husband and imagining myself in his place, laughing on a beach somewhere, as we'd once done.

And yet, every time I had sex with Fiona, every time she called me Martin, every time I felt how wet she was between her legs, it only inflamed my desires more. If the passion of a relationship inevitably declined over time until it became what I had with Sarah, a steady simmer of long-term commitment, the presence of Martin's ghost between Fiona and me kept that passion blazing like a furnace and made each encounter between us more intense than the last. With Fiona, I was no longer the introspective man I was afraid I'd become but someone animalistic and primal, a creature driven purely by sensory experience. It was exhilarating to be that person, and for all the shame

I felt afterwards driving home, I knew there was a part of me that never wanted it to stop.

Eventually, I began to wonder if Fiona and I would be trapped in this cycle for a long time. One day, driving home from her apartment, the smell of her still on my fingers, I put my hand in my pocket and felt the shell from the beach, from all those months ago. As I traced its ridges, I once again imagined the fan, the dollhouse, the court, the woman reclining, and myself as well, seated next to her on the sofa, my hand on her thigh, while someone plays Beethoven in a distant room. I thought about opening my window and tossing the shell into the darkness, as if that might break the cycle and save me from this spiral — but when I pulled it out and stared at it, I found myself mesmerized again by the way it looked, and, in the end, I put it back in my pocket.

Sarah and I eventually broke up, not because she found out about me and Fiona, but because, in her words, "we'd been growing distant." I think she always suspected something but was too wounded to say anything. On our last day together, LA was experiencing one of its rare rainstorms, and the parking lot outside our apartment was gray and misty, like a still from a silent film. Sarah had decided to keep the apartment, and so I'd packed a few bags and was standing by the door. Sarah was on the couch, hugging her knees to her chest and staring at our long shelf, and the empty spaces where I'd pulled my books down. To me, it looked like pockmarked skin, like a patient with scars where tumors had been excised.

Sarah wasn't looking at me, but from where I stood, I could see she was crying. I wanted to say something but couldn't think of what. It felt like we'd long ago exhausted our store of words.

Fiona and I stopped seeing each other around the same time. I think the spark finally faded once Sarah and

I separated. One night in her apartment, while we were having sex, I suddenly felt unable to keep up. The intensity of her gaze was too much, and a heaviness came over me, like something pulling at my chest. I slumped onto the bed and had to catch my breath.

"Are you okay?" Fiona asked.

"I don't know. I feel strange."

We lay there for a while, awake but without speaking. I could feel the warmth of Fiona's body through the sheets, and it reminded me of Sarah. I almost rolled over and kissed Fiona like I'd kissed Sarah, those closed-lipped pecks full of softness and familiarity. Eventually, I got up and put on my clothes.

On the freeway, I passed the familiar string of exits: Arlington, Crenshaw, La Brea, Fairfax, La Cienega. It was only when I reached Culver City that I remembered I no longer lived in my old apartment in West LA. I'd made this drive so many times that my brain now did it automatically. But since the breakup, I'd moved to the Valley, to an apartment in North Hollywood. I still hadn't found an academic job and was working as an adjunct lecturer, making barely enough to live, and everything in Los Angeles was too expensive now.

I got off on National, but instead of turning around, I drove down Venice to Oldfields. Martin and I used to go there occasionally, and after I walked inside and crossed the tiled floor to the old-fashioned wooden bar, I remembered that this was where we'd been the last time I'd seen him, in what now felt like another lifetime. The place had been moderately busy then, and we'd been sitting at the bar. Martin had just come from his office, and he was wearing his blue suit (though he'd taken off his tie, as always). He ordered a brandy after asking the bartender for her recommendation, and I decided to order one too. I found the taste a little strange, too sweet compared to the whiskey that Martin and I usually drank there. We talked about my program for a little bit, and Martin congratulated me for being close to finishing. Then he complained for a while about one of his clients, a developer who was in conflict with the city over zoning rights. The bartender kept coming back to ask if we wanted anything else, and I watched as she and Martin flirted for a while under the moody gloom of the yellow lights.

Eventually, it was close to midnight and Martin said he had to get home. We had one final shot of whiskey ("My treat," Martin said. "You've got to try this one."), and after Martin said goodbye to the bartender, we stepped outside onto the quiet street. It was a rare, cold night for L.A., even in winter, and Martin shivered and rubbed his hands together.

"Sarah's doing good?" he asked.

"Yeah. She's good. How's Claire?"

"She's good."

I had almost said Fiona instead of Claire. By that point, their affair was common knowledge among our friends. I thought of the way Martin had flirted so naturally with the bartender and then enviously imagined him with Fiona, naked in his apartment. In that moment, I felt like I would have given anything to be in Martin's place.

We stood for another minute in silence and stared down Venice Boulevard, past the dry cleaners across the street and along the power lines that stretched into the darkness, like ropes across a vast chasm.

"Anyway," Martin said. "Good catching up, man. I'll see you soon, okay?"

"Yeah. See you soon."

FINISH LINE

SASHA KILDARE

Everything about Lisa was long, except her fingernails. She kept them short and plain.

Having finished stretching, she sat on the side of the black track inspecting her nails while the other runners continued to stretch and pace. As she moved a metal file across the tip of her thumbnail, she was reminded of her mother, who had never let her out of the house until she passed inspection. She wished that her mother were among the thousands watching from the stands.

In profile, Lisa's fine braids graduated in length. The shortest ones just missed her prominent cheekbones. The longest ones fell past her shoulders and dangled against her sculpted back.

Lisa inspected her nails, put away the file, and approached her teammate, Tamaya, who lay on the ground stretching, her face buried in her massive thigh. Lisa crouched and whispered in her friend's ear, "Tay, you know you got it going on. Lighten up."

Tamaya raised her head, but her reply faded into the dry heat of the Technicolor summer day. She finished her stretching routine and stood up. "Lisa, you're strutting around like you're on a permanent coffee break, 'cause you always win, girl."

The sound of the whistle drowned out Lisa's chuckle, and they both took their spots in the lineup for the final of their first event.

"Runners take your marks," the announcer said.

Lisa placed her feet on the starting blocks. Swirls of tropical fish caught her eye where they bordered the stitching of her runner's uniform at her stomach, shoulders, and thighs. Her elongated dancer's legs contrasted with the bulging muscles of most sprinters. The bright yellow background of her uniform stood out among the sea of red, white, blue, and black spandex. It gave her dark brown skin a slight golden glow. Perhaps that's why her three-year-old son had called her team's uniforms "butterfly costumes."

"Set."

Every muscle in Lisa's body tensed.

At the pop of the starting pistol, the runners sped out of the blocks. Lisa exploded into first place, her striking features twisted into a scowl as she pounded her legs into the rubberized track and maintained her lead over her closest competitor, a brawny East German whose caramel braids were coiled behind her ears and resembled pretzels.

Five meters from the finish line, searing pain spread through Lisa's leg, as if the back of her thigh were on fire. When she tried to lift her left heel, it felt glued to the track. A current of pain claimed Lisa's body as she descended in slow motion. The crowd became a blur of noise and movement.

She landed face down, inches from the finish line, just as Tamaya overtook the East German and clinched her first gold medal. The lightning pain had dulled slightly, but her whole body had become an Indian burn. She could taste the blood that dripped down her face. Her nose felt broken, but she could still smell a combination of burning rubber and dust mixed in with her own sweat.

Tamaya held Lisa's bruised and scraped hand as she was lifted onto a stretcher and carried to a vehicle that looked too new and stylish to be an ambulance. But their coach wouldn't allow Tamaya to accompany Lisa to the triage room because she had another heat coming up.

Lisa woke up in a makeshift hospital to the sight of the frowning faces of her coach and a ruggedly handsome silver-haired man who introduced himself as Dr. Rafter.

"Rotten luck, lassie, you'll need to rest your leg for at least a month to prevent permanent damage. You've completely torn the tendon to your hamstring, a grade-three rupture, as severe as it can possibly get," Dr. Rafter said.

Lisa's coach took her hand, kissed it, and held it between both of his. "My precious Lisa, I'm so sorry."

Lisa, about to nod off again, murmured, "Hey, nobody died here. I'll survive."

⌐

Three-year-old Jesse, intently reconfiguring his train tracks for the fifth time, didn't notice his grandma bringing him the phone. "Mommy, Mommy. You fell. Did you get lots of owies?"

"Just one big one. But Mommy is going to be just fine."

Jesse struggled to keep the phone from slipping out of his small hand. "Come home, Mommy. Come home tomorrow."

"I'll be home soon. Rio is far away. Listen to your grandma, okay?"

Aurelia, Lisa's mother, gently pried the phone from her grandson's hand and said, "I'll pray for you, honey."

"Mom, I'm going to be just fine."

"You're going to need the Lord's help to deal with such a disappointment."

"Mom, it's okay. It was just a race."

Lisa finished the call and turned off her cellphone ringer. As she steeled herself for the long walk on crutches back to her dorm room in the Olympic Village, she wondered if the real difficulty was going to be dealing with everyone else's disappointment.

Piles of clothing obscured most of the carpet, patterned in the colors of gemstones, which looked more suited to a Las Vegas hotel or a movie theater than the floor of the tiny dorm room that Tamaya and Lisa shared. Tamaya's clothing was sorted into race clothes, street clothes, and practice clothes, but Lisa's garments were all in one big jumble. As Lisa lay on the bottom bunk, she wished the tiny room would close in on her, detach itself from the massive structure, transform itself into a flight capsule, and transport her home. Now she resented every day spent away from her only child.

Tomorrow she should have been running in the finals of the hundred meters. She had been the favorite to win. It was supposed to have been enough Olympic gold to secure a coaching position at a nice college, maybe in the Northwest. She had pictured Jesse growing up in snow and taking him away from their urban Los Angeles neighborhood that yielded only two seasons a year: fall and summer.

There hadn't been a Plan B because she had been too busy surviving day to day. She wondered if now she'd be forced to return to college to get yet another degree. Three quick knocks on the door were followed by the familiar bellow of her coach, which startled Lisa out of her reverie. Lisa reached for her crutches and navigated her long body out of the narrow bed.

﹁

The kaleidoscope of dancing bodies changed every time Lisa blinked her eyes. Coach Mitchell had sat them at a table in a corner of the Olympic Village disco so that Lisa would not have to worry that anyone would trip over her cast.

The sound of the throbbing techno music dulled Lisa's pain. Coach chewed a tiny ice cube and said, "Don't ask yourself why. You, of all people, deserved to win. You earned it."

Lisa twirled her spaghetti round and round in its oversized bowl decorated with a confetti pattern. If she stared at it just right, it created an optical illusion like her son's pinwheel. She looked at her watch; she had forty-five minutes until her next dose of Vicodin.

Coach Mitchell ignored her inattentiveness as he continued his pep talk. "Try and focus on the positive. In a few months, you'll be healed. Dr. Rafter said you could begin physical therapy as soon as the cast comes off. You'll be back just in time for World's next year."

Lisa put down her fork and shoved her plate away. "I'm done," Lisa mumbled. She tore into a sugar packet decorated with the Olympic logo and became mesmerized watching the sugar dissolve in her iced tea as she stirred it.

Coach Mitchell paused to put his arm around Lisa. Before he could continue, Tamaya broke away from a group of dancers, still clapping to the beat and tapping her feet as she approached their table.

"It's so good to see you, girlfriend."

Coach Mitchell glanced her way. "Isn't it your bedtime?"

"Not to worry. I'm going to get enough Zs. I'm just working off some butterflies before tomorrow's race." Tamaya giggled as she twirled away.

Lisa sighed. "She's still a baby."

"Lisa, she's only five years younger than you."

"It doesn't feel that way. I feel old. Too old for all of this anymore."

"My fault. You've had enough for one day." Coach Mitchell rose to help Lisa onto her crutches. "You'll go home, catch up with your son, and start physical therapy. One step at a time."

"I don't know. It seems like the music stopped playing when my tendon snapped." Lisa wasn't sure if Coach Mitchell had heard her before he had walked off to find Tamaya so he could escort both of them back to their room.

Tamaya shut the door behind her after reassuring Coach Mitchell for the third time that she was going straight to sleep. "He makes me feel like a kindergartner," Tamaya grumbled.

"You'll be thanking him tomorrow morning when you wake up rested," Lisa said.

"Oh Lisa, how selfish of me. You were supposed to be in that race tomorrow, winning your third gold medal. I'm sorry for whining. You've been like my cheerleader, sister, and friend all wrapped into one the past three years, and I just can't stand that this happened to you. I don't know what to do for you, and it's driving me crazy."

Lisa responded, "Just talk to me about anything but running."

Tamaya said, "Hey, did you see that German dude who won the 1,500 meters? Dark hair, light eyes, body to die for — he is fine."

Lisa smiled. "Now that's a nice image before bedtime."

Tamaya helped Lisa settle into her bottom bunk. As Lisa drifted off to sleep, she wondered what it would be like to not see Coach Mitchell, Tamaya, and the rest of the team all the time. They had become her family. She had only had three track coaches in her twelve-year career. She made a mental note to look up her first track coach when she returned home.

Crenshaw High's Coach Guthrie had guided her into the hands of the track club coach who had prepared her to compete at a national level. Those national competitions had led to her first Olympics in 2008, weeks after her eighteenth birthday. Her top five results in two races there had established her as an international talent.

Coach Guthrie had also helped her decide which scholarship to accept when the offers had poured in during her junior year in high school. Originally, she had her heart set on going out of state, not up the road to UCLA. However, choosing UCLA was something she would never regret because it had led her to Coach Mitchell.

All three of her coaches had been heartbroken when she sat out her next shot at the London 2012 Olympics because she had been five months pregnant with Jesse, but they also instilled in her the wholehearted belief that she could return to international competition.

⌐

Coach Guthrie felt as if he had been slapped in the face as he helplessly watched all but one of his sprinters slow down for the finish line. He cleared his throat and screamed, "Fu! Kick, kick, never stop at the finish line. Watch Danielle." He turned to a skinny girl with precise cornrows and said, "Show us how you finish a race. Take it from the fifty."

As the rest of the girls watched, Danielle blasted past the finish line at full speed. Coach cracked a rare smile. "Focus on a spot past the finish line. If you don't, you're going to slow down at the end of a race. You'll give it away." He took a deep breath and stopped himself from giving any further explanation. "Danielle, lead the intervals. I'll be right back, and then we'll work on the blocks."

On his way to the locker room, Coach Guthrie walked past the softball field and saw a blur of long legs and braids round the bases. He was halfway back from the locker room before it registered; he hadn't seen such speed in years. He jogged toward the softball coach. "Terry, that tall girl who just made it to home plate. Let me time her right now. I'll bet you a hundred bucks that she's fast enough to qualify for the state meet in May."

"Stealing talent, now, huh?" Terry laughed. "I never thought of her as a sprinter, but she is really fast."

Five minutes later, Lisa, oblivious to the entire track team staring her down, struggled to figure out the starting blocks and decided against using them.

"Ready. Set. Go."

Twelve seconds later, Coach Guthrie couldn't stop staring at the stopwatch. He followed Lisa to the water fountain. "Don't you want to know your time?"

"I guess," she shrugged.

"Eleven point seven seconds," he said slowly.

"Is that good?"

Coach Guthrie shook his head and began to laugh. "Lisa, my gifted young woman, that is not good. That is *unbelievable*." He tossed his hat in the air and shouted, "Unbelievable."

Lisa giggled.

"That time is national caliber. That time would have won the state championship last year. I want to meet your parents."

﹁

Not quite over her jet lag, Lisa hobbled on her crutches to answer the doorbell. Through the peephole she glimpsed the smug posture and earnest expression of Jesse's father, Tony, and wondered if her pain pills were causing her to hallucinate. His lithe frame was almost disguised by a silver lightweight wool suit that glistened in the sunlight. Italian. Expensive. A vision of male beauty. Her pulse quickened, then her stomach dropped as she remembered how he had abandoned her.

She cracked open the door and said, "Leave it to you to disappear for four years and then return on one of the worst days of my life." Self-consciously, she brushed the scabs on one of her cheeks. She still had cuts and bruises all over her body from the impact of the fall. They comforted her because they were visible. The physical pain mirrored her invisible emotional pain.

She looked him up and down. "Looks like you can afford a phone. Why didn't you call?"

Tony looked her in the eye. "I was afraid you'd hang up. Look. I know I messed up. But it's different now. I'm done with school and doing well, really well. I want to help with our son."

Tears gathered on Lisa's eyelashes. She found herself staring at Tony's impossibly thin loafers that hugged his long, narrow feet, remembering how he had run out on her when she was five months pregnant, too late to have an abortion. He had begged her to keep the pregnancy and then deserted her. The pregnancy had cost her a place at the Olympics that summer. She had watched the games from her mom's living room — her mom's sighs providing an additional soundtrack.

"Tony, you know, I really want to believe you, for Jesse's sake, but it's really not the best time to talk. I just returned last night and I'm heavily medicated."

"Oh, Lisa, I'm so sorry. I saw what happened."

Just then, Jesse burst out of his room and grabbed his mother's good leg. "Mommy, read me story."

Tony kneeled down to Jesse's level and held out his hand. "My name is Tony, and I'm your mom's friend. She doesn't feel too good. Would it be okay if I read to you?"

Jesse's mouth slid to one side of his face, causing his chubby cheek to protrude. He looked down and mumbled, "Yeah."

Tony chased after Jesse as he tried to steal the soccer ball from a nearby practice. Lisa looked down at her leg. No more crutches, but she was still unable to chase anything. Tony returned with Jesse under his arm and placed him on a nearby swing. Tony had picked them up that morning and driven them to Van Ness Recreation Park so that Jesse could see all the different playing fields.

In workout clothes, Tony still looked like the young man with whom she had fallen in love. She limped over and leaned against the metal pole as Tony pushed Jesse's swing.

"I understand you, Lisa. I know you better than you know yourself. You want to move on. Running's been your life for twelve years, but now it's time for your future to begin," Tony said without taking his eyes off the swing.

"Nobody else understands. They think I'm tanking, that I'm still in shock, but I'm not. I wanted to retire after the Olympics anyhow," Lisa said. She couldn't believe she'd forgiven him so easily after so many years. She knew that she would never have let her feelings get in the way of Jesse having a father, but had she sunk to the depths of loneliness by becoming close friends with someone who had so easily betrayed her?

"Well, my education certainly paid off. I can take care of Jesse and pay for your tuition. Let me; I owe you that much," Tony said. He pushed Jesse high and ran under the swing as Jesse squealed, "Do it again, Daddies, do it again."

The words tumbled out before Lisa could stop herself: "Isn't your girlfriend going to get jealous?"

"Lisa, that's none of her business, and if she wants to hold onto me, she'll keep it that way," Tony said as he lifted Jesse out of the swing and onto his shoulders for a ride.

Lisa drew in her breath. "You haven't changed."

Tony laughed. "Not in some ways." He leaned forward, somersaulted Jesse to the ground, and started tickling him. "What do you want to study?" he asked her.

"I have no idea. I majored in kinesiology. I thought I was going to end up coaching."

"Do you still want to coach?"

"Not really."

"What do you want to do?"

"I have no clue," Lisa said. She didn't feel like revealing that being married to him had once been all she wanted. Or revealing that winning races had been such a powerful drive, had kept her so focused on one finish line after another, that she had never allowed herself to find out what else moved her. In some ways, she still felt like that fourteen-year-old girl who had been plucked off a Los Angeles softball field. Twelve years had, it seemed, flashed by in one excruciating day.

¬

Lisa looked around UCLA's Drake Stadium as if to store its essence in her memory bank. Empty geometric bleachers glinted in the sunlight like some kind of postmodern sacrificial tower. Filled with spectators, the bleachers became a mass of collective humanity hungry to be entertained. Lisa, unlike some of her teammates, had never been intimidated by crowds. Her capacity to focus always made the spectators seem far away and insignificant.

Tamaya pumped her legs into the track as if she were trying to destroy its surface. Lisa watched Tamaya run her fifty meters, recover, and repeat the process. Already, Lisa didn't miss training at all.

When practice finished, Tamaya sauntered over to Lisa. Covered in sweat, her skin shined as if it had been brushed with a giant lip-gloss wand.

"Tay, you are the real thing. You give it a thousand percent, girl," Lisa said as she curtsied.

"Girlfriend, you're talking like you're an old lady. You're the real thing, too." Tay curtsied right back.

Lisa looked away.

"You're walking a lot better. When will you be joining us in the locker room?" Tamaya asked.

"I was trying to tell Coach first. I'm retiring," Lisa said, surprised that it had been so easy to say.

Tamaya groaned and shook her head. "No, Lisa, no. I'm not hearing that. I need you."

Lisa laughed and put her arm around her friend's shoulder. "But I need my life back. I can't keep giving what it takes. My son needs me, and I need me."

Three little lines trisected Tamaya's broad forehead and nearly succeeded in neutralizing the beauty of her sharp cheekbones, full mouth, and alert, amber-flecked brown eyes.

Tamaya started pacing and gesturing wildly. "What better life is there than competing to be the fastest woman in the world? Do you know how many people would sell their soul to compete in one world-class race?"

Lisa struggled to keep herself from laughing at the spectacle of her friend, who had been transformed by her tirade. The gazelle now resembled a rhinoceros. "Tay, I'm not young like you anymore. Time is not on my side. I put everything on hold for another shot at the Olympics, and I had my shot. I don't have another four years to give."

Tamaya plopped onto the bleacher and put her head in her hands. "But what about World's next year? You just started running the four hundred; you're bound to win at least one more gold."

Lisa said slowly, "I've been to World's six times. I won five gold medals, three silver, and three bronze. I'm happy with what I have."

Tamaya sat up straight. "Are you sure you're not still freaked out over the accident?"

Lisa sighed. "If I hadn't been pushing myself, I wouldn't have ignored my injury in the heat. I should have sat out the 200 and only gone for the 100, and maybe the relay, but I was just so sick of it all. I got greedy and wanted a chance to triple or quadruple."

Tamaya asked, "But aren't you going to miss it?"

Lisa gazed around the track, empty but for a few runners stretching after practice, and said, "I'm going to tell you something I never admitted to anyone."

Knowing that she had her friend's full attention, she looked her square in her face and said, "I never liked to run." Lisa softly continued, "But once I found out how good I was, I couldn't let go."

Tamaya's face looked as if it belonged to a little girl who had just been told there is no Santa Claus.

Lisa hugged her friend. "Tay, you're not like me. You love what you do. You belong here, and I won't let you forget it."

Tamaya's eyes still looked wide.

Lisa shuffled exaggeratedly and said, "Now, clean up, you're taking me dancing."

TWO TRUNKS

KATE MO

That summer, two trunks, one black and one olive green, sat in the entry, begging to be opened. They smelled of mothballs, sweet and pungent, and a heavier, mustier scent that hung like a dark lining. It reminded Naomi of the quizzes with purple ink on white paper that her teachers handed out at school — surprise tests that needed answers. Naomi had been warned not to touch the trunks, but because she was only eight, the forbidden was all the more delicious.

One trunk, she learned, belonged to Bachan, who had passed away three weeks ago. Naomi's father, the eldest son, drove from their home in Gardena, a community in southeast Los Angeles, all the way to the Coachella Japanese desert farms outside Palm Springs. He went for the funeral and to clear out his mother's small, weather-beaten house. He came back with the two trunks without a word.

That night, Naomi listened through walls for the answers her parents never shared, not even with her brother, Mike, three years older. The truth, if spoken in front of them, would have been babbled in Japanese, which neither could understand. But, eavesdropping, Naomi learned that the olive-green trunk belonged to her father from his days in the army. The black trunk belonged to Bachan, taken on her sea voyage from Japan as a young bride. Maybe the aunties thought her father should have it since he was the only son. There was something about being a boy in the family that was important.

Now, with no one at home, Naomi sat on the floor and ran her hand along the top of the black trunk. Once smooth, the lid was scratched with lines like wrinkles on a face. It was still dusty from years hidden away in the garage. Naomi sniffed. It had an aged, musky smell with a trace of sea. This made her nose itch. She started to sneeze, but it stopped midway, leaving her with that irritating incomplete feeling. She tried rubbing her nose with the back of her hand, but the sneeze was gone and only the pressure remained.

Naomi carefully clicked open the faded black lid of the trunk, designated for Goodwill, and thought, *The past should stay in the past. Nothing good about the past.* As she lifted the lid, the intoxicating smell of mothballs escaped and filled the air like invisible smoke from a genie bottle.

The interior of the lid was lined with pale pink silk, printed with small lavender flowers. Naomi ran her fingers along its smooth, almost slick surface. In one spot, her nail got caught and snagged the fabric. She tried to gently to take her hand away, but it caused a run, much like in her mother's nylon stockings. She didn't mean to damage the trunk. She just had to look inside before it was taken away.

Turning her attention to the contents, Naomi looked at the folded fabrics filling one side of the trunk. So many colors and designs — small white flowers on a field of green, blue polka dots on white, pale blue-and-white stripes, and some green and brown plaids. Yards of material never transformed into dresses, skirts, or shirts. Using only her fingertips, Naomi lifted the top piece — mauve colored, bordered with a white lace trim — and held it to her face. She sneezed at last.

"Mom told you not to do that," Mike said.

Naomi jumped and dropped the fabric back into the trunk. "I thought you were at the park."

"Smells like camphor," Mike said, looking down at her. She saw his nose wrinkle. His hair was shaggy around his squarish face, so different from her own oval face framed by a pixie cut. He wore old blue jeans and a gray T-shirt.

"I don't think it smells like camphor," she said.

"Do you even know what camphor is?"

Mike always said he was better than Naomi because of being the boy. They were like the two trunks. Different colors and sizes, separate and closed.

"I wanted to see if there was anything important before Mom and Dad get rid of everything."

Naomi told her brother to go through the olive-green trunk with their father's initials on it, and that it was from when he was in the army, spending two years in Japan during the Korean War.

"How do you know that stuff?" Mike asked.

"I listen to them talk at night when they think I'm asleep."

"What else did he say?" he asked, not looking at Naomi. She sensed his body tense, like a fist ready to punch. Then, suddenly, his breathing softened. He repeated his question, trying hard to sound disinterested.

Naomi rattled off everything she knew. Their father had been on special assignment. Because he knew how to speak Japanese, the army used him to translate for senior officers and diplomats. He got to visit all kinds of places.

"You made all that up," Mike said. He hated it when she knew more. He never shared secret stories with her.

"Look in Dad's trunk. There might be some stuff from Japan," Naomi said.

"Nothing good, I bet." Mike grunted but turned to the olive-green trunk.

They both sifted through the contents of their trunks quietly and delicately as if excavating a site for artifacts. Naomi wanted to touch and feel every piece of folded fabric. She found a white crocheted sweater and tried it on.

"It doesn't fit," Mike said.

"Someday it will. It must have belonged to Bachan."

"What else is in there?" Mike asked. He reached over and dug into the neatly piled crocheted doilies, quilts, and shawls. Naomi told him to stop. This was her trunk.

"It's mine, too," he said, and she felt an energy building in him.

"It's for girls."

"Boys are more important," he said. "Remember Bachan told us about Boys' Day? It's a national holiday in Japan. For boys." He pushed Naomi aside.

Naomi tried to remember what Bachan said about Boys' Day — purple irises, sweet bean cakes, and paper koi banners. Koi were supposed to be determined fish who swam upstream and later became dragons, and the koi brought good luck to the boys.

Then she remembered something and shot back at Mike. "Dad never flew a paper koi for you."

"How would you know?" Mike said. "He might have stopped after you were born. They planted the iris in front for me."

She knew then that Mike was hurt. Neither of them could remember what the iris symbolized, but she knew the flowers weren't more important than the koi.

Mike continued to rifle through Naomi's trunk. So, she turned to her dad's. She found envelopes and papers, nothing as interesting as her grandma's trunk. But underneath a stack, she found an old photo album. It had a brown cover and was rectangular in shape. The pages were black, and the photos were held in place by four triangular tabs — black-and-white pictures of Japanese children playing baseball, sitting in a classroom, or just lined up for a group picture. She looked at the dates in neat block printing, the type Mike learned in his drafting class. White ink on the black paper: "April 1944."

Mike grabbed it from Naomi's hands, saying, "These are pictures from Poston. Camp pictures. But no cameras were allowed in the camps."

Naomi asked, "What camp?" but her brother waved the question away like a bad smell.

Naomi heard her parents talk about "the camp" at family gatherings: a dance, nurse's aide training, baseball games, communal meals, bathrooms without doors — nothing that sounded like her Blue Bird Day Camp.

"These might be worth something," Mike said.

"Why? We don't know these people."

She wondered how her father was able to take pictures if no cameras were allowed. She tried to take the album back, but Mike refused to let it go.

"What did they tell you about the camp?" Naomi asked, hoping her brother would explain why so many people were living in barracks behind barbed wire fences.

"Nothing," he said as he pried open a wooden box that he found.

"Then how do you know?"

"Mr. Sugu." Mike's history teacher was helping Mike work on a family history project.

"Why were they in a camp?" Naomi asked.

"The government thought they might be spies."

Naomi laughed at the thought of her grandma, her mom and dad, and her uncles and aunts as spies. "No, seriously, Mike, tell me." He ignored her as he picked up a book.

To spite him, she said, "There is no more Boys' Day. There's Children's Day. Bachan said *No more Boys' Day*, but there's still a Girls' Day."

But Mike was still looking at a handmade book, copied from an original — *Momo Taro*, a children's story about a boy hidden inside a big peach. Naomi knew the story. The husband in the story had been gone a long time. The wife was lonely and wished for a child. One day, a big peach floated down the river. The wife presented it to the husband when he returned home. Inside was a baby boy.

Mike closed the book. He wasn't going to tell her about the camp. Naomi pulled out another photo album; this one was white with little lambs on the cover. Inside were her baby pictures.

"What's that?" Mike asked.

"I didn't know that they took pictures of me."

"Let's see." He grabbed the book and flipped through the pages. "They're all of you."

"It's my baby book."

"There should be some pictures of me. I'm older than you," he said and threw the album down. Some loose pictures slid on the ground. "Where did you find them? In this box?"

Mike stepped over to the trunk and began digging and tossing things aside. There were loose pictures and envelopes with birth certificates, army discharge papers, death certificates, medical records. But no more pictures.

"They must have put yours somewhere else," Naomi said, sensing his disappointment.

"Where?"

"Dad is really good at putting things in order."

"Or maybe he didn't save them."

"Why wouldn't he have?" Naomi asked.

"Same reason they want to get rid of all this stuff."

Nothing good comes from the past.

Naomi reached for an envelope that Mike tossed aside. Just copies of official looking records. Then, she found Mike's birth certificate. Reading it, she noticed something wrong and tried to hide the paper.

Mike grabbed it from her. He saw it, too. The father's name had been scratched out, but they could both see the name beneath the marks.

"They made a mistake," Naomi said.

He threw the paper aside and mumbled something about how everything in his life now made sense. Naomi wasn't sure what Mike meant. He kicked the trunk. It made a dull thump that she knew hurt his foot.

"I'll tell them. They'll get another one."

Mike grabbed Naomi by the shirt and shook her. She was too scared to scream. Suddenly, he let go. The screen door slammed.

Naomi heard him yelling and kicking the iris in the front yard. She waited until it was quiet before going outside. He had clawed and scratched the iris blooms and stomped them into the ground, along with their flat green leaves. The flowers lost their soft, sweet scent along with the promise of celebration.

The next day, the trunks and all they held went to the Goodwill. Naomi and Mike never talked about the paper again. They both remained separate and locked.

Shawn,

Hope you enjoy
this!

JP Higgins
(Jimmy)

LIVING, DEAD, AND IN-BETWEEN

J.P. HIGGINS

Johnny O'Neill lay between pieces of cardboard under an oleander hedge along the Los Angeles River. As smudged fingers of creamy streetlights pierced the green and red canopy overhead, Johnny scanned a scrap of *The Wall Street Journal*: a soporific book review that insisted, "Work at what you love."

"Already on it," he said to himself with a smile. One night some weeks earlier, sleeping in the same grimy blue jeans and faded "Happiest Place on Earth" sweatshirt, the idea for his business had come to him whole in a dream.

Johnny loved finding bits of trash on the street, stuff that seemed invisible to most people. Collecting this urban flotsam and jetsam and divining uses for it lifted the shadows that tended to slow his thinking and give him headaches. When such discoveries felt right in his head, Johnny's work would begin in an imaginary windowless laboratory at the theoretical birth of the little object he'd found. He'd see its image there, drawn in blue pencil on a drafting table, always surrounded by the same white-shirted, black-tied, square-jawed men with crewcuts in gray tweed jackets, who analyzed the drawing through heavy, black-rimmed glasses. Johnny imagined himself as the upstart whiz kid among these nameless engineers, the quality control hero with superior intellect and insight.

One recent week "at work," he'd spent nearly every sunny hour alone in the doorway of a vacant storefront, rocking on his haunches, contemplating an empty ballpoint pen casing. His only distractions were finding a place to piss and chasing away haggard competitors for the sunny doorway. The veil of scraggly brown hair that hung down into his beard didn't prevent Johnny from seeing clearly into the windowless laboratory in his mind where an exploded drawing of the ballpoint pen casing sat on the imaginary drafting table. A cobalt blue corona of stylized architectural letters labeled the drawing's structural and design details. One engineer pointed at the drawing with the stem of his pipe and commented. The other engineers joined in: murmuring and chin rubbing, lip pursing, and head nodding. The draftsman made an erasure, redrew a detail, and edited its label. Then another pipe stem, or at times a slide rule or mechanical pencil, would point at the drawing and the process would repeat, again and again until the drawing satisfied everyone in the lab. "Not so fast," Johnny said out loud, rising to his feet in the storefront's doorway with the broken pen casing clutched in his outstretched hand. The design flaw was obvious from his vantage point across space and time. He shook his fist and shouted, "It will fail! Can't you see?" Though ignored by the nameless engineers in his mind, his shouting frightened pedestrians passing him on the sidewalk.

While he slept that night, his lungs worked, straining the air of smog, cooling and animating his brain, where new ideas tumbled like soapy wet clothes in an all-night launderette. At dawn, stiff and sore from a fitful night, Johnny coughed until his lungs cleared, then set to work invigorated by this new nocturnal inspiration.

He scoured gutters and dumpsters for inanimate things with life still in them. He rolled his inventory in his shopping cart to the filthy Mission Street sidewalk, where he displayed it on a grimy pallet balanced against the low block wall of a municipal parking lot. His operation may have looked like litter and junk eddied by capricious Santa Ana winds, but for Johnny it was commerce. His peers would pay him a nickel for a length of good string or a strong rubber band, or a dime for a knapsack without holes. Containers with working lids, like cigar boxes, could fetch a quarter — treasure chests, Johnny called them. He didn't barter. "Cash is king," he'd chant impatiently when he sensed desire or need in a customer. "Cash is king," he'd snarl at non-buying browsers who interrupted his reveries, shooing them when he felt compelled to pursue one of his analytic visits to the windowless laboratory.

One morning, Johnny found a small pistol in a parking lot dumpster. He'd never held one, and when he saw what he'd touched, he shuddered involuntarily. With his thumb and forefinger on the sides of its handle, he lifted it delicately and then sat cross-legged behind the dumpster in the quiet bright light to examine it. He studied how it was assembled, how its parts might swing or slide into each other. With it close to his face, Johnny smelled a strange blend of ketchup, gunpowder, and oil. When he wiped a small blob of the red sauce off the sight at the end of the barrel, he let his fingers trace the scuffed dark metal. He avoided the hammer and trigger and the small lever beneath the barrel. *Maybe it's a safety switch*, he thought, *or a release for the bullet-filled cylinder.*

He shifted the pistol from hand to hand, admired its heft, and wondered what might have created each scratch and dent. He imagined it had been dropped to a concrete garage floor by a nervous new owner, battered by wrenches and pipe fittings at the bottom of a plumber's toolkit, or maybe thrown by an angry woman through a fourth-floor windowpane, hitting the street amidst shattered glass. He pictured it being ground into roadside gravel under the heel of a scuffling policeman.

As the gun warmed in the morning sun, Johnny grew more at ease. He tucked the gun into the front of his pants and leaned back against the dumpster. He felt spiritually enriched by this new possession and closed his eyes to better feel the weapon press the chakra behind his waistband.

Suddenly, from the windowless laboratory, glaring engineers surrounded Johnny. *"Does it work?"* demanded one as he looked over the top of his glasses, pipe clenched between taut lips, face pushed close to Johnny's.

"I don't know," said Johnny into the air. He pushed hair off his face, leaving a streak of red on his cheek.

"Don't you think you'd better find out?" barked the engineer.

Johnny stood up and moved the pistol into a small cigar box in his cart, then wiped both hands a few times on his "Happiest" shirt. Maybe he could test-fire the pistol in solitude down by the river, he thought, so he yanked the cart to the sidewalk and headed back to his campsite under the oleander.

He'd been raised in the San Fernando Valley a few miles north of where he now walked, the third of five children, the only son, his father's namesake. When he was ten, a forbidden candle in a "fort" in his closet started the fire that destroyed his house and killed both his little sisters. The family moved to a new house, and they got mental therapy for a while until John Sr. decided they'd had enough. Life moved on. John Sr. disappeared into his office work in the industrial park by the Van Nuys Airport; Mrs. O'Neill and the older girls took up square dancing in Glendale; Johnny drifted through high school, dreaming under a marijuana cloud that loomed darker than the burnt-out shell of his old house.

In Johnny's senior year, the principal had summoned Johnny's parents to discuss his withdrawn and antisocial behavior. Mr. O'Neill showed up alone, offering only a terse, telling response: "That kid never gets anything right."

On the calm, clear night when the rest of his class was graduating, Johnny was solo stargazing on LSD at Point Dume. He sat cross-legged on hard, rock-strewn sand near the water's edge, soothed by the whisper and rasp of the Pacific's ebb and flow. He piled smooth, round stones on his ankles and in his lap. By placing one stone for each failure of his life, he soon made a mound that pinned his legs. Immobilizing his body seemed to set his mind adrift, and it shot directly to the familiar memory of the contraption he'd rigged in his closet the night of the fire. His bedroom floor had been strewn with model airplane parts that night, broken and smashed by his father in a perfectionist rage. Johnny's incendiary device had been a candle and string soaked in the plastic model cement. But it had been worse than a failure; his baby sisters were dead, yet his father still lived. His screwup proved what his father had so often told him: "You can't do anything right."

The untouched wet stones lying on the sand seemed to mock him as innumerable future failures — more numerous than the stars in the black sky above. Overwhelmed in contemplating the enormous weight of the future, he wept.

⌐

When he got to the river, he pushed his cart through the access gate onto the paved bike path atop the riverbank and found new orange plastic cones had been placed to block the path. A city maintenance truck sat parked beyond the cones, its bed full of freshly trimmed greenery. The huge oleander hedge had been transformed, reduced to clusters of leafless stalks, each about half the height and girth of a phone booth. Six men raked the dusty brown earth between these clusters as it baked in the hot morning sun. There was no sign of his cardboard, his bedding or his inventory, no remnant in the dirt of anyone having ever lived among these stumps. A short, round man in a hard hat and orange reflective vest waved his arms over his head and walked toward Johnny.

"Hey, amigo! Vamoose!" said the man. "Casa no mas, buddy. Hasta la vista."

"Where's my stuff?" Johnny shouted back at him.

"All gone, pal," said the vested man. Even with the hard hat, he was shorter than Johnny, but older, with pencil-thin white sideburns and a close-cropped gray goatee. His face was as brown as the oleander bark. He squinted and frowned.

"What did you do with it?" Johnny repeated.

"Trucked everything to the dump," said the little man. "Orders."

Johnny fumed, and his mind jumped to the new power he'd acquired from the pistol inside the cigar box in his shopping cart. He could shoot all six of these little men!

The nameless engineers suddenly appeared in his mind and one shouted, *"How many bullets do you have?"*

"I DON'T KNOW!" Johnny shouted back, raising his arms. "HOW SHOULD I KNOW?"

"Get the hell outta here, you wacko," said the little man in orange.

Johnny turned and kicked his cart hard, and then muscled and shoved it back out the gate to the street.

"Can't you do anything right, Johnny?" said another of the crewcut engineers.

"Move along," Johnny mumbled over and over through gritted teeth as he walked. It was a calming mantra that helped propel him while walking long aimless distances day and night when he'd first left home. It also kept the nameless engineers out of his mind when he didn't want them around.

As he walked, Johnny focused on the explosive power of the pistol. He stopped, took it out of the cigar box, and slid it in behind the waistband of his pants. *Finally, some real power*, he thought. *Real power can fix anything.* At a little park downriver, he pushed his cart across the grass to a bench and sat down.

"Bring it on," he said as he closed his eyes.

The windowless laboratory appeared. *"Who do you think you are?"* said the engineer with the pipe in his mouth.

"I'm the guy with the power," said Johnny.

"What are you going to do about this?" said the engineer, looking at the drafting table and pointing with his pipe. There stood a drawing of a younger Johnny as he'd looked before he'd moved into the street, before he'd let his hair and beard grow. The cobalt blue labels filled the periphery of the drawing like an aura, with straight lines from each letter to a part of Johnny's clean-cut head.

Johnny peered into the image at the drafting table. One draftsman turned from the table to look directly at Johnny. It was his father, John Sr.

"I see the problem!" said Johnny. He rose and pushed his cart back to the street, mumbling his mantra over and over.

He went down past Figueroa Street to the end of an alley where he knew he'd find Eddie, a fellow Skid Row entrepreneur who cut hair. Johnny had sold him a few combs.

"Hey, Skinny Hands!" shouted Johnny when he found Eddie in the midday shade of the narrow alley. Eddie's shiny, thin, blackened fingers interlocked and jutted proud from the threadbare sleeves of a rumpled brown business suit. Squatting against the wall with his forearms resting on bent knees, Eddie resembled a spider suffocating in a jar.

"How many time I tol' you don' call me dat?" said Eddie, rheumy eyes smiling.

"Hah!" said Johnny. "Cut my hair?"

"Got cash? All haircuts cash today. I'm hungry."

"Yeah, cash is king. I got a dollar, so clean me up?" Johnny stroked his beard and smoothed the knotted mass of his hair.

"Johnny, you a scary mess. Take a whole lot more to clean you up," Eddie laughed. "Siddown here. I'll do you a dollar's worth, and Halloween be over."

Eddie unfolded himself and stood nearly a head taller than Johnny. He opened one large white palm toward the chrome and black stepstool beside him in the shade, like a waiter directing him to sit. Johnny had sold that stool to Eddie months ago.

"Gimme the dollar now," said Eddie.

"Nah, I'll pay you when you're done. You get hungry and quit halfway through, what do I do?"

Eddie was always hungry and talked fast and endlessly about food he wanted, and the restaurants with that food, their proximity, their hours, their décor, and of course the food itself: its color, texture, weight, shape, temperature, aroma, and flavor. He'd chatter on about his stomach's responses to various foods, theories to explain intestinal reactions, and the genetic and allergic predispositions of his entire family three generations back.

"You know my rules, man," Eddie said.

"You really piss me off sometimes," Johnny said. He moved his hand to the butt of the pistol in his pants. He could shoot Eddie right there waiting for the dollar, but then there'd be no one else to clean him up. On the plus side, though, there'd be no more of Eddie's constant yammering about food.

Johnny pulled the pistol from his pants and pointed it at Eddie. "I'm thinking of changing the rules," he said.

"Oh, a loaded thirty-eight?" said Eddie. His eyes widened, riveted to the weapon in Johnny's hand.

"Do things seem different to you now? Do I seem different now?" asked Johnny.

"You want a haircut, you got to put that piece away," Eddie said.

"You thinking about food now?" asked Johnny.

"I'm thinkin' food don't go good with guns, man."

Johnny hesitated, then nodded. "Okay," he said, and put the pistol back in his pants. "Here's your dollar, then," he said as he slapped four quarters into Eddie's palm.

Eddie frowned and counted the coins as Johnny turned to the stool. Then he shook his head and smiled. "All right! Now we cookin'! Eddie's college of kwee-zeen-ee-airy knowledge is now in session," he said with a flourish of his hand and a fancy bow toward the low stool, "and for my first witness, your honor, I call Mr. Johnny O'Neill."

"That's right," Johnny said as he sat down. "Make me look like a cop."

"Cops," Eddie said. "You think they donut eaters, but they real secret is hot dogs. Lemme tell you 'bout some hot dog places I seen the cops."

"Eddie!" Johnny interrupted. "Can you show me how to use this gun?"

"Use it? Ain't you gonna sell it?"

"I gotta test it. Gotta know if it works."

After the haircut, Eddie showed Johnny how to release the cylinder. They counted five bullets in the cylinder. He showed Johnny how to cock the hammer and how to brace his wrist to shoot with two hands. Johnny repeated Eddie's actions until he felt confident.

"Where you gonna test it?" asked Eddie. "You be in a world of hurt if anyone see you."

"I'm going out to where my father lives," said Johnny.

"Where that?" asked Eddie.

"Way out in the Valley ... a million miles from here."

⌐

When he got to the bus station, Johnny reached deep to the bottom of his shopping cart and grabbed a lady's white high-heeled go-go boot, a size 6AA, that zipped up the back. It held the paper money he'd accumulated from his sales, small bills crammed hastily into the boot when he converted his change at a liquor store. He carried the boot into the bus station and went to the men's room, a tiny, tiled space crowded with two stalls, a urinal, and a sink, lit by a single overhead fluorescent. One sash of the room's sole frosted window, tattooed with dark blue graffiti, had been left open for ventilation and more light.

Johnny looked at his short hair and smooth chin in the mirror for several minutes. Eddie had done a good job after all. Backlighting from the open window cast a blue aura around his face. He took off his sweatshirt, turned it inside out, and put it back on. "*Now* who do you think you are?" he whispered to his steel-eyed reflection.

He went into a stall, closed the door, and stood silently, waiting. When he was sure he was alone in the bathroom, he sat on the closed toilet seat and removed the wad of wrinkled one-dollar bills from the white boot, smoothing them on his thighs. He counted fifty-six. He folded ten ones and put them in his pants pocket, then squared up and folded the remaining pile and shoved it back into the boot. Johnny took the pistol out of his pants and used its barrel to pack the paper money flat against the sole of the boot. By mistake he squeezed the trigger. "Oh shit," mouthed Johnny, ears ringing from the blast and the ricochet.

The bullet had smoked a small clean hole through the newly stacked bills, torn the bottom off the boot, and ricocheted off the tile floor between his feet.

As he scooped up the shredded boot sole from the floor of the stall, he noticed its stitching had failed at the impact of the bullet.

With his hand and the gun still inside the boot, he turned it over to check on the money. The bills were still wadded there in the boot. There was a small, puckered hole in the middle of the wad that seemed to bind the bills together as if speared on an invisible spindle. He removed the punctured bills from the boot and held them over his head to peer through them at the dim overhead light. *Like looking up an asshole*, he thought. He tucked the gun into his pants under the sweatshirt and the money into his front pocket. Then, he set the remains of the boot under the toilet's water tank.

The men's room door burst open, and a male voice boomed, "What's going on in here?"

Johnny said through the closed stall door, "I think something just came through the window."

"Are you okay?" asked the voice.

"Yeah," said Johnny. He stood and opened the stall door a crack to look out.

He saw a crewcut security guard, whose thick neck seemed choked by the narrow black tie under his polo shirt collar. "Am I glad to see you," Johnny said, feigning relief, easing the door open a bit more.

The security guard gave Johnny a suspicious once-over but seemed reassured at this clean-cut fellow in the stall.

Johnny saw that the ricocheted bullet had passed up through the sink's counter, ripping out a hunk of the veneer and leaving a delicate black star-shaped depression in the brown Formica. It had come to rest on the ledge in front of the mirror as if it had been placed there by hand.

"There," Johnny said, pointing. "The window."

The guard walked two steps to the open window and stuck his head outside, looking left and right, up and down the alley. Johnny slipped out of the men's room and headed straight to the ticket kiosk in the middle of the crowded lobby. He glanced over his shoulder, then went around the kiosk to an open ticket window on the far side.

"Next bus to Westlake Village?" he said, lifting the currency from his pocket.

"One minute, door six," said the agent.

Johnny was the last to board. He dropped into an empty seat at the back of the bus and slouched until his knees touched the metal seatback in front of him. He had to readjust the pistol in his pocket to keep it from sliding out onto the floor.

An old lady across the aisle stared at him. "Nice to be headed home, ain't it?" she said.

"You talking to me?" he said.

"You're relaxed," she said, smiling. "Not all tightened up like outbound folks." She was small and seemed smaller in the faded cloth coat she wore closed to her neck. A little black hat decorated with netting sat neatly on her head. A gray bun of hair hung behind it. "You ain't been away long, though. No luggage." She smiled with her lips closed and nodded as if she'd just solved a riddle. She had a strong jaw, but a face so wrinkled it looked rubbery.

I've been gone a long time, thought Johnny as he turned his eyes from her. The graffiti on the seatback above his knees read, *You don't know Dick.*

"My things are in storage," the old lady said. She sat straight and held a small, beaded purse on her lap with both hands. "I'll be living with my kids when their house is fixed up for it."

A grimacing engineer appeared in Johnny's mind, asking, *"What's wrong with this woman?"* Johnny turned back to her and noted her dirty athletic shoes and the frayed hem of her coat. Their eyes met; she smiled.

"I'm going to my father's house," he said.

¬

As Johnny crossed town on a bus, John O'Neill Sr. lay shoeless on his sofa in khakis and a gray cardigan, just waking from his midday nap. After Mrs. O'Neill died a few years ago, Mr. O'Neill discovered that naps actually functioned to lessen the negative effects of his insomnia. This changed napping from a gratuitous indulgence — like reading fiction — to a purposeful biological activity. Since then, he'd napped on schedule.

While lying on his side, Mr. O'Neill swung his feet off the sofa and let gravity pull them to the floor. With a slight assist from his arm, this leg motion levered his soft, rounded upper body to a sitting position. Since he was a boy, he had relished finding efficiencies. As a man, the pursuit of efficiency had inspired his career, circumscribed his passions, and driven his compulsions.

He picked up his glasses from the table beside the sofa, and in doing so bumped a tarnished silver frame that held a portrait of his family. The photo had been taken near Christmas a year or so before the fire. All five children wore red V-necked sweaters and white button-down shirts; the older girls and Johnny stood behind Mr. and Mrs. O'Neill, who were seated with the younger girls on their laps. All seven posed against a studio background of indistinct ice blue.

Mr. O'Neill put on his glasses and straightened the picture. He noticed the redness of the sweaters had lost some of its luster, and all skin tones had yellowed. He remembered tying his son's bow tie the morning of that photo and running a lint brush over his daughter's sweater. That same bow tie still hung on a section of his closet pole with dozens of others.

I don't know why I keep those ties, he thought as he released the picture.

He went to change into his gardening clothes.

¬

The old lady in the back of the bus was still talking. "It's been a rough ride for Marissa — that's my daughter — you know? Four kids in six years. Husband just this side of no good. Loves his Bud, his Dodgers, his car, and his family. In that order. Neanderthal in a La-Z-Boy, get the picture?"

Johnny listened to her prattle and thought, *Can't shut up, that's her problem.*

The old lady went on. "She needs me, otherwise I'd stay on my own. I like my independence, my own space, always have. But that Donald, he's useless. Won't change a light bulb. Wouldn't know a paintbrush from a hairbrush from a broom. Marissa's off at work, her kids come home and run wild and hungry, he don't lift a finger. If it weren't for Marissa, they'd all be living in their car down by the river."

Johnny was concentrating on the corner of the seatback in front of him, where a rivet had pulled through the seat cover vinyl. He could see that its problem might have been one of three: insufficient fabric, excessive tension on the rivet, or vandalism, but when the woman said, "living down by the river," his train of thought was interrupted. The windowless laboratory popped into his mind, and the pipe-smoking engineer smirked at him. *"She's mocking you,"* he said.

"What do you know about it?" Johnny burst out at her. "You think you're helping? You think Marissa wants help?

Everything you think is probably wrong. You can't possibly know what's in your kid's mind."

"Or what's in your own mind?" said the engineer, still smirking.

"But I'm her mother," said the old lady.

"You're getting in your own way with ideas like that," said Johnny. "You got to listen more. It takes a committee."

"That's insane," she said.

"Let me tell you, lady, there are plenty of people watching you, with plenty of ways to get into your brain and tell you what to do, and you won't even know it's happening. You'll think it's you, but it's them. Believe me, you *are* the problem if you don't know that you're only part of the solution. Just part of it! You get it?"

The lady stared at him, her eyes had gone small, her head and her little black hat cocked to one side, her brow a mass of confused wrinkles. Johnny went back to examining the rip in the seat cover. *Maybe now she'll shut up.*

He was exhausted but not sure why. He fingered the pistol in his pocket.

The bus exited the San Diego Freeway on Roscoe Boulevard and turned west into Van Nuys. When it passed the Van Nuys Airport, Johnny saw familiar buildings and landscape out the window. He stood up to walk toward the front of the bus, and the old lady spoke to him.

"Young man, I'll remember what you said, even if some of it is nuts. I'm sorry if I bent your ear. Enjoy your visit with your father. He's got a good son." She smiled again, all pale rubbery wrinkles, strong jaw, and closed lips.

Johnny got off at Balboa and stood in the baking sunlight until the signal changed. As he waited, lunchtime traffic zoomed through the intersection. The air smelled hotter, different than the downtown air. He decided it had more of a mineral smell, more dust and particles than the animal and vegetable smells he was used to from downtown, and different too from the stagnant dampness by the river.

He turned west onto Stagg Street, and then onto a small cul-de-sac called Goldmine Lane. At the very end was his father's house, in full and constant view as he walked to it.

John Sr. was using electric clippers to sculpt the crisp right angle of his Eugenia hedge along the driveway. Johnny heard the chattering of the tool, saw its bright orange extension cord, and recognized the pith helmet his father wore when doing yard work. He fingered the pistol as he walked. John Sr., intent on cutting a perfect surface on the dense greenery, was unaware of his son's approach.

Johnny stopped at the sidewalk and waited. John Sr. finally looked up, did a quick double take, then released the trigger, which stopped the electric tool's chattering. It hung at his side like a gunslinger's weapon for a moment, then he set it on the ground at his feet.

"Hello, John," he said.

"Hello, Dad."

"Everything okay? Where you been?"

"You're kidding, right?"

"What's the trouble?" John Sr. removed his pith helmet and took one step toward his son.

"The trouble? The trouble is you. Doesn't matter I'm far away, never see you, never talk to you. You're always there. Always blaming, always criticizing, finding fault. I can't get you out of my head. It's driving me nuts."

"I'm sorry, son."

"Sorry? You think being sorry is all it takes? Sorry fixes nothing, Dad. Nothing."

"I'm more than sorry, if you want to know the truth."

"What do you mean?" This sudden apology by his father, apparently genuine and wholly unprecedented, confused Johnny and made him cautious.

"Here, sit down a minute. There's something I've been wanting to tell you, and since I doubt you've come to stay, and I don't know when I'll see you again, I want to tell you now."

"I don't want to sit down."

"Well, I do," said John Sr. He crossed the driveway toward a small patio nestled behind the shrubbery in front of the house. There was a wrought iron table and two chairs. He sat in the one facing the house, with his back to his son. "Suit yourself, Johnny, but I'd rather look at you while I'm talking to you. Come around here where we can talk."

Johnny stepped onto the patio and remained standing.

"Here's the thing, son. Since your mother died, I've been …" — he lowered his eyes — "… very depressed. Banging around alone in this house, I think a lot. I look at my life and see a trail of mistakes and screw-ups. I've tried to balance it with good stuff, you know, achievements and such. But the truth is, I can't balance it. My life is shit."

"So?" said Johnny. "So's mine. So's everybody's. The difference is, I'm going to fix it. For both of us." He pulled out the pistol.

"Where'd you get that?" John Sr. asked with more curiosity than alarm.

"Compliments of kismet … fate … karma. Take your pick."

"And … what? You plan to use that on me? Ha!" He let out a big belly laugh.

"Typical. You think this is funny."

"No, I don't, Johnny. It's not funny, but I think it's perfect. Go ahead. Kill me. Do me a favor."

"What are you talking about?"

"I just told you. I'm a failure. Wife's dead, two babies dead, and I'm left with two airheads and one homeless nut. Why should I care whether I live or die? You know how to use that thing? Go ahead."

"Is this a trick?"

"No. It's all true. I'm depressed, and I don't care if you shoot me. Wait ... one part's not true: I don't think you're really nuts. Your sisters really are airheads, but you? You're not crazy."

"Why do you say that?"

"You want to kill me. I think that's a pretty sane response to all the trouble I've caused you."

Johnny flashed back to the old lady on the bus ... believing she knew what was in her kid's head ... unable to get out of her own way ... stuck with a fixed idea.

"So, you *want* me to kill you?"

"No, I don't want anything. Except for you to know that ... if you've got problems, well, it's probably my fault. I know how much trouble I've caused you, and your sisters. After the little ones died, I —"

"Don't bring them into this."

"They're already in it, Johnny. We're all in it. Living, dead, and in-between. Tell me, do you still see those engineers in your mind sometimes?"

Johnny felt his face flush.

"Okay, let's say that you do," said his father. "Know what? I see the babies, my dead kids. I see your mother, my dead wife. They talk to me, they complain, they cry, and they wail. They're never happy with me. I cry sometimes for days. Does that make me crazy? I don't think so. You see engineers in your head; I see the dead. You're no crazier than I am."

"Why are you telling me this?"

"I know what your engineers are telling you, and they're wrong."

"How do you know?"

"They're probably telling you that force is power, right?"

"So?"

"They're wrong. I'm an engineer. I've looked at my life and seen the results of believing in the superiority of power. It's a flawed premise. So, I'm flawed. And if you don't get it, then you'll be flawed too."

"Get what?"

"What's senior to power is the decision to use it. Use it, or don't use it, you see? The decision is the senior thing. Either decision, that's the key. So, a decision to not use power is always superior to power itself. I never learned that. Never lived that way. For me it was power all the way. Get it, use it, and then get some more and use that. I pushed you, and look what I got for it. My life is a flop. You, my son, my namesake, want to kill me. I'd say that's proof that my life is a flop, isn't it?"

Johnny felt lightheaded. He sat down in the chair opposite his father. His mouth hung open, and he was panting.

"Seems odd, doesn't it?" his father asked. "The more force you use to fix a problem, the harder the problem pushes back at you. It's simple ... like physics ... like thermodynamics."

Johnny looked at the pistol in his hand, and then at his father's face: unshaven, lightly tanned, with a red mark across his forehead from the pith helmet. Nose slightly off center with small hairs growing on its end. Lips thicker than Johnny remembered. Eyes dark below bushy brows, but clear and ... kind. It was like seeing John Sr. for the first time.

"It's hot out here. Want some iced tea?" asked his father.

THE PANDEMIC SALON

NICK DURETTA

Because I pay attention to signs, and use them to adjust my expectations and actions, I was the first in the company to see it coming. They had been building for months: progressively dire items on my news feed, anxious conversations on the street, articles in the *Times* working their way from the back pages to the front. At rehearsals I would mention what this could mean for our play (cancellations, smaller audiences) but got little response. Nobody was taking it seriously. Suddenly, though, the signs were everywhere: masks, toilet paper shortages, hand sanitizer, social distancing.

Our director called the cast together and told us that the planned opening of *Stripe* was cancelled. He was apologetic but hardly hopeful. No, he didn't know for how long — this was a global pandemic, for Christ's sake. We weren't the only ones facing unemployment. Theaters everywhere were closing, even cinemas.

"Now what?" asked Stefanie, the willowy ingenue cast as my sister, as we gathered afterward in the corner Starbucks.

"We're screwed," said Carlos, who played the suicidal auto mechanic.

Jason, my dissolute brother in the play, said, "It's an overreaction. Everything will be back to normal in a month. Trust me on this."

As the lead actor, and the only one with feature film credentials, I felt the need to be reassuring. Yet I couldn't.

The signs were clear: something had fundamentally changed, and the sooner we accepted that, the better. I suggested that my fellow cast members "consider other options" — industry-speak for non-acting jobs. It was a cliché, but the only one I could think of.

Stripe wasn't to be staged at a large-capacity name theater — we were basically at a renovated warehouse in Hollywood — but it was an Equity production, and we were all getting paid. Even so, most of us had been supplementing our income with side jobs. I worked part-time as a sales rep for an office equipment supplier, which, with what was left of my savings, might see me through the next few months. But beyond that? Experts on the news were predicting a complete economic shutdown for at least a year. A fucking *year*.

¬

Three days later, I received a message. Not an email or a text or a mailed letter, but a typewritten note slid under my apartment door.

"Mr. Brace," it began. "I was looking forward to your performance in *Stripe* and was sorry to hear of its cancellation. For an actor of your caliber, this must be a difficult blow. I am in a position to be of help. I am looking for a stellar thespian such as you to give performances for intimate audiences at my home. Nothing salacious or illegal, I assure you. You will be compensated handsomely, and you might, if I should be so bold to suggest, find yourself enhanced by the experience. Please contact me at your convenience." He signed the note "Allerson" and included a phone number.

I'd never heard of the guy. Was this a joke? He obviously knew where I lived.

"An actor of my caliber"? Come on. Sure, I'd gotten good reviews in a few small roles, but I also had a reputation for being difficult. I was often accused of "not being a team player," the usual euphemism for someone who is more trouble than they're worth. My old acting coach put it most kindly: I was "too tied to the script"; that is, I had the temerity to play characters the way they were written rather than probe the soul inside. Playwrights usually loved my approach, but directors frequently didn't; many preferred actors who would think way outside the box. Well, screw them. It wasn't my job to change what was written. That's why the cancellation of *Stripe* hit me so hard. The director had loved my faithful portrayal of the main character, a son called to assume control of the family business after the sudden death of his father. It was what was expected of my character: he'd been preparing for it, he was ready. Then the world turned upside-down.

Still, for the next twenty-four hours, I debated responding to Allerson's invitation. The whole thing sounded crazy, and perhaps dangerous. Fraudulent, even. "Performances for intimate audiences"? What the hell was that all about?

My curiosity — and the need for rent money — won out. I phoned Allerson and, to my surprise, he answered.

"Ah, Mr. Brace! I am so pleased to hear from you. I feared my strange inquiry might have put you off. It is unorthodox, I confess, but I assure you it is entirely genuine. Rather than discuss it over the phone, though, would you consider meeting in person? Let's say, this Thursday night?"

He spoke in a precise and elevated tone that I was suspicious of. It was as if he were a performer himself, auditioning for a role. I hesitated but agreed to meet. He provided me with a time and an address — a side street off Coldwater.

The next two days passed, and before I realized it, there I was, standing outside a prewar cottage perched on a hillside that afforded a killer view of the L.A. basin, an array of lights sparkling into the distance. I pressed the doorbell and a moment later was greeted by a man who was, on my first estimation, in his mid-sixties, with a healthy crop of slightly graying hair (assisted, I was certain, by artificial help) topping an angular, masculine face, the kind I associate with CIA handlers in spy thrillers. He wore a casual yellow linen shirt and bright green trousers. Beneath the mask over his mouth he seemed to form a smile, and extended his hand. "Mr. Brace! So glad to see you. Please come in."

Despite my suspicions, I managed a smile. He led me into an opulent parlor that belied the plain façade of the exterior. I had stepped into a bohemian *pied-a-terre*, with walls painted a deep blue, intimate lighting from a few strategically placed Tiffany lamps, and bookshelves filled with more *objets d'art* than actual books. An abstract painting that looked like a 1950s' television test pattern rendered in psychedelic colors hung above the white stone mantelpiece of the fireplace.

"Can I get you anything?" he asked in that cultured voice I'd heard on the phone. "Wine? An apéritif?"

"Nothing, thank you."

"Then please make yourself comfortable," he said, motioning to a chair upholstered in chartreuse chintz. He sat opposite on a burgundy-velvet chaise.

I sat and took a breath. "Let me get this straight. You want someone to perform for you and your guests? I'll tell you right up-front, I'm an actor and can work my way through scripted scenes, but I'm not a dancer or a singer."

He smiled — patronizingly or comfortingly? "I understand your concern. These performances will require none of that. Unless you wish to."

I wondered if I was being led into a trap. I shifted uneasily.

Allerson leaned forward. "I can see you're confused, and I certainly don't blame you. I realize this proposal must come across as seriously bizarre. You don't know me. I could be a psychopath, or worse. Yet I knew your father, and what a superb actor he was, and I know he prepared you to follow in his footsteps, which you have been doing admirably. I am proposing nothing sinister, I assure you. Let me outline the stipulations. Number one. Every week or so you will be provided with a script. Sometimes it will be precisely detailed, perhaps a soliloquy from a work with which you are familiar, and at other times it will be a mere suggestion, allowing you to improvise. You will not question your instructions; you must perform the part as shown or written. Number two. There must be no social interaction with the audience. Some of this is due to the possibility of infection, of course, but the primary reason is to assure artistic distance. Finally, number three. You are not to mention this arrangement to anyone. But I assure you that you will be more than adequately compensated for your time and effort." He mentioned a dollar figure that surprised me. "That's the deal in a proverbial nutshell," he concluded. "Do you have any questions?"

The arrangement sounded straightforward and enticing, but unsettling. That bit about improvising — I didn't like the sound of that. I asked, "Are these … 'performances' … to take place in this room?"

"Of course not," he said, standing. "I'm sorry; I should have known that would be a concern, with the pandemic and all. You will be performing in my courtyard. Here, let me show you."

He led me through a small kitchen and onto a red-brick patio that provided a more stunning view of the city than the front of the property. Wrought iron chairs with cushions were scattered about. It was clear where the stage was: a broad deck at the rear, at the point where the yard descended down a slope.

"And how large an audience will there be?" I asked.

He gave a small shrug. "Perhaps ten or a few more. It will vary. The concept is similar to that of the seventeenth-century French *salon*, where the literati gathered to amuse one other with discussions of books or philosophical works. I am proposing nothing so grandiose; this will simply be a gathering of friends interested in theater, and the entertainment and enlightenment it affords."

We stood silent for several moments. I waited for him to make the next move, and when he didn't, I asked, "What happens next? Do I need to sign a contract? Or a waiver?"

Allerson gave me an enigmatic smile. "Nothing so formal, Mr. Brace. We're kindred spirits, I suspect. Just let me know if you're on board with my strange request, and we'll go forward. I assure you — this will not be something you will regret."

How many con artists have said such words? This sounded nuts, as if I were being asked to step blindly off a cliff. Yet, somehow, I oddly trusted the strange man. "I'm on board," I said.

"Very good. I will be in touch."

¬

For the next week, I heard nothing. Just as I was about to dismiss Allerson's bizarre proposal as the sly joke of an eccentric (or worse, a hallucination I may have imagined), a large envelope appeared outside my door. Its instructions were clear: I was to arrive at Allerson's the following Saturday night at six and be prepared to perform a section of a Samuel Beckett play, enclosed.

I remembered the play; my father had performed it once. Because it required portraying the title character at two points in his life — as a thirty-nine-year-old, and then at sixty-nine — it would be tricky. Yet I knew I could do it.

The following Saturday, I arrived at Allerson's fifteen minutes early. From the number of cars parked on the street, I figured some of the audience had already arrived. My host answered the door, elegantly clad in a peach blazer and a red bow tie.

"You're punctual," he said. "That's excellent." Although he wore a mask over his nose and mouth, I detected the perimeter of a smile, and followed him through the house. On the way, he picked up a filled champagne flute from a sideboard and handed it to me. I lowered my mask and took a taste as we went out onto the patio, dimly lit by lanterns placed in the trees. Twelve or so people were seated in a semicircle; all wore masks and seemed to be a balance of men and women. The "stage" was illuminated before them.

Allerson stepped before the group. "Tonight we are privileged. The renowned young actor Richard Brace will perform for us a portion of Samuel Beckett's play *Krapp's Last Tape*." He gave a brief recap of the play's premise and stepped aside, nodding for me to begin.

I closed my eyes and pictured myself in the scene. Had this been an actual theater, I would have been seated at a desk with a tape recorder before me. The scene was toward the end of the play, when the title character listens to portions of a tape he'd made when he was thirty-nine and comments on them. The challenge was not only to approximate an Irish accent but to find the right tone for each persona. The older Krapp was more cynical; the younger still had the hopefulness of youth, tarnished only partially at that point. I drew from my own experience. The life of an actor is never easy, but I had managed to keep up my spirits through all the rejections and downturns. The key was finding the right roles, the ones that fit, and not worry about the ones that don't. By keeping that in mind in my performance, I aimed to communicate the delicate balance between self-doubt and optimism.

Although I focused on my acting, I also kept an eye on the audience, as any actor does, to gauge how engaged they were. The masks made this difficult, but other signs — positions and movements of bodies and heads, and most importantly, the eyes — told me they were at least paying attention. When I finished, there was silence, then applause. It was more than polite; there was energy to it, yet it was not as enthusiastic as I'd hoped.

"Thank you, Richard," Allerson said, stepping forward again. "That was masterful."

I nodded in thanks, uncertain what to do next. No performers were waiting to take my place. Allerson handed me an envelope, which I assumed must contain my pay. I turned, gave a small bow to the audience, walked back into the house and out to my car.

Driving home, I pondered the surreal nature of the experience. There was something not right about it, yet I couldn't put my finger on it. Wouldn't Allerson's friends — if that was who they were — have preferred more uplifting entertainment, such as a singer or a comedian, given the darkness of the times? The whole thing made little sense, yet I couldn't discern any explanation beyond what Allerson had provided. The more I thought about it, the creepier it seemed. I decided to refuse the next summons to perform, should it come.

Five days later another did arrive — this time asking me to perform two monologues from *Long Day's Journey into Night* by Eugene O'Neill. Both featured the mother, Mary Tyrone. I was enticed by the opportunity to perform a woman's role and reconsidered my decision to turn down the engagement. A glance at my checkbook, with its frighteningly low balance, made up my mind. Other actors were delivering food, and here was a chance for me to actually work, without having to audition and print up headshots and resumes. I decided to give it another go.

Getting into this character was more challenging. Not only was she female, she was also a morphine addict, bitter about her life, and frustrated with her family. In the first monologue, Mary expresses her disappointment in her actor husband, her sons (one an actor as well), and her home. She had expected greater things from them, and they'd let her down. In the second monologue, at the end of the play, Mary has been done in by her inability to prepare for the future. She's lost in her drug-laden dreams of the past, clutching her wedding gown and lamenting the lost promise of her youth.

Without the guidance of a director and the support of other cast members, I felt adrift. But O'Neill is such a brilliant playwright — it's all there, on the page — so there was little that would go wrong if I played the part as written. And I was going to be performing for only a handful of people in some guy's backyard, after all.

I showed up at Allerson's, was handed a glass of champagne, and led onto the patio. On stage, I closed my eyes and tried to inhabit the character as best I could, and ended up connecting with my role more closely than I expected. It was gratifying but chilling; the character was disturbed, and it was scary to get that close.

Over the next few weeks, a pattern emerged. Every ten days or so an envelope would appear outside my door with a scene enclosed. These began as monologues but progressed to two-person scenes, from plays and films. Some were from familiar works (Kafka, the movie *The Matrix*, even the Unabomber's manifesto), but many weren't. What they had in common were troubling themes — characters out of touch with reality, besieged by a hostile world, struggling to find ways to adapt. I frequently considered giving up but stayed, wanting to honor my commitment.

Then things took an even darker turn. I began receiving prompts to structure scenes of my own, focused around snippets of lines suggesting hallucinatory delusions, self-deception, and psychosis. This was not what I had agreed to. Was Allerson playing some kind of sick game with me? The whole thing had become perverse, yet I was forbidden to question him about it.

Exploring these disturbed characters began affecting other parts of my life, something I swore I'd never let happen. I would carry a role with me throughout the week, disappearing into it so deeply that I forgot where I was or what I was doing. Contact with the outside world — friends and family, news programs, social media — faded away.

There were times I was nearly overwhelmed. One role required me to portray a schizophrenic who believed he was dead and alive at the same time. In death he was in a calm limbo that was comfortable yet stagnating. Alive he was pressured, strained, struggling to stand out, to succeed at any cost. The not-so-subtle message, I assumed, was that the key to maintaining sanity in life lay in finding a compromise somewhere between the two. Based on the audience's reception, I assumed I succeeded in getting that across, yet found myself preferring the character's dead alter-ego.

As the roles grew more bizarre so, it seemed, did the audience. Who were these people? At first I had found them easy to differentiate. There was the beefy bouncer-type guy who sat with his arms folded, the thin woman in the sleeveless summer dress with the crimson streaks in her hair, the two men with their shoulders pressed together, frequently looking closely at one another (conspiratorially? lovingly?); the bearded professor-type with horn-rimmed glasses; the older couple holding hands; the short black man with a goatee. They always sat in the same seats, in the same arrangement.

Over time, they began to coalesce into a faceless mass, difficult to tell apart. More than once I wondered if they'd been replaced with cardboard cutouts, like the fake crowds at sporting events. The masks and distancing also kept me from making any meaningful connection with them — one of the most rewarding aspects of stage performing. What was most upsetting was that I couldn't shake the feeling that this was all some kind of weird joke, not at all what it seemed to be.

One night I felt a little lightheaded after my usual glass of champagne, which oddly helped me better embody my character, who on that occasion was a firefighter struggling to adjust to the transfer to a new, more hostile work environment. After I finished and the audience went into its applause, I studied them more closely. The crimson-haired woman in particular caught my eye. During my performance she had sat as rigidly as the others, but when I finished, she straightened, raised her hands as she clapped enthusiastically, her eyes alight with appreciation. I had even heard her cheer. I bowed, accepted my pay envelope, and departed as usual.

Except it wasn't as usual. As I was walking to my car the effect of the champagne reasserted itself and a wave of dizziness overcame me. I held onto a lamppost to keep from dropping.

A voice came out of the darkness. "Mr. Brace?"

I looked up and saw the woman with the crimson-streaked hair. I let go of the lamppost and took a step backward. "I'm not supposed to talk to you."

"Why not?"

"Allerson made that clear."

She moved close. "You don't look well."

171

I ran a quick check on my motor skills. I still felt woozy, but I was able to walk. "I'm fine," I said, though without much conviction.

She took hold of my arm. "I don't think so. Have you been tested?"

"Tested? For what?"

"For COVID, of course."

"I was, yesterday," I lied. "The test was negative."

She placed her palm on my forehead. "I'm still concerned. Let me drive your car and take you home. I can catch an Uber back."

I tried resisting but found myself handing her my car keys. At my apartment I felt more like my usual self, but she insisted on walking me to my door. I thanked her, but instead of leaving, she put her hand on the back of my neck and looked up at me.

It is surprising how much a mask can disguise. I could hear her voice, husky and full-bodied. I could make out the contours of her body, thin yet curvaceous. I could see her eyes, violet and hypnotic, the distinctive arc of her brow, the petite indentation in her chin. Yet without a view of her mouth and lips, I couldn't get a complete sense of her. She reached up and pulled down my mask.

I felt as if I was back on stage, being thrown a sudden change in the script. "We shouldn't be doing this," I said. "It's too risky."

She lowered her mask. "Some risks are worth it."

"We really shouldn't."

Her lips were nicely proportioned between full and thin. She pressed them against mine.

⌐

Her name was Millie, and she had a faint accent attributable to her childhood in France, Toulouse specifically.

Beyond that tidbit of information, she revealed nothing about herself and fell into a stony silence when I began asking questions. Even so, she was surprisingly uninhibited in bed — surprising, I suppose, because of her guarded demeanor during my performances. After we made love, she quickly dressed and left. In the morning I felt back to normal, with no traces of the previous evening's torpor.

Over the following days, I berated myself for not getting Millie's cell number, or finding out how to contact her. Yet at the next performance, she was sitting there as always, and when I again felt woozy afterward (damn that champagne, the next time I swore I'd refuse it) she insisted on driving me home. As before, she was passionate in bed, but remained mostly uncommunicative afterward, and left before midnight.

And so another pattern began to emerge. After each performance I'd stagger a little (I was unable to refuse the champagne), accompany Millie back to my apartment, and have sex in a mad rush. It was all disturbing but curiously comforting. Besides the sex, I found myself increasingly looking to Millie for feedback during my performances — gestures or eye movements that told me: less, more, yes, no, deeper, stronger. She became my muse, and rarely disappointed. Just one glance from her (and a loosening of my inhibitions, thanks to the champagne) enabled me to proceed on an artistic course I never would have otherwise. I found myself taking chances that, once I sobered up later and realized what I'd done, both thrilled and frightened me.

The characters in my performances grew even more damaged and troubled, and I became unable to view them apart from myself. At times I struggled to remember who I had been and who I had wanted to become. Was I as good a person as I believed myself to be? Or, like my characters, was someone darker lurking within, waiting to take control?

I had become so consumed by my roles that I had lost touch with the outside world. One afternoon I happened, by accident, to hear the tail end of a news report. I learned that the world had been thrown off-kilter by the pandemic. There was an irony there. I had been untouched by the disease myself, but my world had similarly become off-kilter. My relationship with Millie, at first seductive in its mystery and taboo nature, had grown toxic. I felt exploited, and ultimately disregarded. So expressive during my performance, Millie fell into a silence after our lovemaking before taking her leave. Shouldn't lovers become closer rather than more distant?

One night as we lay in each other's arms (she permitted a small amount of that), I finally had to say something. "Why won't you tell me where you live? Or give me your cell number?"

She ran her finger teasingly over my lips. "It's against the rules."

"Screw the rules. We're breaking them by doing this, aren't we?"

"This is different."

"Not that different."

"Things will change. They say a vaccine is right around the corner." She curled against me, but I didn't know how to respond. Our relationship, such as it was, was going nowhere. There seemed to be no third act in sight.

⌐

It took more time than usual for my next invitation from Allerson to arrive. When it did, my "script" consisted of only three words: *Who am I?*

What was I supposed to do with that? I felt I didn't know who I was anymore, not really. When I was acting professionally, I was ascendant star Richard Brace, son of two-time Tony nominee Peter Brace. But that was before the Big Chill. My credits had evaporated, and although my performances at Allerson's enabled me to say words on a stage, could I really call myself an actor anymore? What was worse, I had so fallen under Millie's thrall that my performances had almost become hers, not mine.

I looked again at my "script." *Who am I?*

I must be someone. I could be someone. An actor can be *anyone*.

¬

Uncertain, I showed up at Allerson's three nights later at the appointed time. From the moment I entered his house I could tell something had changed. Allerson was not his usual self; no welcoming smile, no offered glass of champagne. Outside everything appeared the same, but I quickly noticed Millie wasn't there. Had I frightened her away?

I stepped up to the stage, facing the audience sitting before me, who were oddly silent and still. I stumbled through my performance, rambling through a diatribe about the elusiveness of identity. Was it possible, I wondered aloud, to truly know ourselves, who we are, without acknowledgment from others? I didn't want to exist solely as an actor, which was how Millie saw me. I had more dimensions than that … didn't I? "I'm a real person!" I yelled. "I'm not just an *actor*!"

The audience remained still, unresponsive. Could it be? I stepped down to examine them more closely. Many times I had seen them as cardboard cutouts. And that night, that was exactly what they were — the beefy guy with his arms folded, the goateed black man, the men gazing at each other — they were all replicas, photographs on poster board. Had they ever been real?

I marched over to Allerson, obscured in the darkness. "What the hell is all this about? Are you making fun of me? Has this all been a joke?"

Allerson stayed calm. "Tonight was your final appearance here," he said. "You've been a severe disappointment to me, Richard."

So, he knew about Millie and me. But how? I was thrown, searching for answers. "You always seemed to enjoy my performances," I said. "At least you said so."

"That's not what I'm talking about, and you know it. You violated our agreement."

If he could play games, so could I. I gave an offhand shrug. "Just consider it part of my performance. I improvised." I tried to project cocky self-confidence, but I felt as if I had been caught selling nuclear codes to the enemy. "How did you find out? Did Millie tell you? Where is she, anyway?"

He held up his hand. "No questions. Consider our arrangement terminated. Unless ..." He brushed his hand against my cheek. "Unless you would agree to continuing your improvisation with me ... inside?"

I grabbed the pay envelope clutched in his other hand. "Forgive me, but I don't believe that was part of our 'agreement' either." I turned and walked away.

¬

I returned home and was opening my door when Millie emerged from the shadows. It took me a moment to be certain it was her; she looked hollow-eyed, haunted. She wore no mask.

I reached out to touch her, but she backed away.

"Where have you been?" I asked. "I've been worried."

"It's Scott. He's sick. Real sick. With the virus."

"Who's Scott?"

She looked down. "My husband."

"You're *married*? Why didn't you tell me?"

She shrugged.

"Oh, of course," I said. "The rules."

A guilty look flashed. Did she feel culpable? Was she blaming *me*?

"I don't feel drunk tonight," I said. "That's strange, isn't it? Sorry to hear about your husband, though."

She wrapped her arms around herself. "It isn't just Scott. I … I had a miscarriage."

That gave me pause. "Was it mine?"

"Probably. Scott's had a vasectomy."

If this were a play, I wondered, how would my character respond? "Would you like to come in for a drink?" I asked.

"No," she said. "I shouldn't have come at all."

"Then why did you?"

She stepped forward. "I wanted to see you again. Just one more time."

It was nice to be acknowledged as a full human being at last. Then I thought of her husband, sick in a hospital ward somewhere. It was as if I had been sucked into a wormhole and spit back out into the real world. I entered my apartment. For the first time in months, I turned on the television. The scrolling chyron on the bottom of the screen showed the growing global death toll, in the millions.

Millie had followed me inside. "Turn that off," she said. "I don't want to hear about the disease."

I looked into her mesmeric eyes, now green, again feeling their pull. "The disease is real. Everything else — this, us — isn't."

She moved close. "You're real, Richard. And so am I. Believe it."

I didn't feel real at all. Somewhere along the way I'd lost the capacity to play my most important role: myself. If indeed I ever had been able to. So, I did what every actor is told to do when at a loss for how to tackle his character: I sought my motivation. This scene didn't call for dialogue. I needed to say goodbye and face whatever the next day would bring — all without words.

Millie picked up on my discomfort. "Don't overthink this. It's time for me to be a wife again, and it's time for you to move on also."

I reached out and squeezed her shoulder.

She hesitated, then moved closer and gave me a kiss. "I wish you luck. But you won't need it. Just let yourself go. You'll do fine."

┐

The next day, I received an invite from Jason, my *Stripe* castmate, to catch up with the other players over a Zoom call. I hesitated; they were from another, distant part of my life, and I wasn't sure I wanted to return to it. But my need for connection with others was too strong.

They looked disembodied inside their small video boxes on my laptop screen, yet not, I realized, as much as the audiences had seemed at Allerson's. I didn't mention my experiences there and listened more than I spoke. The others were getting by but were technically unemployed, waiting for audition calls. I was shocked to hear of COVID deaths in the local acting community.

"It's been like a bad dream," Stefanie said. "Without an opportunity to work, I feel like I've lost myself. I keep thinking I'm going to wake up and find everything back to normal."

"There won't be any going back," said Carlos. "Things will never be 'normal' again."

There was a time when I would have debated the point. "Normal" once had a clear definition for me, involving going to work, shopping, attending the theater. Was that gone for good? Perhaps not, but I was now used to uncertainty. The only thing I knew for sure was that wherever "normal" ended up, it wouldn't look the same as it had.

I called my agent, Renata.

"Where in the hell have you been, Richard?" she asked. "I thought you dropped off the edge of the earth. I was afraid you'd gotten sick."

I was about to tell her about Allerson, but she would have demanded a cut. Instead, I asked, "Has anything come up?"

Renata sighed. "It's slow. No stage work, of course. Films are slowly picking up. You were marketable when all this started, and you'll be again. We just have to wait it out."

I hesitated, debating whether to confess that I was different — not the reliable actor she remembered, someone who "would never change his stripes," as she once said. I wanted to tell her I'd become someone new, more malleable, an actor more sought after than one who was merely "marketable."

Unsure whether that was true, I just thanked her and said goodbye.

⌐

That night, I drove to Allerson's. I had received no further invitations, and though that was to be expected, I needed closure. Our last exchange still plagued me. Perhaps we could continue as friends, yet part of me didn't really want that.

There was a light on when I arrived but no cars parked outside. Ringing the doorbell produced no result at first. Then I heard a faint rustling, and the door was opened by a tall, elderly woman. She looked at me expectantly.

"I, um, I'm sorry to disturb you," I said, "but is Mr. Allerson at home?" I couldn't think of his first name. Edward, was it?

The woman said, "I'm afraid you have the wrong house. No one named Allerson lives here." She went to close the door, but I held onto it.

"Are you sure? There's no Edward Allerson who lives here?"

"I've lived here for twenty years," she said with a patient smile. Then a light came on. "Oh. You must be thinking of my brother Charles. He was staying here while I was out of the country."

When she described her brother, I realized he most likely was my mysterious host. I mentioned his weekly salons, the performances, the perplexing "rules."

She smiled. "That sounds like Charles, all right. Or more likely the brainstorm of one of his dilettante friends — they always know how to wrap him around their finger. Everything considered, it's a good thing he didn't burn the place down."

⌐

As winter approached, vaccines were being readied and the end of the pandemic was in sight. *Stripe*, however, would not be produced. Professionally, I was back on the street again with no prospects, the common fate of actors. I managed to get by with the pay from my part-time job and kept going to auditions.

I wish you luck. Just let yourself go. You'll do fine.

Just as I was about to hit up my brother-in-law for a loan, Renata phoned me with news of an audition for a series pilot. One of the producers had asked for me specifically. That wasn't a complete shock, as I had been building a reputation before the pandemic, but months had passed and time is a killer in that business. I studied the script. My character, one of the leads, was well written, but I felt I could do more with him.

The night before the audition, I lay awake, puzzling out different approaches. I showed up for the audition and, amazingly, two days later I was told I'd gotten the part. I filmed the pilot and, although I knew I'd done a good job — much better than I'd expected, as affirmed by other cast members — I didn't hold out much hope.

Two weeks later, I got the word: *The Incredible Smith Family* had been optioned for ten episodes. I was working again. At the first taping, a few network execs were in the audience. After the first scene, I looked to see their reaction. One woman, a hint of crimson in her hair, returned my look with a small, knowing smile.

The director announced the next take, and I took a deep breath, and closed my eyes to place myself in a new persona. When I looked out at the audience again, the woman was gone. Still, I pictured Millie's face, masked, the slight shift in her eyes telling me to go for it, to test my limits.

Then I let myself go.

STEALING AWAY

CRISTINA STUART

The day Sandra is arrested for shoplifting begins as usual.

She stands at the front door, ready to kiss her husband as he leaves for work, their two daughters with him, ready for school. Across the street, she sees her neighbor doing the same and waves. These Silver Lake wives have husbands who prefer their women stay home; it's the man's job to provide for his family. Sandra is content with this arrangement. Unambitious and with a propensity toward laziness, she ensured the man she married had money.

That warm spring morning, in the kitchen stacking the dishwasher, Sandra picks up a favorite wine glass from her single days and casts a short, nostalgic glance back to her youth, when she used to go clubbing, flirt and have one-night stands, and indulge in petty shoplifting for the latest lipstick.

Red rose tattoos no longer trail across her shoulders. Her husband didn't like them; they appeared "inappropriate" so near the diamond earrings he'd given her. Her nose piercing healed too, leaving only an insignificant dot as a reminder of her wild past. But now her teenage daughters have both reached the age when they want their own tattoos. Yesterday, she argued with them.

"Tattooing hurts a lot. You hate pain."

"It's only painful if it's near the bone," they argued back, in unison, as typical.

"It takes ages to remove them," she said. "The skin feels sore for weeks."

Her daughters tossed their long blonde hair, their eyes and minds already sucked back into their phones.

The kitchen door opens, disturbing her daydreaming. Their housekeeper has arrived.

She bustles in, beaming. "Buenos días, Señora. Please, no need you tidy. I do it."

In two strides, she takes over the kitchen.

Upstairs, Sandra slips off her robe before stepping into the shower, wondering whether her young, wild self has been completely tamed, confined by the white picket fence. The fence helps her feel secure.

The previous evening, her husband sat holding the TV remote, running through channels until he landed on a program he wanted her to watch with him. And on the nightstand in the bedroom lies the book he has given her, *The Woman in White*. "I know your taste," he said. "You'll enjoy it, for sure." None of his behavior concerns her. When her father died in her teens, her education was cut short, and now her husband is helping to widen her knowledge.

She doesn't mind that his control extends further. He is willing to pay for breast implants, but she must lose a few pounds first, he says. Only, it's hard for her to stick to diets. Out of the shower, she dries her faded blonde hair, and when it catches in the brush, she pulls it free with a sigh. Is today Wednesday or Thursday? She often forgets what day of the week it is; every day is the same.

It's Thursday, she recalls, and once dressed, she drives to lunch with a friend at the Granville Cafe in Glendale. There, she orders the Thai Ginger Salad with the dressing on the side. After they have air-kissed goodbye, Sandra cuts through Bloomingdales on her way to the parking lot. Inside, the store is uncrowded and inviting, and she has no reason to hurry home; her daughters have after-school activities and won't be back for a while. She lingers, looking at summer clothes and shoes. In the jewelry department, she considers gold cufflinks for her husband's fortieth birthday. When she turns away from the counter, another woman bumps into her. They express mutual apologies, and Sandra hitches her large, unfastened tote bag back onto her shoulder.

When she reaches the exit of the store, a burly man in a dark suit blocks her path. She notices his badge: Security.

"Ma'am," he growls. "I must ask you to accompany me to the manager's office."

He towers over her. Her heart quickens. "What do you mean? What for?"

"I will explain once we are with the manager," he says, his hand on her elbow turning her back into the store.

She wants to protest but is too mortified to make a fuss. An elderly couple has stopped to gape.

In his office, the manager indicates she should sit down and asks to search her purse.

She holds it tightly in her lap, staring at him, her pulse throbbing at her temples. What is going on? They make her feel like a criminal.

"You'll have to explain why you want to look in my bag," she stammers.

"We believe you intended to leave the store without paying for goods."

"That's ridiculous. Here, take it. I have nothing to hide." She can't recall if it contains some tampons. Too bad. Let them be embarrassed.

The manager peers inside and removes her wallet, which he opens to find her driving license, placing it on the desk. Next, he pulls out a floral scarf she carries as protection against excessive air-conditioning. Finally, he plunges his hand back in, emerging with the cufflinks she looked at earlier, held high like a sportsman displaying his trophy to fans.

"How do you explain what these are doing in your purse?"

A heavy weight presses on her chest; she's unable to breathe.

"I have no idea." She takes a deep breath. "There was a woman ... we collided. It's possible ... somehow my sleeve ..." She shakes her head. "I don't know."

"Is there anything you want to say before I call the police?"

She gasps. "The police? That's ridiculous." She looks from the security guy to the manager. "You must believe me. This is a mistake." They stare back without a glimmer of compassion. She smiles hoping to ... she doesn't know. Mollify, perhaps? "I have money to buy the cufflinks. Look at my credit cards. Call my bank." She straightens her back and glances at them again. Neither man is looking at her.

The manager squints at the price tag on the cufflinks. "Just as the salesclerk reported," he says, frowning at her over his wire glasses. "Part of our Classic Antiques collection. Seven hundred and thirty-five dollars. Definitely one for the cops."

She watches him pressing buttons on his phone.

"Suspected shoplifter," he says. "Bloomingdales, Glendale ... yes, immediately please."

She loses all sense of time; her head is light. She is dizzy. They offer her water. She sips from the glass feeling she's caught up in an alternate reality. Only a moment ago, she was making for the parking lot, trying to remember where she'd parked. Somehow, now, they were accusing her of stealing. She wonders about the woman who bumped into her. She seemed to appear out of nowhere. At that time, Sandra thinks the shop assistant was helping another customer ... or was that earlier? Her brain is in sleep mode and not cooperating.

Behind his desk, the manager has resumed his work, staring at a screen and clicking a mouse. The security guard stands at ease, his hands behind his back, eyes focused somewhere above her head, but she expects ready to pounce if she tries to flee.

When two policemen arrive, the cufflinks are placed in a plastic bag and she is arrested, led from the store between the officers. She is not handcuffed; she guesses they checked the height of her heels and didn't consider her a flight risk. In the police car, barricaded in the back seat with little legroom, she calls her husband. At the station, she waits for him in a numb silence on a hard chair in a narrow hallway. She has no control over anything.

When her husband appears, silent and grim-faced, accompanied by his attorney, he warns her to remain silent. In an interview room, he, the attorney, and the police officer conduct an inaudible, lengthy discussion, while she remains in the corridor outside, straining to hear. She thinks she hears the word "parasite." Maybe the attorney can get her freed. He must know she's innocent. If only they'd let her explain what happened.

Finally, the officer calls her in and tells her to sit at the table.

"I am formally charging you with entering an open business with the intent to steal property worth less than nine hundred and fifty dollars. California State Law Penal Code four-nine-five point five."

Throughout the proceedings, no one — including her husband — looks at her. She puts her head in her hands.

"Let's go," says her husband, taking her arm.

"What?" she leaps up. "Are they letting me go?" She has been preparing to spend the night in jail.

"Until the trial," her husband says.

She stumbles out of the station in a fog of bewilderment and asks, "Did you have to pay bail?"

"We argued it was a misdemeanor. No bail needed."

In the car, she relaxes, hoping her husband will break his silence, but he refuses to talk. Once home, he leads her into his study. His choice of room is puzzling until she realizes this is the only room downstairs with a door, which he closes.

She perches on the couch, eyes downcast, repentant. But for what? Causing a nuisance, making him lose precious time in the world of high finance? She's certainly not guilty of shoplifting.

"Sandra," he says, and she looks up.

He stands in front of her, his elegant jacket open and one hand in his pants pocket. Gray hair around his temples adds to his distinguished manner. They lock eyes, and she gives him a half-smile, which he doesn't return. She wonders if this is how he acts in his office, with miscreant employees.

"I want you to tell me exactly what you did," he says, "from the moment you entered Bloomingdales this afternoon."

When she opens her mouth to speak, he stops her with a raised finger and sits at his desk. Holding a pen, he nods for her to commence.

She recounts her afternoon, striving to be as precise as she can, knowing he'll pinpoint any inconsistencies. All the while, he rapidly records her words in black ink.

Finally, he lays down his pen and joins her on the couch.

"Tell me the truth," he says. "Did you steal the cufflinks?"

His eyes are intense, his handsome eyes with their gold-brown dots like tiny grains of sugar sprinkled onto the green iris. He's concentrating on her and nothing else. She can't remember the last time her husband was so engrossed with her. Then a strange sensation. So much has happened so fast; she can't be sure. But yes, she feels animated, vivacious, excited. She pauses, relishing this new force. Her heart beats faster, and she has to repress the urge to kiss him hard on his sexy lips.

"Well?" His tone is impatient.

"I did not put the cufflinks in my purse." She takes his hand. "I did not steal them. Why would I?"

"For fun?"

She shakes her head. "Those days are long past."

"Good," he says and pats her hand. "I believe you."

Suddenly, she's ravenous. In the kitchen, the house-keeper has left a chicken parmesan casserole for their dinner. She only needs to heat it. Alone for the first time since this started, Sandra smiles and instantly covers her mouth with her hand. This is crazy. She could end up with a criminal record, but she's bursting with energy. Her husband comes in and she turns away, her cheeks flushed. She must take control of herself.

That night while her husband reads in bed, Sandra sprays perfume over her naked body in the bathroom. Early in their marriage, he declared he preferred she didn't initiate their love-making, but tonight Sandra decides it is time to ignore his petty rules. She bends to fasten a black lacy garter to her stockings and steps into black stilettos. She rubs her nipples so they protrude and opens the bathroom door.

"Hey there," she says in a low voice.

"What the …?"

She struts over to the bed and pulls off the covers.

"Let's see what you're hiding down here for me."

Her husband places his reading glasses on the bedside table, grinning. He responds to her unrestrained passion.

They make love and it's magical and fun, and later they lie back, shaken, astonished at the power of their emotions.

The following weeks are filled with activity: conferences with the attorney, viewings of the CCTV, questions about the stranger who bumped into her. The attorney is convinced the woman was a parasite.

"What does that mean?" Sandra asks.

"She used you to carry the cufflinks out of the store. Shoplifters employ this method, particularly for high-priced items."

"Wait a minute," Sandra says. "How would she get them back if they're in my purse?"

"She'd have stopped you in the parking lot," the attorney explains. "Maybe pretend to be an undercover cop and ask to search your purse. They have a variety of tactics."

"Would it be worth hiring a detective to track her down?"

"Probably not." He frowns. "She could be in another state by now."

Sandra loves the attention. Everyone is working on her side. She has lost a few pounds and is sleeping better. Her daughters tell her she looks pretty. Normally, they never notice anything. Her husband is attentive and confident she'll get off the charge, but does he genuinely believe she's innocent, or is he pretending?

In bed, she rolls over and stares at him.

"Do you believe me?"

"Of course," he replies, stroking her breast. "I also know that the word 'lie' is in the center of 'believe.'"

She doesn't care anymore if he thinks she's guilty. The tension between them acts as a charge, making her feel alive and powerful. Neighbors eye her with curiosity, and she doesn't care. She and her husband make love every night. They have seldom been closer. She glows under his attention and feels more his equal. She begins paying more attention to the news on TV, occasionally even challenging his views. To her surprise, he's willing to discuss events with her instead of belittling her.

She knows she's innocent, and the attorney is cautiously optimistic, so the day before the trial she has a massage, a manicure, and her hair freshly highlighted and styled. It's as if she's preparing for a party. On the morning of the trial, she dresses with care, choosing a black frock and a tailored white jacket fastened with a huge black pearl at her waist. She winks at herself before setting off with her husband to the court.

The attorney argues that she has no reason to steal and has no previous criminal record. He describes the encounter with the strange woman as a possible reason for the stolen goods being found in Sandra's purse. She is found not guilty. Her husband is elated and, to celebrate, he reserves a table at La Boucherie on 71 at the Intercontinental Hotel in DTLA and invites several of their close friends.

Toasts are proposed in her honor and Sandra delights in their happiness for her. Eventually, the conversation moves on to other things and her pizzazz leaves her. She feels bereaved, deflated. It must be tiredness after all the activity. She's sure to feel better in the morning.

But she doesn't.

A week passes and, desperate to regain her earlier zest, she forms a plan and begins by making a list of objectives.

In the morning, she picks out high heels — the best ones, with Valentino printed on the sole — along with an ivory silk shirt and black pants. She drives to West Holly-wood and parks at Bristol Farms, away from the cameras, though a friend of hers has told her they never work. She picks up a green plastic basket and wanders around the store with posh posture and a superior smile, looking like most other shoppers. At the cheese counter, she discusses the merits of Roquefort and Gorgonzola, eventually ordering a quarter pound of each.

Next, she circles her target for a while before zooming in on a one-ounce jar of sturgeon caviar priced at seventy-nine dollars. She pretends to read the label before slipping the jar into her large tote, covering it with her scarf. She hovers by the display, moving the jars to cover the space where hers had stood. A few minutes later, her head held high and her heart pounding, she joins a short line at the checkout. The cashier has tied her dark hair off her round, worn face. Too much sun in her youth, decides Sandra, trying to distract herself from her racing pulse. Why had she ever decided to do this? It wasn't worth it. If she were caught, she'd lose everything. But isn't this what gives her energy and makes her life worth living?

The cashier glances at her. "Find everything you were looking for?"

Is her tone accusing? Sandra swallows, dumbstruck for a moment.

"Yes, thank you." Her voice sounds strange.

She clears her throat and opens her wallet to take out a credit card. Wait! Leave no trace. Use cash.

The cashier has the cheese in her hand to scan it, but instead looks directly at Sandra.

This is not exciting, it's terrifying! Please God, let her get away from here. Should she walk out and leave the cheese? She could suddenly remember she's late to collect her child from school. Perfectly natural. Or would that arouse suspicion? She glances at her watch without seeing the time.

She looks quickly at the cashier, who smiles at her.

"I'm sorry for staring," the cashier says, as she scans the cheese. "I was admiring your earrings."

Sandra puts her hand up to her ear. "Mmm, yes … they are …" She stops mid-sentence. Don't draw attention to yourself. Must blend in. She doesn't want the cashier to remember her. Over by the exit, she spots a well-built man in a dark suit, his back to her. Not a typical shopper. Was he security? Would he want to search her tote? She hands over a twenty-dollar bill and receives a few coins in change. Her eyes are on the brawny man. She must somehow get past him.

"Excuse me, ma'am," the cashier calls.

Sandra's heart jumps. Should she make a run for it? She's caught between the two of them.

"Don't forget your cheese."

She takes it from the cashier and places it in her purse, urging herself to walk calmly, head up, shoulders back. Not far to the exit, now. The guy in the suit is still facing away from her. Only a few more steps and she will be free. Then he turns toward her. She must get past him. Her heart is thumping uncontrollably. This stress can't be good for her health. What would happen if she fainted or had a stroke and they found the caviar? He looks at her. She pretends not to see. Only three steps more. He moves towards her. Not again. Please God, don't let him challenge her.

"Hi, hon," he says. "All done?"

"Sure thing," says a woman's voice behind Sandra.

One step and she's out. She must not run. She strolls out into the blue-skied hot, sunny day and shivers. Fear, astonishment, and euphoria crash through her. Get to the car. Act normal, the cameras may be working. She starts the car and glides out, her hands damp on the steering wheel.

She checks herself in the car mirror. She still looks like a respectable law-abiding middle-aged woman. Inside, she's bubbling with joy.

At home, she eats the caviar slowly with a small silver spoon accompanied by a glass of white wine. She's still terrified, but the fear gives her a buzz. It's her ecstasy, her intoxication, and her addiction. The stakes are high. Her husband wouldn't support her a second time. She decides she'll never go to the same store twice, vary what she wears, and plan every sting in detail. She sips another glass of wine, speculating how she should smuggle out a bottle of French champagne on her next shopping fix.

BOYS ON MULHOLLAND

JANNA LAYTON

Ruben Kasparyan and Brandon Long are both at the party. They know this, everyone knows this, but neither of them is sure what to do. If they talk to each other, it will become a Thing. People will take photos and post the photos, and then there will be rumors of a rebirth of their old Bruden Bros YouTube channel, or of Brandon joining Ruben at Cannon Blast, the ensemble channel Ruben moved to after Bruden Bros, or of them teaming up to start a new project entirely.

Other fans will take the assumptions even further upon seeing photos of them together and insist that not only is a Bruden Bros revival forthcoming, but that Ruben and Brandon are in love and always have been. That the photos will be of poor quality, due to the fact that they're outside at night, will not deter those fans. They'll easily make out Ruben (taller, thinner) and Brandon (shorter, more muscular). In those grainy photos of a brief meeting between former friends, they will read longing and lust. Multiple fanfics will be written because of those photos, the dormant Brandon/ Ruben shippers awakened.

The possible fanfics don't bother Ruben or Brandon. They did at first, but years ago they learned to ignore it and let the fanfic writers and fan artists do their thing. Now, content creators long for that type of engagement. But as for them working together again, it's unfeasible. There's no point in giving the fans false hope that Bruden Bros will return.

They're also both suspicious of the other's possible intentions in wanting to be seen together. Ruben thinks that Brandon will want the photos because Brandon's new solo channel hasn't done well, and Brandon thinks that Ruben will want the photos in order to continue portraying himself as the good guy.

But they're both here; there's no denying it. If they don't talk at all, that will also become a Thing. They're twenty-seven, they've been in this business for a dozen years, and they shouldn't be feuding like the newer, younger social media stars. Speaking of which, Ruben knows that if he doesn't jump into a conversation soon, he'll end up cornered by some fame-hungry kid who grew up watching Bruden Bros and now lives in a TikTok mansion.

So, when their eyes meet across the crowded backyard of the Hollywood Hills house, Ruben walks over to where Brandon is standing with a small group by the pool. A few onlookers have their phones ready to record.

"Hey," say Ruben and Brandon at the same time as they reflexively go in for a half-hug.

"How's it going?" asks Ruben.

"Pretty good. How's New York?" asks Brandon. He silently congratulates himself for saying "New York" so casually, like it doesn't bother him at all that Ruben fled Los Angeles after their falling out, despite being the one who insisted they had to relocate to L.A. in the first place.

"New York is good," says Ruben, and he wishes they were still friends so he could tell Brandon about the series of apartment disasters he has endured (the rat infestation in East Williamsburg, the addict roommate in West Village) without feeling self-conscious about his decision to move.

Ruben greets the people Brandon is standing with, both of whom he knows. Joshua Choi is twenty-three, tall, gangly — a former dorky class clown from Texas growing into his looks and becoming more passable as the K-Pop stars he sometimes parodies on his increasingly popular channel.

Next to him is Sam Oliver, a twenty-five-year-old video game livestreamer. His naturally blond hair changes color frequently, sometimes to reflect brand deals. It's currently blue. He claps Ruben on the shoulder. "Saw your red-carpet pics from the premiere. Very dapper. Even if the game totally sucks."

The premiere is why Ruben is in L.A. He voiced a minor character in a kid's movie based on a mobile game.

"Hey, man, a job's a job," says Ruben good-naturedly. "At least now I can say I've been a skateboarding ferret."

"Are you in town long?" Joshua asks him.

"I fly back tomorrow night, after a meeting."

"A meeting? Fuck work, play games," says Sam with an ironic lilt, raising his beer in a toast. It's the slogan for his livestream, and the abbreviation "FWPG" is printed on the merchandise he sells.

"Man, the last game I played was when I guested on your stream," says Ruben. "I wish I had more time."

Brandon changes the subject. "Sam, Vanessa's not here tonight?"

"No, she's home sick with the flu. Well, I think it's the flu. She's insisting it's just a bad cold."

"Wedding's coming up soon, isn't it?" asks Ruben.

"Two months," says Sam.

Ruben jokingly asks if they're going to livestream it, and Sam laughs. "No, but we are doing a video, of course. And there will be a sponsored VR bouquet toss!"

A commotion disrupts their conversation: the name "Gary" is stretched out into a war cry by a familiar voice, and a splash follows. Brandon, Ruben, Joshua, and Sam look at the illuminated teal oval of the pool. A large, hairy, bearded man wearing nothing but his boxers has just jumped in among the slim, bikini-clad girls and ripped, waxed boys. He raises his arms in triumph as the crowd cheers.

"Oh my God," says Joshua. "Gary Milton's here? Jahan said he invited him but didn't think he'd actually show up."

Brandon and Ruben have known Gary a long time. Gary Milton is a veteran of the vlogger business. He's been doing it since vlogging became a Thing. He recorded his wild days as a twenty-something and later pivoted to family vlogging once he and his wife married and started having children. Their vlog isn't as active as it once was, but he has a line of grilling instruments he didn't design, and his wife has a cookbook she didn't write.

Gary wades out of the pool, bows to the crowd, and takes his vlogging camera back from the girl he had film his jump.

"Dude's a legend," opines Sam.

Brandon and Ruben notice each other's silence.

"One of the real OGs," Ruben says reluctantly, wanting to both avoid awkwardness and look more gracious than Brandon.

"Yeah," says Brandon, annoyed that Ruben said it first.

⌐

A bit later, karaoke has started in the living room, and everyone is "on," because the cameras are out. The party is just for fun, but the karaoke is not. These videos generally won't be posted on YouTube due to copyright, but clips will be all over Instagram and TikTok, especially for the most recognizable stars. There are two acceptable ways to sing: either very well or badly-but-jokey.

Joshua is up next, and he's debating how earnest he wants to be. The only singing he does on his channel are parodies, generally of K-Pop or country songs. Those parodies have gotten him millions of views. But tonight, he wants to sing Lana Del Rey's "Ride," and not in an ironic way. He wants to give a sincere — but not embarrassing — performance.

After all, his idols are here. He grew up watching You-Tube stars like Ruben and Brandon. Especially Ruben and Brandon. Even though he's only four years younger than they are, they seemed so much older and cooler on their Bruden Bros channel when he was in his early teens. They were still filming in Santa Cruz then, still uploading the occasional skateboarding video along with their skits. Furthermore, Gary Milton is here. Joshua doesn't want to come off as cringey at a party where Gary Milton is. Maybe he should sing something funny instead.

All too soon, it's his turn, and he steps up to the mic. He selects "Ride" before he can talk himself out of it. He's been agonizing about how he's going to perform the opening lines, which are addressed to a man — if he's going to slyly arch an eyebrow or do an otherwise vampy or goofy look. But from the first notes, he knows he's going to do it unironically. He figures that he's already out as gay, and even if he weren't, why should it matter?

And then the words are flowing effortlessly from his lips and he's on. He knows it. He can feel it in his voice and in the audience's faces. A group cheers during a pause, and his heart swells. When he breaks into the chorus the first time, he can feel the elation from the crowd. He's Joshua Choi, he's at a party full of industry greats, and he's killing it.

⌐

By two in the morning the party is winding down. Brandon wishes that his girlfriend, Mandy, were with him, but she's a pro cosplayer and at an anime convention in Atlanta. He veers off into a corner by himself for a moment, looking at his phone. One good thing about being a content creator is that you don't look pathetic standing alone and staring at your phone at parties; you look like you're doing work, even if you're just scrolling through social media, which is what Brandon is doing. Already, photos and videos of the party litter Brandon's feed, including a clip Sam Oliver has uploaded of Joshua singing Lana Del Rey.

> *My man Joshua Choi aka JoshPop can SING! I'm sad that Vanessa's home sick cuz she would of loved this. :sadface: Oh well I'm sure we'll have karaoke at our wedding #Joshuachoi #JoshPop #vanessamwedding #fwpg*

Brandon scrolls through a few more posts and then, even though he told himself he wouldn't, he checks to see if anyone has used the #BrudenBros hashtag tonight.

> *OMG someone posted a photo of Brandon and Ruben talking at a party! :hearteyes: Maybe a #BrudenBros reunion is coming???*

> *tfw you run into your ex and your pretending you didn't use to fuck #BrudenBros*

> *There's a photo of #BrudenBros hugging tonight and my heart I can't. :crying: Thank you @Jahan_Game_On and @ GamerKweenNasreen for bringing our soft bois back together!*

> *Guys, they're just being polite. :rollingeyes: They still hate each other. Smh this fandom #BrudenBros*

> *I hope Ruben gets Brandon on Cannon Blast. Brandons channel sucks. #BrudenBros #CannonBlast*

The last comment was made by someone who doesn't even have a profile photo. Nevertheless, Brandon knows he won't forget it, and he berates himself for checking the tag. He knows he's been floundering with his mishmash of content: vlogs, movie and TV reviews, workout challenges. He hasn't found his niche and fears he never will.

He decides to head home. He's a little buzzed and could sober up here in the living room, but he's had enough socializing for one night, so he plans to hang out in his car for half an hour before the drive to Long Beach. He can sleep in tomorrow because, unlike Ruben, he doesn't have a meeting to go to.

Outside, he sees Ruben standing under a streetlight with Sam and Joshua, probably waiting for rideshares. He wonders what Ruben is telling them, if he's claiming the Bruden Bros breakup was all Brandon's fault. He doesn't really want to go and chat, but he doesn't want to slink away, either. Maybe he'll just yell, "Later, guys!" as he walks to his car, like he doesn't care about their opinion at all.

"Trying to make it in showbiz?" a voice asks from above, startling him.

Brandon looks up and sees that the neighboring house has a balcony. An old woman is leaning on its railing. Even in the dim light, he can see her face is deeply lined, her gray hair is frizzy and brittle, and that her tie-dyed tank top has seen better days.

"What?" he asks.

She fixes him with an appraising stare. "Are you trying to get famous?"

Brandon doesn't want to explain that with certain demographics, he's already famous, or at least *was*, so he says, "I guess."

"Well, be careful. That business will chew you up and spit you out. Stay focused on what matters."

"Thanks."

He looks back at Ruben and the others, still considering what to do, when a sports car pulls up and Gary Milton's aging frat-boy voice calls out from the open window. "Hey, who's up for a nightcap? Ruben? Sam? It's way too early for the party to end. Brandon, get over here!"

Since he's been spotted, Brandon walks over to the others. "What's this about?"

"Nightcap?" Gary asks again.

"Where?" Sam asks.

"My place."

"I'm not going all the way out to Malibu," Brandon says.

"Not Malibu," says Gary. "My little hideaway. My mancave. It's a secret," he adds, holding up a finger to his lips. "Over in Beverly Hills."

"I'm up for it," says Joshua, looking at Sam.

Up close, Brandon can see Joshua is still flushed with alcohol, and Sam's a little unsteady as well. Twenty minutes ago, they were jumping around and singing Toto's "Africa" as a jubilant, drunken duet.

Sam looks intrigued, but explains, "I hate to be a killjoy, but Vanessa's sick."

"If she's sick, she's probably sleeping," argues Gary, "and you should let her sleep."

Sam makes a show of considering, and then acquiesces by yelling "shotgun" and jumping into the front passenger seat.

"Come on," says Joshua, looking at Ruben and Brandon with pleading eyes. "It'll be fun."

Ruben hesitates. He's tired; he wants to go back to his hotel, and tomorrow he has the meeting to discuss a gig as a guest commentator at an extreme sports competition. Instinctively, he glances at Brandon and is relieved that he also looks unwilling. Then he remembers they're not here together.

"Come on, Ruben," says Gary. "We hardly see you any-more since you moved to New York. You've got a weekend in L.A., and you're going to go to bed like an old man? Brandon?"

"My car is parked here," explains Brandon.

"So? Rideshare back," says Gary. "You not getting enough ad revenue these days? Come on. Surely the Bruden Bros can have one nightcap together. You can't hate each other that much."

Neither Ruben nor Brandon want to go. They're tired, and they've never liked Gary. But Sam and Joshua are going, and they're both worried about being left out if the other one goes.

"Come on," says Gary. "One nightcap. It'll be nice. Just a small group of legends and rising stars."

"Okay, fine," says Brandon, and Ruben follows him around the car as the others cheer.

⌐

It's weird being in the car together, pressed up against each other with Brandon in the middle seat and Ruben next to him. They haven't even talked for over a year, and now their thighs are touching as if they're in high school again, piled in a friend's backseat for a late-night trip to the diner. As soon as the door closes, Gary takes off. The car has a kick to it.

"My seatbelt buckle is under your butt," says Ruben to Brandon.

"You don't need your seatbelt," says Gary. "It's like fifteen minutes, tops."

Joshua, Brandon, and Ruben buckle up anyways.

"What is this place, exactly?" asks Ruben.

"My Beverly Hills mancave," says Gary. "A little bungalow I'm renting. If we film, we're gonna have to say it's your Airbnb, Ruben, okay? When you've got a wife and four kids, you gotta escape sometimes, for your own sanity. Sam, I heard you're getting married soon, and that's cool, but don't have kids, man. At least not right away."

Sam laughs. "We're gonna wait at least a year."

"No, no. More than that, man. Wait like ten years. You're lucky you're gay, Josh," Gary adds, turning to look in the back seat. "No accidental pregnancy for you."

"Eyes on the road, dude," says Ruben, trying to keep his voice teasing.

Gary whistles. "Damn, this one's a stickler."

Brandon says nothing. Soon they're on Mulholland, a road that reminds him of Highway 17, the twisty, mountainous, treacherous route between Santa Cruz and Silicon Valley.

Ruben grips the door handle as they go around a turn too fast. It feels like they're barreling down a gaping maw. He thinks back on the party, trying to remember how much he saw Gary drinking, if he saw Gary's eyes when getting in the car, if his pupils were dilated. He remembers being at a vlogger party with Brandon when they were seventeen, and Gary telling them he had cocaine and did they want some, and only realizing months later that he hadn't been joking.

Sam laughs as they take another turn, even though it throws him against the door. "Damn, you suck at Mario Kart!"

Occasionally the lights of Los Angeles are visible on their left, beyond and below. The turns keep coming, and Gary seems to savor them. But then, abruptly, the wheels are on dirt instead of asphalt, and then there's a jolt that jolts everything as Gary hits the brakes: every bone in their bodies, their eardrums, the air in the car. Brandon feels his hips and chest slam against the seatbelt. The headlights illuminate the steep hillside they were inches from hitting.

"Whoops," says Gary.

There's a pause, and then Ruben undoes his seatbelt. "Get the keys," he says to someone, maybe Sam, who has been thrown against the dashboard and is saying, "Holy shit" over and over.

Ruben opens the door, climbs out.

"Where are you going?" asks Gary.

"Get out," Ruben says to Brandon.

Brandon doesn't move. Although Gary continuing to drive doesn't seem like a good idea, and he remembers that party when he and Ruben were seventeen and other parties afterward, he's still low-key fighting with Ruben and wants to defy him out of spite. Besides, Gary has supposedly cleaned up. Next to him, Joshua reaches for his own seatbelt but stops, looking similarly conflicted.

Ruben feels the same hesitation. He worries that he's overreacting since they didn't actually hit anything. But something about the way the road ahead looms makes his heart pound, so he leans back into the car, unlatches Brandon's seatbelt, and takes his wrist. "Get out."

Brandon obeys, both annoyed that Ruben is making a big deal of this and thankful that someone is giving him an excuse to escape the car. When his feet touch the firm ground of the turnout, he feels a wave of relief.

Ruben yanks open the driver's side door. "Dude, you're in no shape to drive," he says. "Give me the keys." Gary argues with him, half-laughing still, asking what his deal is and pointing out that the airbags didn't even go off. Then Ruben leans over to get the keys and Gary hits reverse.

Brandon sees Ruben scurry to back up with the car while still trying to wrestle the keys out of the ignition. He sees him lose his footing, fall to one knee, and get dragged backwards through the dirt and gravel. He hears Sam and Joshua shouting. The car pauses, and Brandon grabs Ruben and pulls him away just as Gary hits the gas. The car shoots back onto the road, both driver's side doors still open, and within seconds the taillights disappear around a curve.

¬

From the backseat Joshua asks, "Did you hit them? Did he hit them?" But neither Gary nor Sam answer. Sam begs Gary to stop or at least slow down, all teasing humor finally gone from his voice, but Gary still argues that he's fine. The driver's side doors are still open.

Joshua leans across the seats, but with his seatbelt on, he can't reach the door handle to pull it shut. The cool air brings in a woodsy scent that reminds him of summer camp. He can close the door when they stop, he thinks. They can't be too far away.

His phone vibrates in his pants pocket. Brandon's texting him, asking if they're okay. Joshua replies that they're okay so far and asks if he and Ruben are okay.

> *Brandon: We're fine. Ruben says get the keys.*

┐

Brandon and Ruben sit on the dead grass at the far end of the turnout where the hillside rises like a wall. Neither of them is sure what to do. Ruben asks if they should call the cops.

"And tell them what?" Brandon asks. "They'll never get there in time, anyways."

"Have Joshua or Sam texted you back?"

In the immediate aftermath, once they had staggered over to where they're now sitting, their first reaction was to text. Ruben replied to a recent group chat with a few others who were at the party, giving a stunned, matter-of-fact, punctuation-less account of what had happened. Responses have been flying in, but they're all things like "!!!" or shocked emojis or laughing emojis.

Brandon checks his phone again. "Joshua texted. He says they're okay so far."

"Tell him to get the keys."

In the group chat, Jahan, the party host, asks where they are. Ruben opens his map app, sees the blue dot that represents him and Brandon. He sends the location, and soon Jahan says he and Nasreen are coming to pick them up.

With that problem solved, Ruben shines his phone's flashlight on his right knee, which has started burning as his adrenaline fades. There's a hole in his pants from where he was dragged backwards by the car, showing a dirty, bloody abrasion below.

"Fuck," he says. "I just bought these jeans."

"Shit. You okay?" asks Brandon.

"Yeah," he says, flicking a piece of gravel from the gore. "I definitely got worse in our skateboarding days."

"Now your jeans are 'distressed.' People pay extra for that."

Ruben takes a blurry flash photo of the damage and shares it to the group chat.

> *Ruben: FML these were expensive*

"I haven't been skateboarding in forever," says Brandon, and they both think of the skatepark by the San Lorenzo River, of the hours and hours they spent there in the foggy summers of Santa Cruz, dreaming up stories of two rival skateboarding gangs that would eventually become humorous skits. They remember walking and skating side-by-side along the Boardwalk, the wharf, Pacific Avenue. They remember going past all the dingy motels on Riverside and wondering why tourists came to their cold, boring town.

And now they are somewhere in Los Angeles on a warm, clear night, in near-total darkness. Brandon wants to thank Ruben for getting him out of the car but doesn't because he fears it might be too sentimental, especially if Gary gets the car to Beverly Hills. Really, he thinks, he should be mad at Ruben for making him miss the nightcap at Gary's, which would have lent him some clout.

They wait, their flashlights angled at the road to help Nasreen and Jahan find them. They don't mention it, but they're listening carefully, listening for the sound of a distant car crash. They don't hear anything besides crickets.

Brandon keeps looking at his text to Joshua and Sam, waiting for the three dots to appear that indicate someone is typing. There's nothing.

> *Brandon: Where are you now?*

"Look!" whispers Ruben.

Brandon looks up from his phone to where Ruben's flashlight shines. There are two glowing eyes and brisk movement. It's a coyote on Mulholland Drive, trotting along the opposite shoulder. Like most coyotes, it only glances at them briefly, not even breaking stride as it continues on its way. Still, there's a thrill of fear; they're facing a wild animal with claws and teeth, and the only thing stopping it from attacking is its own disinterest.

"Remember when we saw that coyote in, like, fourth grade?" Ruben asks.

Brandon can see it, the sauntering canid so similar to the one in front of them. They had been walking to Ruben's house after school.

"And we told everyone it was a wolf," says Brandon.

Their parents had told them it couldn't possibly have been a wolf, that there were no wolves in California, but he and Ruben had remained insistent. Much of the summer after fourth grade they spent in the woods, or what they considered the woods, looking for more wolves. They narrated to each other a whole story about the wolfpack they imagined was there, and how they would gain their trust. For that whole summer, it felt like the wolves would be just behind the next redwood. It seemed impossible that when summer ended, they would be sitting in fifth grade instead of running wild through the mountains.

Jahan's car finally pulls up, with Nasreen driving and Jahan sticking his head out the passenger window.

"Holy shit, you guys," he says. "Gary just fucking drove off?"

"Yeah," says Ruben as he and Brandon dust themselves off before climbing into the back. "He floored it. Doors still open and everything. Do you think we should call the cops?"

Nasreen says they should, but Jahan says, "What? Don't do that. Don't be a narc. What are they going to say, anyways? That their ride ditched them?"

"But what if they crash?" Nasreen asks. "Have you heard from them?"

"Joshua texted me a while back," says Brandon. "Nothing since then."

"Should we look for them?" Nasreen asks. "Where were they going?"

"Beverly Hills," says Brandon. "I don't know more than that."

Ruben looks at his own phone. He has no texts from Joshua or Sam, only texts from the group chat. He adds an update that Jahan has picked them up.

> *Mike-O: Jahan is the man!*
> *Tony: Rate him 5 stars on Lyft :laughing:*

"They probably got to Gary's place and aren't checking their phones," says Jahan.

Nasreen says they should look, just in case, and drives west, winding around the dark turns. Brandon tries actually calling both Joshua and Sam, but neither picks up.

"Which road down do you think they took?" Nasreen asks. "Coldwater Canyon?"

"We don't know," says Ruben.

As they return to Jahan and Nasreen's place, Brandon glances at the neighbor's house to check if the old woman is still there on the balcony.

There's no balcony. Only flowerboxes. Brandon doesn't know he's staring until Ruben makes eye contact with him, questioning. Brandon shakes his head that it's nothing, tells himself it's been a long night.

Brandon's car is nearby, but it's late, and Nasreen says they should stay the night. No one has a contact for Lara, Gary's wife, but Nasreen is able to message Sam's fiancée Vanessa on an app they're both on. There's still nothing from Gary, Sam, or Joshua. No one on the group chat has heard from them either.

"Someone's passed out in the guestroom," says Nasreen when they're all tired of news failing to arrive, "but are you two okay sharing the sofa bed? If not, we might have a sleeping bag somewhere. One of you could sleep in the gaming studio."

"It's fine," says Brandon.

⌐

Brandon texts a quick summary of the situation to Mandy, knowing she'll be fast asleep in Atlanta, then sends a final text to Sam, Joshua, and Gary before getting into bed.

> *Sorry if we're overreacting but please text us as soon as one of you gets this.*

He puts his phone on silent and settles on the thin mattress. The springs yelp and groan. Ruben is already under the covers.

"It's just like at your grandma's," says Ruben.

Brandon's grandma had a house over in Aptos, and sometimes when they were kids, they would spend a weekend there. This does feel like that, Brandon thinks, like he and Ruben are in his grandma's seashell-and-driftwood living room, on her querulous sofa bed, whispering together until late. Before Bruden Bros and arguing about Bruden Bros and lawyers dividing up future ad revenue from Bruden Bros.

Neither Ruben nor Brandon think they'll be able to fall asleep, but they both do within minutes.

＿

Joshua doesn't know how long he has been walking. Some time ago, he was in the car with Gary and Sam, and Gary was driving like a maniac, and then the car started moving in a way it shouldn't. The car bumped, it lurched, there was a slam, something like an explosion near his ear, and then the thumping, roaring, rushing, metal-and-screams sound of a roller coaster. Then it was still and quiet and pitch-black. The whole right side of his face burned. He called for Sam and Gary, but no one answered.

An attempt at movement caused pain to burst through his right shoulder. He couldn't use his right arm. His head throbbed, as if his skull suddenly remembered that it should hurt. There were still no noises from the front seats. His left arm was fine, so he undid his seatbelt, and even though his shoulder was in agony, he leaned forward to reach between the two front seats. Gary's bulk wasn't in the driver's seat. Sam wasn't in the passenger seat.

He opened his door and, cradling his right arm, climbed out. He had expected flatness, but the ground was slanted and slick with dry grass. He fell and screamed and there was a click in his shoulder and he knew the joint was once again in place.

After dry heaving for a few moments, he had circled the car by touch, stumbling over rocks and bushes and uneven terrain he couldn't see. No one was there. Had Sam and Gary gone to get help? Where was his phone? His phone had been in his hand when the crash happened. He felt around the backseat but couldn't find it. He had started walking and shouting, walking and shouting, pushing his way through what felt like a sea of scraping, hard-branched scrubs.

Now he sees lights. They're up on a crest, and it feels like he's been trying to reach them for hours. First, he had to walk down a ravine, and now he's climbing the opposite side. Are they coming from a home? Are they streetlights for a dusty side road or some little-used maintenance building? He can't tell.

Suddenly, he's looking down at the lights, which doesn't make sense. The change in perspective hits him with a wave of vertigo. He wants to give up, but the lights look closer now, so he keeps going, staggering downhill. Soon, he can see that the source is a house. He's looking down into a backyard with a glowing oblong pool. He calls for help and breaks into a jog.

The black bars of a fence stop him at the edge of the property. Gentle outdoor lighting reveals a manicured lawn, palm trees, and a large, white mansion. Several windows are illuminated, but more importantly, a group of people are in and around the pool.

"Help!" Joshua yells. "Help!"

Faces turn toward him. A dozen or so young people are gathered, all traditionally beautiful. There are curves and muscles, smooth skin, sharp jawlines, dark eyelashes. But no one otherwise reacts.

"Please," he calls. "We were in a car crash. I don't know where my friends are. Someone call 911."

He looks into the eyes of the person closest to him, a young man with tan skin and dark hair. He's standing in the pool, water up to his waist. The pool is close enough that Joshua can smell the chlorine and hear the filtration system, but the boy doesn't seem to see him. Desperate, Joshua looks to the next closest person: a blonde girl in a pink bikini, sitting on a lounge chair. She's looking in his direction, but her expression is blank.

A sliding glass door opens in the mansion, and a man steps out. He's wearing trousers and an unbuttoned button-down that reveals a torso covered with scraggly gray hair. Heavy gold chains hang around his neck and wrists, and his fingers are armored with rings.

"Get inside," the old man snaps, and Joshua startles at how mean his voice sounds.

The beautiful young people wordlessly obey. As the boy Joshua had tried to make eye contact with leaves the pool, he looks over his shoulder in Joshua's direction, but his vacant eyes don't quite land on him.

The old man is now outside alone, and his eyes meet Joshua's effortlessly. His ruddy face breaks into a grin. Instead of feeling relief, though, Joshua feels a stab of fear.

"Come on in," the man says.

The black bars of the fence melt away in his hands, and Joshua stumbles backwards. He turns and runs back into the darkness, the grasses, the bushes. He crashes into something more like a tree, and disoriented, pauses for a moment. He can't hear anyone following him, so he risks a glance back at the mansion. It's in the distance now. Only one window is lit up, but then that light turns off as well.

Joshua is suddenly overcome with fatigue. He'll rest for a moment, he thinks, sinking towards the ground. He'll rest and then find some other house to go to for help.

⌐

Ruben is confused when he wakes. The feel of the mattress, the scent of the sheets, the angle of the sunlight on the ceiling: everything is unfamiliar. Then he rolls over and sees Brandon. Brandon also stirs, awakened by the movement.

"Hey," says Ruben.

"Hey," says Brandon.

They're quiet for a moment, remembering why they're there, groggy from the late night and alcohol.

"Did they text you?" Ruben finally asks.

Brandon sits up and twists around to grab his phone off the side table. As he does so, they both tell themselves that this will be it: the end of the drama. Joshua, Gary, and Sam will have had a crazy bender at wherever Gary's rental was. They'll laugh. It will be a funny story. Someone will say, "Remember when Gary ran off the road and Ruben freaked out and dragged Brandon out of the car and tried to take the keys and then Gary floored it and left them stranded on the side of Mulholland Drive?"

It's 9:23 in the morning, and Brandon has too many texts, phone calls, and voicemails for his half-awake mind to register. They're from friends, his girlfriend, people he's not sure he knows. All he can see are question marks and urgency. But none of them are from the people in the car. It seems impossible that there are so many texts and yet none from them. When he opens the last text he sent to Sam and Joshua, there is a red error message: delivery failed.

He calls Mandy first. In Atlanta it's nearing 12:30, and she's been frantic.

A whole Thing started overnight, after they had gone to bed. At around 3:00 a.m., Tony from the group chat Ruben texted began writing about the saga on social media. *Guys, maybe I'm worried over nothing, but this is freaking me out*, the first post began. The posts include screenshots of the group texts, including the location of the incident, the photo of Ruben's knee. Tony ends with a plea for anyone to share any info they have and a promise that he will update as soon as he gets more information.

A few other night owls and fans on other continents shared the posts and time zone by time zone, they have spread. Hashtags have started: #WhereAreGaryJoshand-Sam, #FindJoshuaSamAndGary, #WhereAreSJG, #WhereAreThey.

Ruben retrieves his fully charged phone from the kitchen and tries to get caught up while Brandon talks to Mandy. He stares at his words from the night before, at the blurry photo of his own bloodied knee, presented for public dissection. He doesn't even really know Tony; he just happened to be on the group chat. As far as he could tell from the party, Tony didn't know Joshua, Sam, or Gary well either. He holds up his phone for Brandon, who is still talking to Mandy.

"Lara DM'd you?" Brandon asks. "Jesus. Ruben's showing me the posts from Tony. Shit, shit, shit. So, no one's heard anything? Fuck."

Nasreen comes out of her room. "Any word from them?" she asks.

Ruben shakes his head.

"Yeah, you can give her my number," Brandon says to Mandy. "I don't know what we could tell her, though. Okay … I will … I love you." He puts down the phone, turns to Ruben. "Gary's wife wants to talk to us."

Eventually Jahan stumbles out of his room, more hungover than they are. He's already seen the viral posts.

"Shit, guys," he says. "You should make a joint video. Issue a statement."

Ruben shakes his head. "Not now," he says.

"People will want to know you're okay," Jahan says. "And you can get your side of the story out there."

"Tony already put out everything," says Ruben.

Ruben's hotel is downtown, and Brandon says he'll drive him on his way to Long Beach. When they get on the 101, Ruben remembers how dark the road was the previous night, how different it was from this bright, loud freeway. Brandon's heart pounds. How does he know all these other drivers aren't like Gary, that they won't career into his lane at any moment?

Brandon's phone rings from the cupholder, and he spares a quick glance: it's a number with a local area code. "Probably Gary's wife. Lara," he says.

Ruben answers it.

Lara Milton's voice is full of fury, but also on the edge of tears. Ruben runs through the timeline of the night, but she keeps interrupting. "What place in Beverly Hills?"

"I don't know," says Ruben. "He said he was renting it."

"And he didn't give an address or anything?"

"No."

"Are you sure? Did he say what it was by? A street name?"

"No, nothing. He just said, 'Out in Beverly Hills' and that it was a bungalow."

"Fuck. Fuck. The kids are asking about him, you know. They want to know where their dad is."

"I'm sorry. I don't know."

"What about Brandon?"

"He doesn't know anything either."

"Can you ask him?"

Ruben sighs and looks at Brandon, who is focusing on the road, steering wheel gripped tight.

"He doesn't have any more information than I do," says Ruben.

"His phone's not working either. I can't even get voice-mail," says Lara. "What am I supposed to do?"

"I don't know what to say."

"He fucking dragged you with his car," Brandon mutters. At the time, getting Ruben away from the car had been simple instinct. Even afterwards, the scene had been too fuzzy to feel real. But now it hits him that Gary had thrown the car in reverse with Ruben half in it and had been about to take off down Mulholland Drive.

Brandon's phone buzzes, and an image of Brandon's mother appears.

"Look, I've got to go," says Ruben to Lara. "Brandon's mom is calling him. We'll let you know if we hear anything." He hangs up on her, answers the new call. "Hi, Mrs. Long. Brandon's driving, I'll put you on speaker."

"Oh, Ruben," she says, and the familiar sound of his childhood best friend's mother saying his name makes Ruben want to cry.

Once Ruben has relayed the previous night's incidents again and Mrs. Long has been assured that they're all right, she urges Ruben to call his own mother, which he does. When they finally reach the hotel, he's had to explain the previous night three times since they left Jahan and Nasreen's house. He's exhausted, and Brandon's knuckles are white from the drive.

"Do you want to come up?" Ruben asks.

⌐

The landscape is confounding when Joshua wakes: a brilliant blue sky through the red branches of a manzanita. He sits up, and it feels like every muscle in his body has been wrenched. His neck is too stiff to allow his head to turn. The right side of his face is swollen, and the weight of his arm is too much for his injured shoulder.

The memory of the crash snaps into his mind, and he pushes himself to his feet, looking for the car in the sea of scruffy green brush over the hilly terrain.

"Sam!" he calls out. "Gary!"

No one responds. How did he get so far from the car?

Then he remembers the mansion, the old man, the hot guy in the pool. He had been able to see the mansion from this spot last night, but there's nothing now. No fence, no yard, no palm trees. Had he hallucinated, perhaps due to a concussion? It's the only explanation, but he can still feel the cool metal bars of the fence in his hands, still smell the chlorine.

As he wanders the area, searching for the house and calling for help, a new sense of dread forms in his chest. He's been hiking in the hills before, and nothing ever felt as remote as this. There were always other hikers, or a distant housing development, a view of the city below, power lines, the sound of traffic, something. There's none of that here. How far had they driven? The crash couldn't have been more than a few minutes after they left Brandon and Ruben, and that had been somewhere around Laurel Canyon.

His heart thumping, he starts climbing a nearby peak to get a better view. His progress is slow, and he wonders how the others are doing, if they're in better or worse shape than he's in. He hopes that somehow, when he reaches the top, everything will make sense again. He'll see the city and be able to orient himself. He'll see Sam and Gary, alive, and shout to them.

He reaches the top and sees nothing but an expanse of green-and-tawny mountains.

⌐

They get a toothbrush for Brandon at the hotel's front desk.

"Jahan made a video," Ruben notes in the elevator. He doesn't watch it.

They continue scrolling as they walk to the room. Ruben doesn't look at his mentions, but he can't help but see comments about himself as he scans for new information. *I know this isn't the most important thing but Ruben and Brandon slept in the same bed??? :hearteyes:* one fan has typed. Jahan must have mentioned that in his video. Someone else has asked, *Why didn't Ruben get Joshua and Sam out of the car too? :sadface:*

He tells himself he tried, that when he said, "Get out," he directed it at everyone.

In the room, Brandon crashes face-down on the white duvet of the king-sized bed. Ruben sits and leans against the headboard. After a few moments, Brandon rolls on his side and continues looking at his phone.

"Jesus," he says, "kids are going out to the hills to look for them."

"The homeowners are going to be pissed," says Ruben, imagining teenage fans climbing over fences, marching through roses and hydrangeas. "I hope Gary just pulled over in someone's mile-long driveway and they all passed out," he adds. That seems possible, and he feels a flicker of hope. Maybe Gary got lost in the twisting, dark roads and finally stopped somewhere. Soon they'll be found. There will be a photo posted online of Joshua, Sam, and Gary looking bleary-eyed and sheepish, posing with their thrilled fan-rescuers. "Do you want to eat?"

They order room service and take turns using the shower while they wait, washing away the smell of beer and sweat, the dust of the Mulholland Drive turnout.

In the mirror, Brandon studies the faint seatbelt bruise that is forming across his chest. He knows that if he took a selfie right now, it would be wildly shared: the towel around his hips, the carefully trimmed trail of hair that runs up to his navel, his defined abs, and then the faint brown-purple smudge between his pecs. He looks good, but the context would mean no one could call him vain. The photo would elicit concern instead — a concern tinged with lust. He could take a selfie in this hotel bathroom mirror, and it would trigger an explosion on social media, especially if he mentioned that it's Ruben's hotel room. There would be tragedy, eroticism, voyeurism, and fanservice all in one perfect image.

The idea to take a selfie feels automatic and sensible, but also remote, as if through a fogged window. He doesn't take a photo.

He does show Ruben the bruise, though.

"Damn," says Ruben, suitably sympathetic and impressed.

They eat pancakes on the bed while checking for news, wrapped in the hotel's white terry cloth bathrobes. Nasreen texts that she's spoken with Sam's flu-stricken fiancée Vanessa, and Sam didn't come home last night. Ruben ends up talking with Vanessa, too. She's congested, confused, and scared. She says that when she calls Sam's phone, she gets an error message. Ruben forces himself to be patient while he once again explains what happened. He tells her his hope that the three are passed out in the long driveway of some mansion, their phones' batteries dead. After that call, Ruben cancels his meeting. Then someone from Cannon Blast's parent company calls and says one of their lawyers is going to call him, even though he insists that isn't necessary.

Nasreen texts that Joshua's parents have contacted her. Brandon offers to handle that conversation. It's the worst one. He hates talking on the phone to strangers anyway, and Mr. and Mrs. Choi are clearly crying. They want to know where their son is. They want to know why no one called the cops. They keep asking the same questions phrased slightly differently, as if the answers will be different if they get the wording right. When he's making videos, Brandon is perfectly articulate, but now he's tripping over his words, stumbling with long pauses.

Ruben eventually takes the phone from him, introduces himself, confirms what Brandon said, and gently convinces them to get off the phone and file a missing person report.

"Shit," says Brandon when Ruben hangs up. "This is really happening, isn't it?"

"Yeah," says Ruben, rubbing his face. "It's like they fell into a black hole." There are bags under his eyes, and his jawline is marked with stubble. His skinned knee is starting to scab over, but still oozes some blood after being scrubbed in the shower.

Ruben's phone rings again. "That'll be the lawyer," he says with a sigh.

Brandon takes Ruben's phone, answers it, says Ruben is sleeping, and hangs up.

￢

Joshua rests under an oak tree he saw from the peak. At first, he had wanted to stay where he was, so he could easily be spotted by rescuers, but it was hot, and the shade had beckoned. He keeps replaying his memory of the mansion but trying to understand where the mansion has gone or how he got where he is makes him dizzy, so he tries to think of something else. He wonders if anyone has noticed he's missing yet, if his parents and sister know. Maybe Sam or Gary have had better luck finding help, and soon he'll hear a helicopter whirring above.

Then he does hear something. Someone or something is coming toward him through the brush.

He sees a gray coat, long muzzle, pointed ears — a dog. He sits up straight, heart leaping in his chest. A dog will have an owner nearby. He's about to call out when he sees the animal more clearly.

The animal is massive. He keeps telling himself that it's a Malamute, it's a husky mix, it's a German Shepherd mix, it's something that will be followed by a person with a leash and a tennis ball, but he knows it's not. He knows it's not even a coyote.

It's a wolf. Wolves are extinct in California, but the creature in front of him is a wolf. Its small yellow eyes are not like anything Joshua has seen in a dog, and when the wolf stops and stares at him, he can't breathe.

The wolf is going to eat him, he thinks. Or maul him, leaving him to slowly bleed out here in the wilderness. His body would never be found. His parents would never know what happened to him, and the expressions he imagines on their faces make him decide that he isn't going to die. He's going to stay so still that the wolf will leave. He will be a statue. He will be a tree. He will be one of those monks who meditate until they mummify.

As suddenly as it stopped, the wolf moves on. Joshua waits for a long time, breathing as shallowly as he is able. He waits until he is sure the wolf must be far away before taking gasping, deep breaths. Then he forces himself up again. He walks downhill, because downhill has to lead somewhere, eventually. He will keep walking until he can tell his parents he's alive.

⌐

Brandon and Ruben are both stretched out on the bed, looking at their phones. There's no new news, except that Joshua's sister has confirmed online that the Choi family has spoken with the LAPD, as have Vanessa and Lara. The hotel room's TV is playing a local news station, but the disappearance hasn't been picked up there yet. For now, it's strictly a social media story, spread and elaborated on by people who weren't there. Fans are out on Mulholland and its environs, posting photos of tire tracks, skid marks, dented guardrails, trash.

Brandon and Ruben still haven't posted anything.

Brandon goes back into his text to Sam and Joshua. He's tried to resend the failed text, the one that reads, *Sorry if we're overreacting but please text us as soon as one of you gets this*, several times throughout the day, to feel like he's doing something. He's gotten the red error message every time, but he tries again. This time, it goes through with the usual sound effect, and the word "delivered" briefly appears.

"It worked," he exclaims, showing Ruben.

Then Ruben gets a text from an acquaintance. It's a shocked emoji and a link. Ruben clicks it, and a video pops up. The title is "Hills Discovery." The POV is of someone holding a phone, and there are three young men in the frame.

⌐

When Marco Rey is asked, again and again and again, why he didn't stop the livestream, why he didn't turn the camera away, he'll give different answers. For a while he'll say he thought it was a prank, or he'll say that because of the glare on his phone's screen, he couldn't even tell what the object was at first. Later he'll say he was in shock, and even later than that, he'll believe it. Trung Nguyen, who in the video is the quickest to realize the severity of what is happening, who blanches and darts out of the frame, gets the least amount of social censure, but still has to explain those few minutes of his life endlessly. Matt Knowles, who is one of the two seen laughing and nudging the severed arm with his shoe, who is the one who actually bends down and touches the arm, drops out of UCLA and dies of an overdose a year and a half later. Scott Foster, the other boy seen laughing and kicking at the arm, seems unscathed. When asked, he just shrugs and says he thought it was a discarded Halloween decoration.

¬

Still in their robes, Brandon and Ruben are ushered up several floors. The manager escorting them says a staff member will bring their things.

"Won't we go back to the room after it's clean?" Ruben asks.

The room is being cleaned because Ruben couldn't make it to the bathroom in time and threw up on the carpet. Neither of them is sure how long they let the vomit sit there, under a towel Brandon threw on it, before it occurred to them to call the front desk. The drying vomit hadn't seemed important.

"That won't be necessary," says the manager, opening the door to a new room. "You can stay in this suite, no extra charge."

The suite is nicer and bigger. It's a pity upgrade, Ruben thinks as he and Brandon settle on white leather couch in the living area. Fans have determined it's Sam's arm. Comparison collages have been posted. The news has picked up the story, reporting that human remains and a wrecked car have been found.

Brandon's phone rings with Mandy's ringtone, and he takes it out of his robe's pocket. She tells him she has a red-eye flight booked for that night. "Okay," he says. He's cried and screamed and he feels empty. While Ruben was vomiting on the carpet, Brandon was kneeling beside him, saying, "You saved my fucking life," repeatedly with stunned and grieving reverence.

"I saw they've got search and rescue out there now," Mandy says.

When Brandon doesn't respond, she hesitantly adds, "Are you guys … are you going to make a statement? I'm getting a million questions about you and Ruben. Everyone's waiting for you to say something."

Brandon feels a clenching behind his sternum. Ruben has overheard the question, and their eyes meet. If the Bruden Bros released a video now, somber, sad-eyed, gravelly voiced, what a moment it would be.

"We don't want …" Brandon begins, "we don't want this to just be …"

"Content," Ruben finishes.

⌐

The songs everyone used to sing while hiking at camp keep running through Joshua's head as he walks, but in fragments, mixed together. The ants go marching two-by-two, hurrah, hurrah. You take one down and pass it around, thirty-three bottles of milk on the wall.

As those chants skip and repeat and blend on one tab in his mind, he also rethinks his whole life. If he hadn't dropped out of UT Austin to do YouTube full-time, maybe he would be in grad school by now, either still at Austin, close to his family, or somewhere exciting. He could have just done a video occasionally for fun and extra cash instead of making it his career.

Or what if he had never started posting videos at all? He would be a private citizen. He would never have to worry about video viewership metrics, and he wouldn't be hiking down this mountain in agony.

But he likes his job, he concedes. Instead, what he shouldn't have done was get in Gary's car. Or at least he and Sam should have gotten out when Ruben and Brandon had. All four of them could have called a rideshare and then gone and had late-night pizza. It would have been fun, just the four of them, and maybe Brandon and Ruben would have even become friends again. The night would have been legendary. It would have been the night that kick-started the Bruden Bros reunion, and he would have been part of it.

He imagines that after their pizza night, the video Sam took of him singing "Ride" at karaoke would go viral. Maybe it has already. He doesn't know since he doesn't have his phone. In his mind it goes viral, and Lana Del Rey herself sees it and shares it. It'll be a huge boon for his career. He'll start doing more music, record an album, tour, pay off his parents' mortgage, buy his sister a house. He'll do interviews and laugh with TV hosts about his journey from college student to "funny guy on YouTube" to hit recording artist. One day, he'll be riding the subway in New York for business, and then a hot guy will look at him surreptitiously a few times before saying, "You're Joshua Choi, aren't you?"

Or maybe it will be at Sam and Vanessa's wedding where he meets someone. He switches to this scenario and revises the pretext. This time, the crash did happen, but it's in the past, and they're all fine. He imagines himself sitting at a table at the reception. He's telling his captivated tablemates about the accident. Sam and Vanessa are making the rounds and are standing nearby. "It was crazy," Sam says, in a tuxedo but with his hair still spiked neon (maybe green or pink by then). "None of us knew where the others were. We all thought the worst." And across from Joshua will be an attractive man, struck by their tale of survival. He won't be someone in "the industry." He'll be someone who does something good, like a pediatric oncologist. The doctor will invite Joshua to dance.

Joshua is so caught up in his imagination that he almost doesn't notice that the harsh shrubs are gone. He's standing on a dirt path.

It's a hiking trail, and it has come out of nowhere. He looks back from where he came. The landscape behind him looks less vast than what he traversed, and he can see power lines that weren't there before. It's as if he's been spat back out to reality. He calls for help again, noticing how rough and strained his voice is, as if he's had a cough for weeks. His mouth is bone dry and full of dust, but he makes himself walk a little quicker, trying to work up saliva to moisten his throat.

The ants go marching seven-by-seven, the little one stops to pray to heaven.

Even if there aren't people on the trail, he thinks, he has to reach the beginning of it at some point. There will be a parking lot. There will be a road. There will be cars and houses. He won't have to walk all the way to his apartment. Someone will help him before then.

And then he can hear the sounds of people from around a bend: a laugh, footsteps. "Help!" he calls.

The footsteps stop. He hears anxious chatter. No, the people can't leave, not when rescue is so close.

You take one down and pass it around, one bottle of milk on the wall.

He follows the trail, doing his best to jog, and there they are: a startled-looking young Asian couple in stylish hiking gear.

He stumbles towards them. "Help," he says again. "Car accident. There was a car accident."

They seem frightened, and Joshua wonders what he looks like. The pair talk urgently to each other in a language that Joshua thinks might be Cantonese, but the man is holding a slim guidebook of L.A. hikes, the title written in English.

"English?" Joshua asks. He tries Korean, too, although he knows it's a long shot.

"Some English," the man says. "What happen?"

"Car accident," Joshua says, waving his good arm at the hills behind them. "The car went off the road."

"Your car crash?" the woman asks.

"Yes. My friend's car."

He feels dizzy and tries to ease himself down. The tourist couple hurry forward and grab his arms, helping him to sit by the side of the trail. It's as if all the adrenaline and willpower he used to reach them has disappeared. The woman unzips the man's backpack and pulls out a metal water bottle.

"Thank you," he manages to say with his dry tongue. Then he drinks, and the water is the most beautiful thing he's ever tasted. He's going to be okay, he realizes. Here are these kind people giving him water, and somewhere hopefully other kind people are giving Sam water. Soon he'll be in an air-conditioned hospital, getting pain medication, his parents on the phone, the accident already receding into the past.

LOVER'S LEAP

CATIE JARVIS

> "At its strongest and wildest and most authentic, love is a demon. It is a religion, a high-risk adventure, an act of heroism. Love is ecstasy and injury, transcendence and danger, altruism and excess. In many ways, it is a divine madness."
>
> — Cristina Nehring, *A Vindication of Love: Reclaiming Romance for the Twenty-first Century*

When they wheeled me out of surgery, I cried the way a baby cries, without knowing why or how to stop. The morphine still had hold, so I couldn't yet feel the physical pain, but every pent-up emotion from the weeks and months that had led me here burst forth. I could hear the sad whimpers from my throat, feel the puff and deflation of my chest. I had no control of it. It was strange to be almost thirty and to feel a helpless child.

"Are you in pain, dear? Is there anything we can get for you?"

I shook my head, or at least tried to.

Outside, a slender palm tree arched with the breeze. It reminded me of something I'd heard years ago from a hairdresser back in New Jersey where I grew up. The city of Los Angeles had ruined her, she had told me between snips. *I gave it ten years and left in pieces.* It seemed to me ridiculous to blame a city for one's own failures.

"Go get her boyfriend from Waiting. Bring him up," the nurse said.

Boyfriend. The word struck me like an angry lover's slap. So full of possibility and so terribly empty of commitment. I wanted my familiar old love to wrap itself around me, a revival.

New love did not mix well with broken bones. But what had I expected? That my husband would come running through the hospital door and save his damsel in distress after I had tossed him aside like a wet towel at a Vegas pool party?

My crying stopped.

I was propelled back into my strange new reality in which I was separated from Mr. Till-Death-Do-Us-Part and had started dancing with the Devil. Only now, I wouldn't be doing much dancing. The break in me extended way beyond my shattered heel bones, to everything that had ever been mine.

⌐

One week earlier, I lounged on a stranger's outdoor couch on a roof deck in the Hollywood Hills. It was a hot afternoon, no breeze. The sun burned everything out of the sky but the blue. I wondered what L.A. would be without it. The sun had drawn me here from across the country, kept me here, lit within me fires that may have otherwise gone unignited. I was wearing that bright orange TRIANGL bikini and matching orange Frogskins sunglasses that Troy had gotten me for my birthday the year before. Back when nothing had yet begun or ended. My skin burned and it was only noon.

I sat reading *A Vindication of Love*, a book Troy gave me the day after I showed up at his apartment with tears and two suitcases. Every line seemed to apply. I folded page corners into tiny points, marking phrases to return to. In between chapters, I looked out at the expansive view: the brown-green hills like a wilted Shire. The iconic Hollywood sign tiny in the distance. The layer of smog, abutting the clear blue, making L.A. not unlike myself — looming clouds and a bright, clear day all at once. All the downtowns rising to dwarf the winding urban sprawl that crawled right up to where I sat, making me feel such a tiny piece in this large city. Or maybe I was no piece at all. I could disappear and L.A. would go on without skipping a beat.

On the pool deck, Diego whacked at overgrown trees with a machete that he wielded dramatically like a sword in battle. He voiced "swoosh, swoosh" sounds as the branches fell to the ground. He was spirited and scrappy, with wild brown hair and a distinct limp from a motorcycle accident that he'd been lucky to survive. He was a year or two older than Troy and me, but seemed to have held on to all his childhood energy — a charming quality.

Troy swept the fallen branches and leaves into neat piles with an industrial-sized broom. His lean arms swirled with tattoos of skulls and flowers and crying girls. Neon-green tank clung to that dramatic arch in his back; a line of sweat formed down the center as the bristles scratched forward and slid back with a steady rhythm. I watched him in that way I had been watching him for months now. Zooming in so that the past and future seemed to disappear to a blaring present, as if this extended study would somehow reveal to me the truth of him, the truth of life itself. But it never quite did. He saw me watching, smiled, and blew a flamboyant kiss.

"Lover boy," Diego said, mockingly.

Diego pretended to wield his weapon and chop off Troy's head. Troy played at decapitation for the briefest moment, then pardoned himself from the game.

They were friends through the Ducati Owners Club that Troy headed, and they were cleaning up for a DOC party they were hosting the following afternoon. Diego did odd jobs, one of which was being a caretaker for this property in the hills. The owner, a heart surgeon named Larry, whom I'd yet to meet, said they could use the roof for their party but it needed some tending to first. I was along because Troy and I found it difficult to be separated for more than a few minutes, and when we were, all I did was cry.

Troy came over to check on me. We were electric with newness, and his mere approach flipped my stomach like a ten-story drop.

"Babe, stop doing that. You're ruining the book," he said as he caught me tagging another page. I shrugged. I was a corner folder. In nearly all things we were different.

"I'll get you a pencil. You can mark all the lines you'd like in a civilized way and read them to me later." He was full of corrections, as if he might mold me into something he could bear for a long time.

I smiled, nodded, waited anxiously for his skin to touch mine. Somehow my own body was no longer enough. He leaned over and kissed me, deep and hard. It was difficult to pry our mouths apart. I'd never felt so feral in my life.

I felt him scan my face and then down my body. I was skinnier than ever; love and loss had made me angular in a youthful way, with almost no breasts to speak of … I know Troy would have preferred there were. As he examined me, Troy's expression was a mix between *I want to fuck you right here* and *I wish I could throw you over the edge of this four-story balcony and be done with you.* He'd been looking at me this way for the last three weeks. Since I left Victor. His best friend.

"How do you like the book?" Troy asked. He'd read it a few years ago when his ex broke up with him. He hadn't dated anyone long-term since.

"It's perfect." I paused and wiped the sweat from under my eyes and upper lip. "There's a part of me that wishes I could undo it all, but this book reminds me that it's my duty as a woman and an artist to define and redefine love for myself. To live, experiment, feel, see; it's what life is for."

Troy smiled, lips thick with that cupid's bow dip in the center. I wanted them. I needed them. He had an angular face, heavyset brows, and the striking green eyes of a could-have-been movie star. Since we lived in L.A., people were always thinking they'd seen him in something. Certainly no one took him for an accountant, which he was. When we walked together, the gazes lingered on him, rather than me. I liked this. But in the grand scheme, I hadn't thought I'd care so much about looks, which were bound to fade. I was always trying to figure out what exactly about Troy had inspired such desire. What had propelled me to become the villain in my own love story?

"It really is nice how you can occupy yourself by reading," he said.

A checkmark on the pro side. Troy was having similar deliberations as I. For a person who thought he could get anyone, why did he have to choose me? No one wants to be a wife-stealer. It's too complicated. He felt shitty; he'd lost friends.

"Bleach time!" Diego yelled out with his hint of accent. He spoke nearly flawless English, but he had grown up in Mexico. "Would you like a drink or something while you wait?" he called. "There's some beer in the house."

I didn't respond until Troy nudged my shoulder, whispered, "He's talking to you." I hadn't expected his consideration, assuming he'd been talking to Troy.

"I'm okay, but thank you!"

"Kat doesn't drink beer," Troy added.

"I'll get you an ice water after we take care of this. Then, we swim."

It was nice to hang out with someone who didn't know Victor. Who didn't look at me the way my "real" friends did now, with that toxic mix of judgment, jealousy, and skepticism, which I undoubtedly deserved.

Diego handed Troy two huge canisters of bleach and took two for himself. They recklessly tossed it over the concrete pool deck, stained from dirt, pollen, leaves and what-not. I considered telling Troy to be careful, not to get it on himself or in his eyes, but the warnings felt too domestic. I didn't know what I was to Troy. What he wanted me to be. Besides, I was a reckless person now. Who was I to caution others?

Diego started scrubbing the stains out on hands and knees while Troy hosed the deck down again. They worked hard as I lazily watched. I might have offered to help, might have said in my slightly ticked-off feminist voice, "Just because I'm a girl doesn't mean I can't do manual labor." But I didn't have the energy for that right now. Since I'd left Victor, left my apartment and most of my belongings, my sweet calico cat named Lalia, and my understanding of who and what I was, I'd become lethargic with my self-made tumult. It wasn't my party anyway.

When the areas around the pool were clean, Troy skimmed the pool in elegant swipes.

Diego cleaned off the tiles along the side with a wet rag.

"Are you buying kegs for tomorrow?" Diego asked. "I have a hook-up if you need."

"Nah, just cases of beer, hard seltzer, and some Veuve Clicquot," Troy answered.

There were two kinds of people in the DOC: those like Diego, who spent all the money they had in the world on perfecting their expensive Italian motorcycles, and those like Troy, who had resources to tap into — in his case, family with money. Troy, and the other dudes like him, felt they should use these resources while they were still young on things like sport bikes, track days, upgraded golden wheels, and fancy exhaust pipes. I had only met the members of the group a few times, and I tended to like those in the former category more. I could say of all of them, though, that riding was in their hearts. I respected that.

That first time riding two-up with Troy, up the PCH, Topanga Canyon, winding through Mulholland, it seemed impossible that I wouldn't fly off and tumble to my death amidst the traffic. I held tight to his leather jacket and trusted him with my life. That was months before we started sleeping together. Months, even, before I had raised the subject of our problematic mutual attraction that had been building to the point of painful breach.

"What will we do about this?" I asked.

We had been out to dinner together at Plan Check in Santa Monica. Victor was away on a business trip.

"What?" Troy asked.

I gestured to his hand holding mine across the table.

"Nothing, just like we have been," Troy replied.

But it wasn't true. I had punctured the façade. He didn't take me home that night. Or the next. But three days later as I sat on my balcony in the Marina, looking out at hazy streetlamps, the breeze thick with salt and that stagnant stench of sea lions, a text from Troy lit up my phone. Two hours later he was deep inside of me. What would my life look like now if I had never gotten on his bike, if I had never gone to that dinner, never said a word?

I stood up, feet hot on cement. I gripped the handrail, it felt like touching fire. I held tight, looking out at the only city that had ever felt like home to me, for reasons I understood no more than my absolute attraction to Troy. Los Angeles had beauty (yes), grace, and confidence with a touch of possibility, but so did NYC and San Francisco, yet those cities hadn't held me. It was something else, perhaps an alluring mix of the natural and the manmade. The perfectly peeling point break at Topanga below the backed-up traffic of the PCH. The plentitude of sunshine beating down on solar-paneled roofs. Houses on stilts over the ocean and tucked into winding canyon roads. Hollywood, its industry of art imitating life, and the glow it cast upon all in its vicinity. The fact that you might sit next to Arnold Schwarzenegger or Goldie Hawn at lunch on Montana Ave. The outdoor playgrounds and paths coated with the sweat of those trying hard to stay forever young. It's strange in this life what we are drawn to.

Part of me felt sure I should never have come here, to this place so full of wanting. Victor and I had been happy on the east coast. There, we'd still be together; I was positive. I wanted that future with my kind, gentle, smart, funny college sweetheart, as much I wanted Troy. Each morning when I awoke, I hoped that something would compel me to walk out Troy's door, drive home, and beg Victor for forgiveness. But I never did. Instead, I'd roll over and kiss Troy in that way I thought I'd forgotten how to kiss. Troy's energy woke me up, and I couldn't find it in me to go back to sleep. Too bad, because the old dream had been a nice one.

I was trying hard to dream new dreams now. I grabbed my phone to text Hannah: *We have to go for a beach city. Even if the apartment is small.*

Hannah replied immediately: *Venice, walking distance to the ocean!*

236

Hannah was the sister of my best friend from college. She was two years younger, moving to L.A. from upstate NY.

Hannah: *Anyway, how are you doing?*

Kat: *Oh ... you don't want to know.*

Hannah: *I want!*

I sighed, took off typing a paragraph that Troy would deem way too long for a text: *One part of me is in love, fucking high on it, so excited for the future, seeing the world in technicolor, buzzing with life. Another part of me is sobbing on the floor for the beautiful love that I irrevocably destroyed, my very best friend whom I hurt so deeply, the life I gave up. It hurts. Sometimes it's like I can feel Victor's pain along with my own. This morning I pictured the pair of dirty beige flip flops he always left by the door and I turned into a ball of misery. One part of me is pulsing with life, the other with death. And since I can't be both things at the same time, I flip back and forth. I'm one or the other. Nothing in between. I'm the highest and the lowest. The change can come on at any time. It's maddening. Bizarre. Thrilling. I've never experienced anything like it.*

Hannah: *Oh, Kat. That's some real Jekyll and Hide shit. I can't wait to hug you.*

Kat: *I can't wait to hug you too! Sorry for always talking about myself. How are you?*

Hannah: *I'm only excited. To come out there. To start a new life.*

Kat: *Please don't turn on me like all my other friends.*

Hannah: *I would never.*

Kat: *I may be a horrible person who deserves to be punished, but at least I'm self-aware.*

Hannah: *LOL. You'll get through this my love, I promise.*

Hannah was the perfect person for me right now. I should have been so excited. I was trying. Trying to be excited to sleep alone in bed each night for the first time in ten years. To finish writing all the novels I'd started and abandoned. To support myself fully for the first time. To have more female energy around me, after having lived with a man for so long. There was a whole new life ahead of me; I could almost see it, and I wanted to see it. But when I was honest with myself, which I think it's important to be even if the truth makes you seem like a pathetic girl with codependency issues, I didn't want to be free. I wanted the opposite, in fact. I wanted Victor *and* Troy, in different ways, for different things. It didn't make sense to me that loving two people meant that I might lose both.

Hannah: *I've firmed up my plans, count me in for the start of August.*

Kat: *Perfect. I'm going to start looking at places tomorrow!*

Hannah: *I cannot wait. Find us a surfer-girl apt!*

I should have started searching for places already, but I didn't have the drive. I knew that it was inappropriate to leave Victor's bed and move directly into Troy's, but I thought of all those days that Troy and I kissed goodbye for too long, in parks, at gas stations, in hidden restaurants, wishing that we could be together, wishing that I wouldn't have to leave and go back home to Victor. Victor, who played guitar while I sang, cooked me gourmet dinners, loved me. If I wasn't with Troy, I had ruined a deep love without good reason. I was petrified that I wouldn't end up with Troy and petrified that I would. I couldn't decide which would be the more tragic ending to the story.

Something touched my shoulder and I jumped. Diego stood behind me, handed me a water bottle and laughed at my scare.

"We got things all cleaned up, you want to swim?"

"For sure. I'm boiling!"

The pool was a narrow rectangle, now sparkling clean. A dramatic black-diamond slope ran from the deep end to the shallow. I dove in, my whole body saying "ah" as the cool water touched skin sucked dry by the hot desert air. I floated on my back and heard the mumble of Troy and Diego chatting as they drank a beer by the ledge.

"Thanks for helping me clean up, man."

"You're doing me a favor. This is the best location we've ever had for a DOC party. The guys are gonna love it."

"Well, I got two birds with one stone, if that's what they say. I'm hosting a sex party here the following weekend," Diego said. "We do them every month, but we haven't used the deck yet. We'll heat up the hot tub, it will be great."

"What's that like?" Troy asked, completely unfazed, as if sex parties were a thing he heard about all the time.

"We set up some beds, open bar with girls we hire to serve drinks, charge 200 per couple and I split it with Larry."

"I mean, what's it *like*?"

I swam under water towards them and emerged in time for Diego's answer.

"I've gotten some good fucks for sure. Everyone has a good time. Some are swingers, some like the big group orgies. Lots of girl on girl. Lots of older dudes with younger girls. I'd let you and Kat come for free; you'd be the hottest couple here and everyone would love you." He looked at me. "But Kat isn't that kind of girl. I mean, she's good, too good."

I wiped the water off my face and wondered what kind of girl I was. I used to be a "good girl," whatever such a signifier means. But now?

"Did you know that Kat is married?" Troy asked Diego, knowing full well that he did not.

"Married!"

"Kat's been sleeping with two men for the last three months. She's practically a polygamist." Troy let out a dry, sadistic laugh.

"This is true?" Diego asked me.

I nodded. It was a strange thing, having sex with two men that I loved in such different ways. I remember one night in the dark, half asleep, not knowing who it was that I was fucking. That shook me. So did the fact that my sex life with Victor improved greatly after I started sleeping with Troy. After years with Victor, I'd begun to think of myself as simply not being a sexual person. But Troy changed that. Never in my life had I felt anything like this brave, creative, desirous kind of yearning. This all made me think long and hard about monogamy, something I'd suspected was doomed but now knew for sure.

My sex drive had rocketed, but my sense of self-worth was shattered. The first day I drove home from Troy's bed and back to Victor's, I felt myself begin to crack like a brittle bone. As the days and weeks went on, the cracks turned to caverns, to craters, that split and shattered until I was a fractured woman wondering *Who am I? What is love?* I was begging for answers. None came.

"Men cheat all the time," Diego said. "Never let anyone make you feel bad." I felt a rush of tears for his kindness and pushed them back.

"I still know you are good. Too good for this asshole." He gestured to Troy with a childish giggle.

Diego threw back the rest of his drink. He pointed to the concrete wall that rose behind the pool. "Want to jump?" he asked Troy. "I have to take some cool pictures for my parties. Maybe jump up and pose in the air above the pool, make it look like you're having the time of your life. Yeah?"

"Sure," Troy said. He finished his beer and hoisted himself out of the pool.

"I'll jump too!" I said.

The wall wasn't too high, maybe five feet above the water. I had a long history of cliff jumping: every summer with my sister in Lake George, and into the Gorges at Ithaca at the start of each term. The cliffs were sometimes twenty feet high; this was nothing.

Troy grabbed my hand and helped me up out of the water, up the hot concrete slope, where we stood tall above the world, looking out.

"I love this city," Troy said, his hand around my waist, my skin tingling with his touch. I leaned toward him like a palm tree to the sun. He looked down at me. Perhaps thought of saying that he loved me too, but instead he kissed me on the forehead, then nose, then lips.

He had admitted his love for me only once, in our emergency therapy session with Dr. Sharon, when I was on the verge of cracking. "I do *not* want her to leave her husband for me," Troy told the therapist, who was his therapist, not mine.

"Well, then, walk away and let her mend her marriage," Dr. Sharon urged him. Troy laughed. I cried. Troy had no intention of giving me up; he simply didn't want to be the reason that I left Victor. He wanted me to leave because I wanted to leave, but I didn't *want* to leave Victor at all.

"What do you expect me to do?" I sobbed. "I can't keep living this way. I can't keep lying." Troy slid away from me on the therapy couch. He hated it when I cried.

"Leave him because you're not in love with him anymore, but don't leave him for me. It's too much pressure. I don't want it."

Dr. Sharon passed me the tissue box. "I understand that you don't want to be the reason that Kat's marriage breaks up," she said in her calm, trained way, "but in this life you don't always get what you want. Actions have consequences. You are part of what is happening here, you share the responsibility with Kat. You may not want this responsibility, but unless you excuse yourself from the situation and decide not to see Kat anymore, then it is yours all the same."

"How could I not see her anymore? That's ridiculous. We're in love," Troy said.

"Well, then," Dr. Sharon replied, "you've made your decision."

"Smile!" Diego called up to us. I smoothed back my hair and adjusted my bathing suit. Troy pulled my body in close, my head nestled like a puzzle piece under his chin. Diego stood below at the edge of the pool, eyes squinting in the sun, and snapped a picture of our wet joined bodies. Me smiling up at Troy, Troy looking out past the overpriced houses of the Hollywood Hills. The whole of L.A. was there, hills, city, ocean in the distance meeting the open sky, memorializing us this way. Before.

"Hold hands while you jump!" Diego directed. He squatted down to prepare his angle of view.

Troy switched sides with me so that I was closer to the deep end, out of harm's way. He interlaced his fingers in mine, my hand encompassed.

"On three. One, two, three!" Troy called.

We jumped. Troy whooped and flashed his exaggerated opened mouth smile. I rushed with the wildness of being airborne, a thing I was drawn to. We fell in with a splash, Troy still holding my hand beneath the water. When I came up, I felt a little rush of endorphins as I swam to the shallow end.

"Do it again," Diego called. "I think I can get a better angle over here." He scurried to the opposite corner of the pool.

We climbed back up. This time we had less inhibition. It hadn't been a very far drop. Things had worked out fine. I found myself on the opposite side this time, closer to the shallow end, and thought nothing of it.

"Try to pose in the air for a good shot," Troy said to me. "One, two, three ..."

242

We leaped, lifted our linked hands towards the sky, smiled. Troy released me to land as I may. I didn't know that I had jumped too high. Too far towards the shallow-end slope. I could have tried to adjust, to tuck my knees way up, but all I was thinking of was a pose and a smile.

The bottom of the pool met the soles of my feet unexpectedly. There should have been more water. There should have been more time. Everything slowed down. I felt the jolt rise. A long slow reverberation that began at my feet and spiraled up like an earthquake in my bones. I stayed under water, too long, trying to make sense of it. Once I had, everything in me screamed, but only I could hear. Only I knew the damage I had done. Then I couldn't breathe, time sped up, and I rushed to the surface.

"I broke my feet," I screamed as soon as my head popped up from the molecules of water to the molecules of air.

No one seemed to understand. No one came to my rescue.

I used my arms, half drowning, to get myself to the side of the pool. I pulled myself partially up before Troy appeared behind me in the water, boosting me the rest of the way.

Poolside, I pulled my feet into my body, covered them with my hands, panting, screeching, like a wounded animal.

"Kat, Kat. Let me see!" Troy beside me, dripping, frantic.

I batted him away twice, the damage private, still mine for a moment more. I knew it couldn't stay that way. I uncovered my feet slowly for us both to see. My right foot was frightening, bulbous, discolored, three times its normal size. I grabbed back onto it. Holding helped. Moaning helped. People that I didn't know were there came running out of the house. Larry and two of his friends. They had heard my cries.

"Call 911," Diego yelled, and that was my cue to take control.

As a gymnast, I had broken bones before. As a coach, I knew the protocols. I'd seen snapped elbows, protruding ulnas, exploded ankles. I knew when the ambulance was and was not needed. Ambulances were expensive. I had a divorce to pay for, and a life in L.A.

"Don't call 911," I commanded. My voice was surprisingly authoritative and calm. I rambled off tasks, the men around me complied. "Two large ice packs. Three Advil. Water. My clothes. Someone pull my car up. Troy don't you fucking leave my side."

Troy held my hand, chanting his mantra, "I'm so sorry, babe. I'm so sorry, babe."

I put on my tank top. Troy was against the shorts, but I wasn't going to the ER in bathing suit bottoms; I had my pride. To lift my legs, to get my exploded feet through the holes of the short jean shorts that Victor had helped me weather fashionably with a cheese grater, was arduous. But I managed with minimal screams. The ice came. It helped. I let it numb me for maybe five minutes. Larry, the heart surgeon, came over to inspect me, had nothing much to say other than, "That looks bad." I asked him, along with Troy and Diego, to help me up.

I tried to put pressure on my left foot as they lifted me, but it was a no-go. I collapsed in pain back to the ground. The left was not nearly as bad as the right, but it was undoubtedly broken too.

"You'll have to carry me," I told them.

It was agony when they lifted me, my feet dangling down with the pull of gravity. Angry, anxious blood rushed to the site of the injury.

I broke my knee tumbling when I was thirteen. My dad had carried me out of the gym, the joint unhinged. I remembered that trip to the car, in his arms, as one of the most painful of my life. This beat that. By a lot. I wished that my dad were alive and holding me now, instead of two strangers, one acquaintance, and one lover. Their nervous clammy hands on my injured body as if they might break me further with their touch.

They took me to the elevator that led the four stories down to the garage. We dropped in silence, floor by floor, and then they loaded me into the backseat of my leased SUV.

Larry thought that I would sue him; it was painted all over his face as we drove away. He didn't know me well enough to know that I wouldn't. Troy thought I would hate him forever, that everyone would think it was his fault, as they had our affair.

"This would never have happened with Victor," he said, panicky.

This was true. Vic was afraid of heights, couldn't have been paid to jump off any sized ledge. But Troy didn't know me well enough yet to know that my childhood nickname had been "Calamity Kat" and that this was just the type of thing that *would* happen to me. Everyone was surprised that I cheated on Victor, shocked that it was with Troy. But no one would be surprised that I had broken my feet. No one except me. Of the possible paths that I had laid out before me on that summer afternoon, this was not one I had foreseen. The twisting roads of the Hollywood Hills were tedious as I jerked around in the back seat, adjusting my ice and crying now, really crying, as the reality set in.

We waited in the Beverly Hills Emergency Room for five hours. It was clean and cold. I shivered in my wet bathing suit covered by skimpy clothes. Diego got me new ice packs every twenty minutes; they sustained me. He got me a towel to cover my shoulders and keep me warm. Troy held my hand. I squeezed so tight. I wouldn't let go.

¬

The calcaneus bone is the largest bone in the foot. The injury of this bone is most often caused by high-energy impacts, usually falls. Because of this, a calcaneus fracture has been called the "Lover's Fracture" or the "Don Juan Fracture," with the implication that lovers will jump from great heights for their beloved. The classic setup is the "lover" jumping off his mistress's balcony to escape the angry husband, and bam, heels broken. The scoundrel is literally swept off his feet.

A calcaneus injury is one of the most severe foot injuries that one can incur, and perhaps the hardest to rehabilitate. The calcaneus can be compared to a hard-boiled egg with a thin but hard shell on the outside and softer, spongier bone inside. When the outer bone collapses, it usually fragments; in my case, it split into so many pieces that the surgeon couldn't count them.

Even though you might not think or know it, the calcaneus is one of the most important moving joints in the foot. It forms the subtalar joint, which is responsible for normal foot movement and is the foundation of the whole back part of the foot. Of course, I wish that these were things that I didn't know …

I had fractured my left calcaneus and obliterated the right one. One week after my leap into the pool with Troy, expert UCLA podiatrist Dr. Little put a plate and seven screws into my right foot that will remain there for the rest of my life.

Ironic? Karmic? Purely coincidental? I simply could not decide.

⌐

On the day of my surgery, I came out of my sedation slowly, coasting into the dock of my awakening. Once the tears stopped, I settled smoothly into a state of bleak, exhausted, acceptance. I didn't try to analyze or comprehend. I simply saw it, my life.

The path forward had narrowed. Victor was lost to me; so was the prospect of an apartment by the beach with Hannah. Troy was what I had now, and we deserved each other. The "punishment" fit the crime. My outside now matched my inside: broken. In some ways it was a relief. I hadn't had it in me to choose what came next, and now I didn't have much choice. My life would move forward the only way it could. There I was, lying at the start of the thing. Naked and helpless, but not alone.

"Babe, we did it. It's all over. It's all good," Troy said. His hands in my hands, his face on my face, he draped his body across my hospital bed until the weight of him made me feel connected. He had that way. "Babe. My babe. It's good. We're good," he chanted. His voice was happy, high-pitched, and so sure that I almost believed him.

My right leg was nerve blocked, entirely paralyzed. "Dead leg" they called it. An awkward sensation, but I wasn't in all that much pain. I felt for my leg with my hands, comforted to find it still there. I believed that it would come back to life. I wanted to believe that I would too.

The surgeon approached my bed looking alert, almost excited.

"We didn't know how badly the bone was destroyed until we got in there," Dr. Little reported. He addressed his comments more to Troy than to me. "But we were able to make the smaller incision and get all seven screws locked on, which was not easy."

"Great," Troy said. "That's great. Thanks, Doc."

I nodded to agree. I felt weak but appreciative to be focused on the physical, easier to heal from the outside in.

A gigantic machine, the dirty tan color of old computers and '80s sci-fi robots, was wheeled out to me. The technician manipulated my leg gently to take X-rays of the long-hinged plates and screws that had been placed in my heel to repair my shattered calcaneus.

Dr. Little watched the digital images rise up. He bent forward, leaned into the small square screen, and brought his hands together in a soft cheer. "I'm very pleased with it," he said to my X-rays, to the technician, to Troy, and then to me. "Very pleased!"

I thought about what that might be like, to be pleased; it seemed something from a different life.

In that moment, I could see myself clearly, maybe for the first time since the whole thing started. I was a woman blurring in and out of different realities, one moment beautiful and the next hideous. One moment full of new love and the next full of unrest, loss, and self-hate. A woman hanging onto the edge of my girlhood so that people would pause on me, deciding which category fit. I was a woman conjuring my bravery, building it up with every breath, because I knew it to be the only way through this, and I wanted to make it through. I was a woman who had lost my understanding of what bravery was. One moment sure that bravery meant truly letting go, "following your heart," and the next certain it meant the opposite, that bravery was fighting to save what you most valued. I was a woman who had been so sure my whole life, but now no longer had a clue what I most valued. I had lost all my definitions, all of my truths, and was sifting through the dust cloud of the erasure, trying to make sense of the particles flying about in every direction, looking to bring the chalk lines back together, and knowing that when I did, I would understand things about myself, about this city, this world, this life, that I hadn't before.

When Dr. Little departed, Troy waited by my side, brought me water, stroked my clammy forehead.

"I'm sorry," he said. "For all of it. I'll carry you every-where." I thought I saw tears in his eyes, but it may have just been the drugs still pulsing through me.

"Look," he said, and held up a pencil that said UCLA Medical Center on it.

As we waited for my approval for discharge, he read me the remaining chapter of my book with his most expressive actor-voice. Underlined the important parts that seemed most to apply to us, to the courage it takes to love.

"'Not only are grand passions as rare as masterpieces; they are masterpieces,'" Troy read Nehring's words as if he had written them himself.

I listened and stared with an unfocused gaze out past Troy, past my swollen feet, past the nurses and the hospital walls, looking for some world hidden beyond and behind. A world with less pain. A world where I had made different choices. But I knew that what lay outside was only the city of Los Angeles, its beauty and flaws. Its flare for painful passions, embraced, and turned to art.

BIOGRAPHIES

EDITORS

SARA CHISOLM

Sara is a speculative fiction writer based in the Los Angeles area. Her urban fantasy short story, "Serenade of the Gangsta," was featured in the second volume of the Made in L.A. fiction anthology series.

GABI LORINO

Gabi Lorino is a writer, editor, and organizer of people, tasks, and information, currently based in Fort Wayne, Indiana. Her articles and short stories have been published in newspapers, newsletters, magazines, and books. She has self-published one fiction book, *A Magical Time Called Later*, in addition to a journal series, and serves as an editor for Made in L.A. Writers.

ALLISON ROSE

Allison Rose is a novelist and screenwriter born and raised in Los Angeles. *Tick*, the first in her young adult science fiction series, tackles mental illness, artistry, and violence — themes close to Allison's heart. It has been followed by *Vice*, part two of the Tick Series. Both novels are based in near-future L.A. While Allison's stories vary in genre, her focus centers on the struggles of complex female characters and the deconstruction of clichés and tropes about women. She has used her twenty years of graphic design experience to create her own book covers, including every volume of Made in L.A. She is a founding member of Made in L.A. Writers. Read more on Allison's website at thegirlandthebook.com.

CODY SISCO

Cody Sisco is an author, editor, publisher, and literary community organizer. His LGBT psychological science fiction series includes two novels thus far, *Broken Mirror* and *Tortured Echoes*. He is a freelance editor specializing in genre-bending fiction and an editor for Running Wild Press. He is a founding member of Made in L.A. Writers. In 2017, he started BookSwell, a literary events and media production company dedicated to connecting readers and writers in Southern California and beyond. He currently serves as the Website Chair for the Editorial Freelancers Association and is a board member at APLA Health. Read more on www.codysisco.com.

CONTRIBUTORS

NICK DURETTA

Nick Duretta is a writer based in Pasadena, California. He has worked as a newspaper reporter, screenwriter, and a corporate communications manager, managing communication programs for Fortune 500 corporations. His current project is the Rick Chasen series of mystery novels taking place on English walking paths. When not hunched over his keyboard, he is out enjoying his second-favorite pastime, walking in the Southern California mountains.

J. P. HIGGINS

J. P. Higgins writes fiction and poetry intended to arouse a reader's curiosity, interest, reflection, understanding, humor, inspiration, and enjoyment (usually not all at once, but, of course, anything may happen). Higgins lives in Los Angeles. "Living, Dead, and In-Between" in this volume of the Made in L.A. anthology is Higgins' first fiction in print.

KATE MO

Kate Mo writes and lives in Los Angeles. She writes fiction, creative nonfiction, and plays about Japanese Americans and the effect of intergenerational trauma (incarceration camps, anti-miscegenation laws, model minority myth). She has published creative nonfiction in Out of Anonymity as well as literary articles on Ai, Harriet Doerr, David Henry Hwang, and Terrence McNally in the *Encyclopedia of American Literature*. Her short stories "Java Defense" and "Dead-End Street" appeared in *The Crescent Review* and *Blue Guitar Midstream* respectively.

KARTER MYCROFT

Karter Mycroft is an author, editor, musician, and fisheries scientist from Los Angeles. Karter writes on the beach by asking the dead fish for ideas. You can find them on Twitter @kartermycroft or online at kartermycroft.com.

CATIE JARVIS

Catie Jarvis is an author of fiction, a yoga instructor, a competitive gymnastics coach, and an English and writing professor. She received her BA in writing from Ithaca College, and her MFA in creative writing from the California College of the Arts. She grew up on a lake in northern New Jersey and now lives near the ocean in California with her husband, daughter, and lots of surfboards. She finds the world to be a strange place and loves writing that examines the ambiguity of "reality." Her debut novel, *The Peacock Room*, is available on Amazon. Find more about the author and her writing at catiejarvis.com and 30inLA.com.

SASHA KILDARE

Sasha Kildare, author of *Intact: Untangle the Web of Bipolar Depression, Addiction and Trauma*, is a speaker, mental health advocate, educator, and mom. Some of her feature articles have appeared in *bp Magazine* and *Esperanza*.

Visit her storytelling blog that delves into the creative process and how to stave off depression and compulsivity at DrivenToTellStories.com.

JANNA LAYTON

Janna Layton was born in San Jose, has lived in San Francisco and Oakland, and now resides in Walnut Creek, near the base of Mt. Diablo. Despite being a lifelong resident of the SF Bay Area, she loves and respects Los Angeles (the fact that she is not a baseball fan probably helps). Her fiction has been published in various places, including *The New Yorker's Daily Shouts*, *The Colored Lens*, *Luna Station Quarterly*, *Andromeda Spaceways Magazine*, and the anthology *Five Minutes at Hotel Stormcove*. She tweets at @jkbartleby.

AATIF RASHID

Aatif Rashid is the author of the novel *Portrait of Sebastian Khan* (2019). He has published short stories in *The Massachusetts Review*, *Arcturus*, *Barrelhouse*, *Triangle House Review*, and *X-R-A-Y*, among other places, and nonfiction in *The Kenyon Review*, *Lit Hub*, and *The Los Angeles Review of Books*.

TISHA MARIE REICHLE-AGUILERA

Chicana Feminist and former Rodeo Queen, Tisha Marie Reichle-Aguilera (she/her) writes so the desert landscape of her childhood can be heard as loudly as the urban chaos of her adulthood. She is obsessed with food. A former high school teacher, she earned an MFA at Antioch University Los Angeles and is a PhD candidate at University of Southern California where she is an Annenberg Fellow. She also works for literary equity through Women Who Submit, an organization that empowers women and nonbinary writers to send their work out for publication.

LUCY RODRIGUEZ-HANLEY

Lucy Rodriguez-Hanley is a Dominican American creative nonfiction writer, award-winning filmmaker, and mother of two. Her work has appeared in Harvard's *Palabritas*, NYU's *Latinx Project*, and *Gathering: A Women Who Submit Anthology*.

She writes from the feminist point of view of the bilingual, bicultural brown girl and woman. Her memoir-in-progress, *Late Bloomer*, is a collection of essays about a Dominican mother/daughter relationship. Lucy advocates for representation of BIPOC women and non-binary writers. She is the Chapters Liaison for Women Who Submit, and leads the Long Beach, California chapter of the organization.

AMY JONES SEDIVY

Amy Jones Sedivy grew up in Los Angeles and currently lives in the NELA neighborhood of Highland Park with her artist-husband and their princess-dog. She has a Master's in English with an emphasis on writing, and she now teaches English at a small independent school in Pasadena. Her favorite activity besides reading is driving through the different neighborhoods of L.A., especially the roads less traveled.

Most recent publications include "This Does Not Exist" (2017) and "Anaphora" (2018) in *Write Launch* online literary magazine, and "The Rhinos of Josephine" in *(mac)ro(mic)*, July 2021.

CRISTINA STUART

Born and raised in the United Kingdom, Cristina is now a long-term resident of Atwater Village, close to Griffith Park. Travel has always been in her blood, and her first job was in Hong Kong as a radio journalist. Since then, she has visited in over sixty countries on business and for pleasure.

During her career as managing director of an international training company in London, she authored three non-fiction books on public speaking and media relations. Recently, she completed her first novel and has written several short stories, and she is delighted that one of them is included in this anthology.

RACHAEL WARECKI

Rachael Warecki has attended residencies at MacDowell and Ragdale and holds an MFA in fiction from Antioch University, Los Angeles. She is also a 2021–22 Book-Ends Fellow and an emerita member of the Women Who Submit leadership team. Her novel-in-progress, *The Split Decision* — set in the same world as "The Long Drop" — was a finalist in the 2019 CRAFT First Chapters Contest. Her short work has received the Tiferet Prize, semifinalist honors in the American Short(er) Fiction Contest and the Boulevard Creative Nonfiction Contest, and a Best of the Net nomination, and her stories have appeared in various publications.

DEBORAH WEISS

Deborah Weiss is a Los Angeles-based lawyer and writer who teaches legal writing and analysis at the University of Southern California Gould School of Law. She lives in Topanga with her husband, son, parrots, goats, dog, cat, turtle, and chickens. She is the program liaison for Habele Foundation, whose mission is to enhance STEM education for K-12 students in the Federated States of Micronesia. When she is not litigating or teaching, she spends her time hiking with her dog and cleaning up countless different types of animal poop. Deborah's work has appeared in the *Independent*, *Salon*, and *Westways Magazine*.

HAZEL KIGHT WITHAM

Hazel Kight Witham is a mother, teacher, slam poetry coach, and writer who was made in Los Angeles and still calls it home. She has published work in *The Sun*, *Bellevue Literary Review*, *Integrated Schools*, *Mutha Magazine*, *Cultural Weekly*, *Rising Phoenix Review*, and other journals. She is a proud public-school teacher in LAUSD and was a 2020 finalist for California Teacher of the Year. Since November 2008, she has shepherded more than two thousand students through National Novel Writing Month.

MADE IN L.A. WRITERS

Made in L.A. Writers is a collaborative of Los Angeles-based authors dedicated to nurturing and promoting indie fiction. While our styles, themes, and story locales differ, our work is both influenced and illuminated by our hometown and underpinned by the extraordinary, multifaceted, and often surreal culture and life in the City of Angels.

As indie authors, we face formidable challenges: fragmented audiences, intense competition in a crowded market, and traditional publishers' deep pockets.

If you enjoyed this book, please leave a review. Rave about us to your friends. Find us online and tell us how our stories made you feel. We're looking for connection; we hope to hear from you.

www.madeinlawriters.com